READING ORDER

The Sands of Achten Tan

Speechless in Achten Tan – Book One
~ In the Heart of the Storm (Short story)
~ Pirate in the Desert (Short story)
The Bone Master – Book Two
Tar and Bone – Prequel/ Book Three (Forthcoming)
The Magic Within – Book Four (Forthcoming)

Children of the Stars

The Goodbye Kids – Book One
The Girl from the Sky – Book Two

THE GIRL FROM THE SKY

Children of the Stars book 2

Debbie Iancu-Haddad

Contents

Chapter 1

Sleeping Beauty

Haley

Jorden is sleeping.

I watch the steady rise and fall of his chest, brushing strands of hair out of his eyes. Touch the stubble on his cheek. For the past few weeks, he's been in a medically induced coma to allow him to recover from the head injury he sustained when the pod exploded, blowing him against the bulkhead. Combined with the lack of air from the time I opened the airlocks to minimize the blast, he's probably got brain damage. The doctor doesn't know if he'll ever wake up.

I look around, but I'm alone. The doctor is visiting patients confined to their quarters. Sometimes it feels like I'm always on med duty at these quiet times.

I touch Jorden's soft lips, remember his kiss, the way he looked at me and held me. How he said he hadn't wanted to hurt me. Right before I killed him.

Okay, I didn't kill him. I tried, and that's the same thing as far as it goes. I was prepared to kill him to save the station and the travelers on the jump ship. I made a choice. And so did he.

He looks so peaceful lying there. He looks younger. Just a boy, asleep and dreaming. I wonder what he's dreaming of. Probably some Earthly meadow, filled with fluffy clouds. Or a quiet forest, walking peacefully under the trees, the sun dappling his skin, playing on his tanned shoulders and sandy hair, tree tops reflecting in his green eyes.

I hope he has nice dreams. I don't want him to suffer. Even though he hurt me and then I hurt him back.

Are we even now? I don't know.

At first, I avoided the med center. I couldn't bear to look at him lying here. It hurt too much. But, eventually, Dr. Peters told me if I didn't turn up for shifts, he'd remove me from med training. He was kind, but firm. He knew Jorden and I were together, before.

I couldn't lose this, too, so I started taking shifts again.

I tell myself to be professional. Treat Jorden as I would any other patient. Dr. Peters enters the room and his kind eyes crease at the look on my face.

"How's he doing?" he asks, but I think he's asking more about me.

"The same." I try to look indifferent. As though the boy lying in that bed didn't mean the world to me. As if he didn't break my heart, and the guilt and pain aren't crushing me to dust. Hopefully, I have a brilliant career ahead of me in medicine, or as a pilot, because Dr. Peters' expression tells me I won't make it as an actress.

His expression is sympathetic as he places a palm on my shoulder, steadying me.

"He's young and healthy. That improves his chances. The body heals itself. The next few weeks will determine his condition. Now that he's off the meds, he should gradually wake up and gain consciousness. Though he may progress into a different state of unconsciousness called a vegetative state or minimally conscious state. We can try to help him out of it gently."

"What should I do?" I ask.

"Talking helps. You can talk to him about your day. Some people remember events that happened around them while they were in a coma, while others don't. Touch is a great stimulus. Just sitting and holding his hand or stroking his skin can be beneficial."

I blush, hoping the doctor doesn't notice. *Okay then, so, if I touch him, it doesn't mean anything. It's the doctor's orders.*

"Can he hear me if I talk to him?"

"Possibly. People have reported feeling enormous reassurance from the presence of a loved one when coming out of a coma. They can feel them in the room with them. When you arrive on duty, announce who you are. Tell him you're here."

I don't react when he mentions "a loved one". Did I ever mean anything to Jorden, or was it all just a lie? But since Dr. Peters recommended stimulating the senses, I get permission from Bianca, the head of security, to bring the box with Jorden's personal items into the med center. It feels so intimate going through his things. The shirts still have his scent. I resist the urge to sniff one, but the smell still wafts around me, making me think of sunlight and fresh air.

Rooting until I find the communication device he brought from Earth, I figure out how to access the songs saved in the memory. Placing it by his bed, I play them on the speaker, listening while going about my other duties. I don't know most of them, Earth music is so diverse, but I like what I hear. It feels like him. I can imagine him going about his chores on the farm, listening to the music, tapping the beat out with his fingers.

The talking part is harder. There are so many things I want to say. Ask why he hurt me the way he did. Why he suddenly pushed me away. Why he destroyed Nano.

I want answers, but he can only listen, not respond, so I just talk as I go about the room. Eventually, I sit down by his side and take his hand. He makes a good listener. I find myself asking him questions, telling him about Nano, and what he meant to me. He wasn't just a robot dog. He was my only friend for years before Jorden and Dawn arrived. I end up pouring my heart out. It's strange, but talking makes me feel closer to him again.

I wonder if he can hear me. What he'd say if he ever woke up?

When I finish, I rub my hand guiltily on my sleeve, rubbing away the evidence, as if someone could tell I touched Jorden's sleeping lips.

I don't know why I did.

Chapter 2

SPIRAL

Jorden

I lie there, barely awake, watching her from under half-closed eyelids.

The whole time I was unconscious, I could hear her and smell her. I felt her hand in mine. It was like being in a dream together. I didn't want to ever wake up.

As I drift closer to consciousness, my brain loops into a never-ending spiral, listing my failures. I failed at my mission. Nancy threatened to hurt Haley if I didn't go through with it; I tried and failed. Nancy is probably en route to New Horizons, but her threat still lingers.

Things I once cared about, like proving myself to my father or going down in history as the one who stopped the migration from Earth, don't seem important any more. But they're still on my list of failures. My father will never forgive me. He entrusted me with this mission and I can never face him again. What will my friends think, all the people on the Farm? I can never return home.

It doesn't really matter. I heard the doctor say that, if I recover, I'll return to Earth to stand trial.

Last but not least, while trying to protect her, I hurt Haley to the point she was willing to kill me. I lied to her, so she'll never trust me again. I kissed her, one last time, but now we'll never be together.

I try to shake the oppressive thoughts out of my head, but they're strong. The only way to escape them is to wake up. I push against the boundaries of my consciousness, fighting to break free. Drifting ever closer to the surface, I'm so close I can almost press through.

Haley's shift is coming to an end. She moves around quietly, putting things away. I watch her movement. It's soothing, like a lullaby putting me to sleep.

I close my eyes, listening for her, just out of sight. I think of kissing her, imagine her quick breathing and burning lips. Running my fingers through her hair. But there's no point. She must hate me.

I don't blame her.

Chapter 3

Humpty Dumpty

Haley

The ranger ship arrives from Earth four weeks after the attack. They're going to take Jorden.

Standing on the bridge outside the pod deck control room where my final confrontation with Jorden took place, I view the ranger craft with new eyes. The ship is sleek and black, a small, fast craft designed for quick hops. Unlike the cumbersome passenger transports, this ship can take only 2–4 passengers. It comes equipped with sleeping quarters, a food printer, basic facilities, and not much else. It's built for speed and efficiency.

As I discuss the make and model of the drive with Stacey, the deck chief, all I can think about is *they're here to take him away*. Ending my reprieve. Once more, I'm faced with saying goodbye to him forever.

Ignorant of my inner turmoil, David, one of the older pod pilots, points at the ranger ship. "Imagine being cooped up in that tiny thing for three weeks. You'd go mad."

"Probably kill the person you were with too. Or they'd drive you crazy," Stacey smiles at him.

"I can think of something scarier than that..." I say. David raises his eyebrows in question. "Losing a year and a half of your life in transit. Three for the round trip. Getting home with everybody older, and life has moved on without you."

They nod solemnly. People who sign on at the station take the time slip into account. Contracts here are for at least a decade.

"Anyway," I continue, "it's probably scarier to actually be on Earth. All that open air and weird weather. Oceans, tsunamis, earthquakes, and wild animals." I shudder.

David smiles. "Station kids are funny. You've been cooped up on this station your whole life. No wonder being outside scares you."

I shrug. "You can't understand, if you grew up on Earth."

When I report to the med center for my shift, Dr.

Peters is talking to the two rangers who arrived from Earth-Space-Control, or ESC for short.

One of them is short and bald, with a wide, round face and bulging ears. He reminds me of an egg. I christen him Humpty Dumpty. The other is taller, lanky, with short brown hair and glasses, like a giraffe from the old Earth vids.

Giraffe stands by Jorden's bed, eyeing him like a bug under a microscope. I pretend to be busy arranging equipment, keeping to the side, out of the way.

"How is he?" Giraffe asks the doctor.

Dr. Peters frowns. "He's been in a coma. He's been improving gradually but he's not fully conscious yet."

"Can he walk?"

"We've been using neuromuscular electrical stimulation to prevent muscle atrophy, so that shouldn't be a problem, but I want to wait till he's fully alert before I release him into your custody."

"Why not just take him semi-conscious?" Humpty Dumpty asks, scratching his bald head nervously. "Less hassle."

Dr. Peters frowns. "We need to stabilize his condition. That's my concern as a medical practitioner. It should be yours, too, if he's to stand trial. That's the goal, isn't it? Or do you think Earth authorities will prosecute a kid in a vegetative state? How would that look to the press?" The doctor looks down his nose at the ranger. "Imagine the headlines - Brain damaged teen tried in court."

"No, no. Of course not," Humpty Dumpty hurriedly agrees.

"Anyway, we're helping him heal. I'll release him when I'm convinced his condition is satisfactory. Forgive me if I'm not concerned with your convenience."

After Dr. Peters and the rangers leave, I sit beside Jorden and take his hand. It's become part of my daily routine.

His hand is warm, large, and strong. I trace the lines of his fingers, running my fingertips lightly up and down his hand. For a moment I think I feel movement, but it passes and I'm sure I imagined it.

Then slowly, very slowly, his hand closes over mine, squeezing it.

Surprised, I look up at him. His eyes are open. He's back. His eyes have the same warm, intelligent, green gaze I thought I'd never see again. He can't speak, but he smiles at me and the weight that's been crushing me for the past month lifts from my chest. I can finally take a deep breath again.

He's alive. He's okay. I didn't kill him.

I need to get the doctor and tell him that Jorden is awake but, before I can let go, he holds on tighter, giving a slight shake of his head. So, I keep sitting there, staring into his eyes until he drifts back to sleep.

Chapter 4

AWAKE

Jorden

Over the next few days, I wake up more frequently. It takes some time, as if my body has forgotten some functions, but now I can sit up in bed, talk, and have some food. The tubes have all been removed and my body is readjusting.

There are other junior assistants in the med center who take shifts, but I spend my days waiting for Haley. Though she treats me professionally, as she would any other patient, I watch for a glimmer of something else. Anything to show she still cares about me.

There's an impassable gulf between us. As far as she knows, I chose my mission and she chose to save the station. We don't talk about what happened, even when we're alone. I want to say something, to apologize, explain, beg for her forgiveness, but I'm worried that, if I mention it, her detachment will dissolve and the anger will erupt. At the moment, she's holding back. There are words swirling beneath the surface, but she's holding them in and I don't want to force them out of her.

At lunchtime, she brings me some soup. I try to eat by myself, but my hand is unsteady and I spill some on the covers. She looks around, trying to find anyone else to help me, but there's no one else. Scowling, she takes the spoon from me.

"Let me do it."

She tries to stand and spoon it into my mouth, but the angle is uncomfortable so, in the end, she gives up and sits on the bed next to me. Her leg presses against mine.

"Thank you."

She looks up at me, blushes, then nods and feeds me the soup.

It's oddly intimate. She's looking into my eyes, her body pressing into mine as she leans forward. Neither one of us speaks. I can hardly breathe with her so close. When I finish the soup, she puts the bowl down on the bedside table and sits for a moment. This is my chance to say something. Since I woke up, she's stopped holding my hand, and I miss it, so I reach out and take her hand.

"Haley..."

She pulls away, standing up abruptly.

"Don't. Just... don't."

Her eyes say she's standing on the edge of an abyss and I'm liable to push her in. But I'm running out of time; the men from Earth grow more impatient every day. They're urging Dr. Peters to sign the release and let me go with them.

"I'm sorry." I shake my head. Then I swivel and place my feet on the floor. She darts forward.

"What are you doing?"

I grin. "What goes in must come out." I gesture towards the bathroom door. "It's okay, I can make it."

"No, you can't." She's adamant, but I try anyway. Pushing up off the bed, I manage to stand but, before I can take a step, my knees buckle and I fall back onto the bed.

"No. I can't. You're right." I look at her pleadingly. "Help?"

She exhales in frustration but nods. "All right."

I rise again. Stepping forward she slips under my arm, holding me up around the waist, and guides me slowly to the bathroom door, putting my hand on the guardrail there.

"I'm not coming inside," she glares at me.

"It's okay, I can manage."

When I'm done, she helps me back. I don't say anything, just enjoy having her close. Walking at a snail's pace to draw out the time. After she helps me back into bed, I wait until she's drawn the covers over me and touch her hand, brushing it with my fingers.

"Thanks."

She nods, tight-lipped, but her eyes flash to mine. I think there's hope.

Over the next few days, my health improves. I can feed myself, and get dressed. I still get dizzy if I push myself too much, but Dr. Peters is working with me on walking, keeping my balance, and managing the effects of my head injury.

About a week after I woke up, the doctor and the two rangers from Earth enter the room. The doctor places my clothes and shoes on the end of my bed.

"Jorden. It's time. Get dressed, and then these rangers will escort you down to the pod deck. They'll return you to Earth. You're going home."

He tries to put a positive spin on it, but I know the truth. My time is up. I'm going home to stand trial. Earth authorities will make an example of me. My heart is pounding. My mouth is dry and my head spins even though I'm sitting.

Haley isn't here. *I won't even get a chance to say goodbye.*

"What about my things? There was a box with my stuff." Haley got my player out while I was unconscious.

"Your things are already on the ship," the stocky ranger says gruffly.

I search the room for a way to escape, but where

would I go?

"Can I at least get some privacy while I dress?"

The tall one laughs unpleasantly. "You're going to prison, son. Might as well get used to guys seeing your ass and pray all they do is look. Though it's not likely. Pretty boy like you." He smacks his lips. The short one chuckles.

"That's quite enough," Dr. Peters intervenes. "This young man is my patient for the duration of his stay on this space station, so you'll grant him basic respect, including respecting his right to privacy. Wait outside while he dresses."

They look doubtful.

"He's not going anywhere." The doctor sounds annoyed. "The room only has one exit."

The rangers exchange glances. "Whatever you say Doc, but then we have him for three weeks. That'll be fun."

Dr. Peters leaves the room, waiting for the rangers to join him outside. As they leave, the short one leers at me. I shudder; I don't want to be alone with them for five minutes, much less three weeks. After pulling on my clothes, I search frantically for something, anything, I can use.

The medicine cabinets are locked and require a security clearance. The drawers full of equipment contain bandages, splints, nothing useful. Then I notice a jar in the sink with a scalpel in it, waiting to be washed. I grab a paper towel out of the bathroom and wrap it around the scalpel, slipping it inside my sleeve. My black top is form-fitting flexi fabric, and it holds the towel and scalpel tightly. With my luck, I'll cut my wrist. Then I layer on an overshirt to hide the bulge in my sleeve.

I exhale, feeling more prepared. At least I can defend myself if the rangers come at me. Smoothing back my hair with my left hand, I keep minimal movement with my right. Taking a deep breath, I pull the door open. The rangers are standing a bit further up, the doctor closer to the door. As I approach, the taller ranger holds up a pair of silver bracelets. If he cuffs me, he'll feel the scalpel up my sleeve. I flinch and Dr. Peters notices my reaction and puts out his hand to stop the ranger.

"I'm sure that isn't necessary. Where could he go?"

"It's protocol." The portly ranger scowls.

The doctor stands very straight, staring down his nose at them. Apparently, he's had enough of these rangers and he's pulling rank.

"Then do it when he's in your custody. Not mine."

I'm surprised he's so protective of me, but I guess nursing someone back from death's door will do that, no matter my crimes. *Thank God for the Hippocratic oath.*

The doctor takes my elbow, steering me down the hall. "Come on, I'm going to see you to the dock."

The rangers follow, grumbling to each other. We make our way toward the elevator. As we walk, Haley turns into the hall before us. Her eyes widen, moving from me to the rangers and finally to the doctor, and her steps falter and stop.

She stares at me in silence. Her expression is too complicated to understand. I wish I could read the emotions swirling in her honey-colored eyes.

"I didn't know you were leaving today," she finally says.

All week she wouldn't talk to me, and now we've run out of time. The rangers behind us huff impatiently. The doctor watches our interaction with a patient smile.

There are so many things I want to say to Haley, so many things I want to do, but there's only one thing I can do.

"Can I at least say goodbye?" I ask the doctor, then glance back at the rangers.

The rangers huff again but don't object. The doctor says, "Of course."

He turns to the rangers. "Haley has been caring for him. Didn't leave his side all this month."

Haley blushes at that revelation. She didn't think I knew, but I felt her there. Her expression is a mixture of annoyance and regret. There are lots of things I regret, too. I'm probably going to regret this moment.

I step towards her and give her a hug.

At first, she resists, standing stiffly in my arms, but then she slowly relaxes, leaning into me. I hold her for a minute, breathing in the cherry scent of her hair. Then I bend my head to her ear and whisper, "I'm sorry, Haley. I'm sorry for everything I've done, and for what I'm going to do."

She tenses, lifting her head to look me in the eyes. My hands are behind her back, shielded from the rangers and the doctor. Extracting the scalpel from my sleeve, I hold it in my right hand. Then I run my left down Haley's arm until I find her hand, spinning her around and pulling her back against me, pinning her arm down with mine.

I press the scalpel to her neck as carefully as I can. I don't want to hurt her, but this is my only chance.

She whimpers and struggles against me. The rangers draw their guns, yelling, "Let her go!"

The doctor is aghast. "Jorden, please, don't do this."

Funny, considering that's exactly what Haley asked me before the explosion. If I didn't listen to her then, there's no way I'm listening to him now.

I press my mouth close to her ear.

"Don't move. I don't want to cut you." I hate doing this to her. She doesn't reply, trembling against me. I lock eyes with the rangers.

"Lower your weapons."

They don't, pointing them at both of us. The doctor glares, barking at them, "What are you doing? You're endangering an innocent girl."

They grimace, but persist. I retreat slowly, pulling

Haley with me until I hit the wall. The rangers follow, walking at the same pace.

"Back off! I mean it!" I cry and press down on the blade, just grazing Haley's neck. She gasps and the rangers stop.

With no more space behind me, I slide along the wall, pulling her with me, heading for the door separating the common area and the personnel area. It takes forever to reach. When we finally get there, I position us just in front of the panel.

"Open it," I order Haley. She tries to shake her head, but the pressure of the scalpel stops her. Her breathing is fast and her shoulders are shaking. Though she's trying to control it, her voice wavers.

"No. Go ahead. Kill me. I'm not letting you reach the pod deck a second time."

I want to laugh, and kiss her. She's so brave in this impossible situation. But I can't do either of those things, so I whisper in her ear, "Help me. I just want to get away."

Without looking at me, she retorts, "You have a knife to my neck and you want my help?"

"I don't want to hurt you, but you need to work with me."

She sets her jaw, refusing to answer. The rangers are around the bend, but the clock is ticking. Holding the knife in my teeth like a pirate, I use my free hand to grab her wrist and place her palm on the scanner. If she moves her head, this will end badly for one of us. She bucks, but the door beeps open. Grabbing the scalpel again, I press on the door and pull her through, slamming it behind us as I tug her over to the elevator. Sadly, I don't have time to be gentle.

"Do I have to do that again, or will you do it yourself?" I challenge, hoping she'll listen to reason.

She huffs, but places her hand on the scanner and the elevator opens. A siren wails, loud enough to make me flinch, alerting the station. There's nothing I can do about it now except pray that there's no one from security downstairs.

"You've triggered an alert. They're coming for you," she hisses. Her voice is low and angry.

I pull her into the elevator and press the key for the pod deck. The door whooshes shut and my mind conjures up the first time we kissed in the elevator. Back then, we were close in more ways than one. Now, even though I'm holding her to me, we've never been further apart. But I can't let go. Holding on to her is the only thing keeping me upright as my head spins. Haley is trembling, but her tense shoulders and the line of her jaw indicate she's also furious.

I lean back on the wall and close my eyes momentarily to get my head to stop spinning, concentrating on my breathing. Her body pressed to mine is so soft and warm, she fits in perfectly under my chin. After all this time I can finally hold her, but it's twisted, all wrong. If only things were different. I want to hold her, knowing she wants to be near me, instead of feeling her tremble in fear.

The speaker on the elevator crackles to life. "Haley?"

She moves forward, straining towards the control panel. I don't let her get far, but I lower the hand with the scalpel.

"Mom? Mom?" Her voice cracks.

"Please don't hurt my daughter," her mother's voice pleads from the wall, and I hate myself for being this person. "Where are you taking her? Don't hurt her. Please. She's all I've got."

I don't answer her.

The elevator reaches the bottom deck, and I resume my hold on the knife, expecting resistance. Exiting slowly, I push Haley in front of me, my back to the elevator, scanning the area. The rows of pods are below us. The damage from the explosion I caused is still evident. Scrapes and dents mark the walls where pieces of the exploding pod hit the cargo bay. Wondering which dent my head made makes me want to laugh.

"Where are we going?" Haley sounds calmer, more composed. Probably assuming I've trapped myself in a dead end, and her rescue is moments away.

As I walk her towards the stairs to the lower deck, Stacey and David emerge from the control room. Stacey looks grim as death. Since I knocked her out on the day of the attack, I'm not surprised that she glares daggers at me as she plants herself in our path.

"Why don't you let Haley go and face me?" she hisses.

"You know, I'm kinda busy right now, but I'd love to renew our acquaintance at another time."

Her expression suggests she's envisioning kicking me in the balls, or possibly in the head. I'm too dizzy to fight her, so I gesture with the scalpel.

"Haley has such a pretty face. Do you want it on your conscience if she ends up with a nasty scar?"

At first, I think Stacey won't yield, but Haley whimpers when I put pressure on the knife and Stacey retreats with a venomous glare, allowing me to get past her.

There's an unfamiliar sleek, black craft docked at the other end of the row, which I assume is the rangers' ship. I navigate the stairs carefully, holding Haley, taking my time as there's no immediate threat.

We're almost at the ship when the elevator opens, and a squad of armed men swarm out, followed closely by the two rangers, all aiming weapons at us. I'm forced to raise the scalpel to Haley's neck again.

The rangers step into the front line. "Where do you think you're going?" the bald ranger yells.

I gesture towards the black ship at my back.

"Yes, well," the tall ranger drawls, "You can't get in

there without clearance."

I chuckle. "Lucky for me, the two of you have it."

The ranger growls. It's *now or never*. I have to be convincing or I'll never escape.

"I'm not playing games," I snarl. "Come down here and give me access or I slit her throat."

Haley's knees almost give out. I grab onto her waist tighter. It kills me that she believes I'd hurt her, even though I'm trying my best *not* to hurt her.

The ranger huffs. "Try it, and you're dead before she hits the deck."

A man pushes to the front. His uniform and stance mark him as a high-ranking station official, possibly the captain.

"That's not an option," he barks at the ranger. "I won't risk Haley's life by continuing this standoff."

He turns to me. "If they open the ship, do you promise to let her go?"

I nod, knowing that once I let her go, nothing will prevent them from firing on the ship and destroying it.

"I'll let her go," I promise. *But I don't say when.*

The captain gestures to the bald ranger. "Get it open."

Baldy climbs down, taking his time to convey his irritation as he stomps towards us. Before opening the door, he sneers, "I'll catch you. No matter where you go. I'll hunt you down. That's a personal promise from me."

He can threaten but, by the time another ship arrives to pick them up, I'll be home safe.

Baldy disarms the craft security and the door hisses open. I step onto the door ramp.

"Let me go now," Haley's pleads, tension pouring off of her.

I take a deep breath. "I'm sorry, but I can't. Not yet."

Stepping back, I draw her onto the ship and slap the door button. The door slides closed with a sigh, sealing us in.

Once we're inside, I release Haley, slump into the control seat, and place the scalpel beside me as I check the flight computer. The ship's computer has a return course for Earth pre-programmed. All I'll need to do is take the ship off auto pilot before we arrive at the ranger base, and land somewhere else.

Haley stands frozen in place, breathing in short, ragged pants. She touches her neck gingerly, her fingers hovering over the scratches inflicted by my scalpel.

I swivel my chair to face her, and she flinches when I speak. "Sorry about your neck. I really didn't want to hurt you. All I wanted was to get away."

She exhales, her shoulders slumping, and examines our surroundings. "Genius move. Now we're trapped in here." *She smiles. Does she think I'm stupid?* "You're not going to get far in this thing. It's not a pod ship. You have to know how to fly a ranger vessel."

"I do," I say, and her mouth pops open in surprise. "You'd better sit down."

She crosses her arms and glares at me obstinately as I place a hand on the accelerator, but she knows enough about flying to realize she'll be thrown off her feet when the ship moves. When I don't relent, she plops into a seat and fastens her seatbelt.

What I don't tell her is that I've only ever done this in a simulator, which is painfully obvious as I scrape the side of the craft leaving the dock. Next, I ease the ship into the airlock chute, holding my breath till we're through. At least they haven't locked us in. They are probably worried they will endanger Haley if they annoy me. Keeping her with me was the right move.

Once we're out of the airlock, I position the craft according to the instructions on screen and accelerate. Once we're on route, I shift into auto pilot and lean back, running my fingers through my hair, feeling Haley's glare boring holes into my skull.

"How do you know how to fly this thing?" She sounds calmer and surprised.

"Part of my training."

"At terrorist school?"

So now she wants to talk about it? I don't face her, focusing on the controls.

"I didn't go to terrorist school."

"Sorry, terrorist boot camp," she corrects.

"I'm not a terrorist."

She snorts. "I'm sorry. What do you call it when a person tries to blow up a ship with families and little kids on it?"

She's right. Even though, in the end, my reasons changed. I won't say I was trying to protect her. Even if she hates me for it, that's my burden to carry.

"I had my reasons." Glancing over my shoulder, her expression flattens me. She's looking at me like I'm a monster, and I feel like one.

"We're not going to see eye to eye on this," I say softly. "Sometimes the cause justifies the means."

She regards me with contempt. "Sometimes it doesn't."

For a few minutes, she's silent. When she speaks again, her voice is curious and wary. "Where are we going?"

"Earth."

"What?" she gasps. "Don't do this. Take me back."

"I can't. I'm not going to jail."

"TAKE ME BACK!" Her fists clench, but she's trembling. I swivel around in my chair to face her.

"I'm sorry, but no."

Her lower lip trembles. "They know what you've done. The space station will notify ESC. They'll be waiting for you when you land. You can't escape."

"Actually, since we took the rangers' ship, unless more rangers turn up unexpectedly, they won't be waiting for us when we get to Earth. We'll have a head start."

Her eyes flash in defiance. "You keep saying 'we' like we're in this together. We aren't. You kidnapped me."

"I'm sorry, Haley, but you're in this with me now. I should never have told you who I really was."

"You didn't tell me. I figured it out," she snaps, then squares her shoulders, sitting up straighter. "And I told security everything. Who you really are, where you grew up, who your father is. They know all about you."

Her face is bold, but her eyes say otherwise. *No. I don't think she told anyone the full truth.* Did she tell them I kissed her, at the end, or has she kept that to herself as well? I stay silent while she glares at me like her gaze is going to burn a hole in my skull.

Eventually, she gives an exasperated yell and launches herself out of her chair. At first, I think she'll attack me, but she shoots by me in the low gravity, aiming for the small sleeping berth at the back of the cabin. When she gets there, she locks the door from inside. Locking me out. *So much for conversation.*

Good thing she didn't attack me. I wouldn't have stood a chance. Now that we're away, the adrenaline is draining out of my system, leaving me weak as a kitten. There's another sleeping berth on the other side of the cabin. I drag myself there, my head spinning from the exertion.

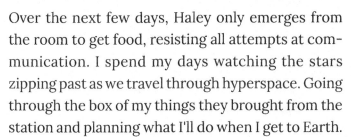

Over the next few days, Haley only emerges from the room to get food, resisting all attempts at communication. I spend my days watching the stars zipping past as we travel through hyperspace. Going through the box of my things they brought from the station and planning what I'll do when I get to Earth.

After a week, I can't take it anymore. The solitude is driving me mad, but even worse is seeing how much she hates me.

I've been giving her space, but enough is enough. The next time she comes out to use the food printer, I step in front of her, blocking her path as she heads back to her room.

She gives me a look that could kill. "Move," she hisses.

I plant my feet and stare her in the eyes. "I need to talk to you."

"Well, I don't need to talk to you. I did all my talking when you were unconscious. It was very therapeutic." It's true. Though I can't remember what she said, I heard her voice when I was sleeping. I grin, and her expression darkens. "What's so funny?!" she fumes.

"Not funny. Sweet. You talked to me."

"It was the doctor's idea. Give him the credit." She huffs. She's holding a steaming hot bowl of spaghetti and she looks so angry I'm worried she'll throw it at me.

"Okay, will you sit down? Or at least put down the food?"

"What for? What's the point?" she sighs, her shoulders drooping.

"The point is, I want to apologize for everything."

Her eyebrows crinkle quizzically. "For kidnapping me?"

"That too." My list of offenses keeps getting longer.

She shakes her head. "Don't bother. Really. I don't want to hear it. Nothing can excuse the things you did."

"You're right, but I'll feel better if I apologize."

Standing in her way is just causing the opposite effect. So, I sit down. I want her to listen. She sets the bowl down near the door and stands in front of me, her hands on her hips. I take a breath, but she holds up a finger and I wait.

"How can I believe you? Everything you did from the moment you met me was a lie. Manipulating Dawn, getting her to lie to me, too. Poisoning people. You destroyed Nano—" her breath shudders, and a tear runs down her cheek. She gulps and stares at the deck, scuffing her shoe. Taking a deep breath, she peeks at me from under her hair, barely meeting my eyes. "We were going to leave together.

I thought I meant something to you. I thought—"
She stops, turning her back to me, her shoulders
shaking. "Do you have any idea how much you hurt
me?"

Rising from my seat, I cross over to her. Taking her
elbows, I turn her towards me. Brushing the hair out
of her eyes with the tip of my finger, I use my thumbs
to wipe away the tears pooling in the corners of her
eyes, lifting her chin gently so I can catch her eyes
with mine.

"You meant everything to me. You still do," I whisper.

Her breath catches. Gazing into my eyes like she's
trying to see the depths of my being, to glimpse the
truth beneath my words. Her eyes shimmer with an
ocean of hope and pain.

I take a breath. "Which is why I couldn't let you
come with me. Because I knew I'd have to destroy
the jump ship."

She falters. "But why? Why go through with it?
If we were leaving together? We could have had a
fresh start on New Horizons. Get away from it all.
You didn't have to do it anymore."

"I didn't want to, but Nancy, Dawn's mother,
threatened to hurt you if I aborted the mission," I
blurt out the detail I hadn't meant to tell her. Her
eyes go wide.

"Nancy was involved?" She shakes her head. "Why
would she threaten me? What did I ever do to her?"

"Because she knew how I felt about you. How I really felt about you. She knew I'd do anything to stop her from hurting you again."

She studies me for a few seconds. Then her hand reaches out, caressing my cheek. I lean into her touch, starving for any affection.

"Oh, Jorden," she whispers. "You were going to die and kill all those people to save me?"

"I —" I begin, but falter.

Her brow creases. "Let's say that's the truth this time, and I believe you. Did you really think I'd want you to sacrifice them all for me? For you to die too? That's insane."

"No. I know you wouldn't, but I couldn't make any other choice." I place my palm on hers. "Is there any way you can forgive me? That I can earn your trust again?"

"How can I ever trust you? After what you did." Her voice breaks.

"I know. You're right. But I won't stop trying." I stand and draw her into my arms, holding her close, praying she believes me. "From now on, I promise you. No more secrets, no more lies."

For a moment she lets me hold her, standing stiffly in my arms, but then she recoils, pushing me away, shaking her head.

"No. Don't touch me. Don't you dare." Her face reddens and fresh tears brim in her eyes. "You've lied to me so many times... I don't know what's true any more. Even if what you just told me is true, Jorden. The truth is even worse."

She backs away from me. "Sorry. I'm not here to make up. I'm your hostage, forced to be here till we reach Earth, but I want nothing more to do with you. Don't talk to me, don't touch me. Leave me alone."

With that, she grabs the bowl of food she'd put down and locks herself in the room again.

Chapter 5

PASS THE POPCORN

Haley

My mind doesn't believe him, but my heart does.

Over the next two weeks, I gradually relax my guard. Keeping to myself was driving me crazy. Once we entered hyperspace, we lost contact with the station and my comm stopped working. I've never been cut off from everything like this. Luckily, when Jorden grabbed me, I was carrying my bag with my art things. So, I sit and draw mindlessly to pass the time, and a face emerges on the paper. His face.

I stare at it for a few moments and then crumple it up.

Walking over to the door, I open it just a crack. He's sitting at the console, staring out into space. Holding the necklace with the tiny globe dangling from it. As I watch, he spins the globe with his fingertips.

He doesn't know I'm watching him. His face is unguarded like it was when he was asleep. He looks so lost, so alone. I slide down to the floor and lean my head near the crack to watch him. After a few minutes, he glances towards my room, as if he can feel me watching, and I duck away.

Over the next few days, I venture out more, lingering.

I've been listening from my room as he uses the ship's entertainment center. I can hear the voices, but I can't really follow and I'm so sick of being bored and of denying myself just to punish him. The next time I leave my room, I dawdle, watching over his shoulder.

Without turning around, he says, "You may as well sit down."

I'd give him a gruff reply, but I'm tired of being in my room all the time. So, I sit off to the side where he can't see me and watch the rest of the movie. There are parts I can't help laughing and he peeks over his shoulder at me, smiling.

It's hard to laugh and be mad, but I still scowl at

him.

When the film finishes, I retreat into my room.

The next day, I come out as soon as I hear voices. We still don't talk, but the air is clearing.

The day after, instead of voices, the smell of popcorn fills the ship. I stifle a laugh. Next comes a little tap at the door. When I emerge, there's a bowl of popcorn where I usually sit. Jorden is facing the screen, not looking at me, but he's grinning.

It's a friendly gesture. Pity he's such a sweet, manipulative, lying, murderous, good-looking bastard, who's making it harder for me to hate him like I should. As a reminder, I touch the scratches from his knife on my neck, now almost healed. My smile falters, but I sit down and pick up the popcorn.

No use in letting good food go to waste.

Over the upcoming days, we develop little routines. Jorden is following my rules to the letter. He doesn't talk to me or touch me. Just coaxes me out like a timid kitten, offering snacks and entertainment, using my need for company against me. It's like a game we're playing. I set these rules and I'll determine when they change.

I'm not scared of him. Though, I don't know why,

because I can still feel the edge of the scalpel on my neck when I close my eyes. But even stronger than that, I feel the press of his body holding me against him. He could have been rough, but he wasn't. He could have hurt me, but he didn't. I've been with him for over two weeks and he hasn't touched me.

We must be approaching Earth by now. Does he know how to land this ship? He got us out of the dock and on route, but that's the easy part.

Examining the complex controls, I quickly realize the ship's computer requires programming. If we're using the pre-plotted course, it will bring us to a predestined location, the ranger base, which will end badly for Jorden. Landing anywhere else requires rerouting or setting down manually.

"Where do you plan to land?" my voice rasps. I haven't used it in weeks.

Jorden lifts his head in surprise, sitting up in his chair with evident relief. "She speaks."

"Yeah, well. I need to know where you're going," I gulp. "So, I can figure out how to get home from there."

His face floods with guilt. Home isn't just far away. Three years will have passed by the time I return.

Hyperspace travel is only fast for those in the craft. Outside, time crawls by as usual. When we land, we'll have been gone eighteen months in space station time. My parents will have been missing me for a year and a half. In the outside world, I'd be eighteen and a half. Instead, I'm turning 17 in a few weeks.

Jorden scratches his neck. "Well, there are a few problems. The ship will drop out of hyperspace in the next couple of days. Then we have another day or so into Earth's orbit. They programmed the ship to land at the ESC base, but I'll try to divert it." He doesn't say where. I guess he doesn't trust me enough.

I fix him with a steady look. "Do you know how?"

"Yeah, sure..." His grin falters, "I think."

I raise my eyebrows.

"Well, worst-case scenario, you know how to fly," he continues optimistically.

Is he mad? "I fly a cargo pod. They don't have navigation systems. All you do is accelerate, turn, stop. You don't need to plot a course or find coordinates."

He wrinkles his nose at me. "Okay then, I guess I should find the control manual."

"It isn't funny. We can crash and die!" I yell. He nods, but he's still smiling. I want to punch him. "I thought you learned this craft in sim."

He shrugs. "Yeah, but that was mostly maneuvering. It was a while back and now all the instructions are muddled together in my brain. You know, I had a head injury."

"I'm about to give you another one," I mutter as I sit and put my feet up on the seat next to me. "Great. I'm going to die because you weren't paying attention in class."

Jorden stifles a grin as he skims the information on the ship's computer till he locates the instruction manual. I relocate to the co-pilot's seat, so I can see the screen, and he raises his eyebrows.

"What?" I say. "I'm going to learn how to land. Did you think I'd leave it up to you? My life is on the line here, too."

Jorden shrugs. So we figure out how to set up the computer to find our location and calculate our speed and trajectory. Eventually, he'll have to share where we're going, but he's not sharing just yet. Jorden picks the navigation stuff up quickly. I always knew he was smart, not just a pretty face. There are some concepts I'm more familiar with, from my studies on the station, so I explain them and soon we're chatting freely, even laughing. I keep forgetting to stay mad at him.

At some point I look up from the screen and he's gazing at me intently, his face inches away from mine. I blush and drop my arm.

He opens his mouth as if he wants to say something or do something but I swivel my chair away, putting distance between us. "Okay, well, we made some progress today. I'm going to rest, and we can pick this up tomorrow."

Nodding, he gives me a tender smile as I flee to my room and shut the door, taking deep breaths to calm my racing heart.

The next day, we're in the final stages of programming, working on the formula to calculate our approach speed, when the ship's computer springs to life.

"Hyperspace terminus reached. Prepare to decrease velocity," it announces.

It's the closest point to Earth we can go at this speed. From here, the ship will decelerate, taking another day to reach Earth. It's the last leg of our flight, and the most critical one. Landing on Earth isn't like maneuvering in space: we'll need to take into account winds and terrain, other aircraft, and possibly law enforcement waiting to intercept us.

Jorden grips the back of the chair, his knuckles white. "Now we'll see if they managed to get a message through," he says.

If they have, it's bad for him and good for me. A rescue attempt might be in the works. Though if they push him, it could end poorly for me, too.

As the vessel decelerates, the stars stop zipping past and we re-enter normal space. I gasp at my first glimpse of Earth. It hangs above us, filling half the window like a bright blue, green, and white ball floating in space. It looks close enough to touch, even though we're still at least a day away. I walk up to the window, staring in wonder.

Jorden joins me, the Earth reflected in his eyes. Just for now, I let myself touch his shoulder and say, "It's so beautiful."

He smiles, his eyes shining brightly. "Yes, it is. I can't believe I'm seeing it again."

It's such a gift to see this. I'd thank him for bringing me here, but I can't. Not under these conditions. Instead, I take his hand. He squeezes back and we stand there, watching Earth grow nearer.

The ship's com squawks and we both jump, then laugh. We're being hailed by Earth control.

"Vessel 1910-SZ4, please come in."

Jorden sits at the control panel and responds to the call. He sounds completely professional as he answers, "This is vessel 1910-SZ4."

"Please confirm your trajectory."

His speech sounds formal and military as he replies without hesitation, "Vessel 1910-SZ4 on route to Peterson Air Force Base, Colorado Springs."

"Confirmed. Vessel 1910-SZ4, you may proceed."

They don't know we aren't the rangers assigned to this vessel. They aren't waiting for us yet.

"What's at Colorado Springs?" I ask.

"Well," he grins. "Colorado Springs is where NO-RAD and the Air Force Space Command headquarters are located."

"Is that where we're going?"

He looks very pleased with himself. "Of course not. We're going home to the Farm."

"Well, won't they notice when we veer off instead of landing there?"

"They won't have much time, all things considered." He lowers his voice conspiratorially, even though we're the only ones here. "The Farm is right under their noses. On the only land still safe from development. In the Colorado national park."

Now that we're out of hyperspace, we can reset the computer. Jorden takes charge of manually flying the craft towards Earth as I cancel the preset coordinates and take the ship off auto pilot.

The maps of Earth in the ship's database help me pinpoint our new coordinates. Jorden points to a location on the map, just north of Boulder, Colorado.

"That's the best place to touch down. Any farther east, and we'll have to go through the city."

"The city of Boulder?" I grin. Such a funny name

for a city. Calling it a rock.

"Well, the entire area east of the Rockies is now the Denver metroplex. Spanning from Boulder through Denver and past what used to be Colorado Springs." That means nothing to me, and my expression must convey my cluelessness. "It's big. Over 1000 miles of solid metropolitan area. And it's still small compared to other cities nowadays."

"Okay, so let's land on the right side of the city." I examine him curiously. "Is the farm far from the city?"

He smiles. "Kind of, the whole point is that we're off the grid. It's hidden. Only a handful of people live outside of cities nowadays. It's too expensive, and since the corporations took over, there are no municipal services out there. Homes must be totally autonomous. It's just super rich folk and subversives like us."

"But how did you get permission to live in a national park?"

He smiles mysteriously. "My dad has connections with pull and money. That's all I know. You'd be surprised how many people support us. Even inside what's left of the federal government."

Talking about the Earthers makes me uncomfortable. It's obvious he still thinks they're the good guys. Meanwhile, outside the windows, the shapes of continents appear, coated in an almost unbroken swath of twinkling lights. The black area around them must be the oceans.

As we enter the ionosphere, we're surrounded by vibrant swaths of red and green, purple and yellow light emanating from the upper atmosphere. It looks like a tenuous bubble of light that closely encases the entire planet. We breach the atmosphere and the colors fade from the black of space to navy, gradually brightening into the most amazing blue I've ever seen. It's breathtaking.

The descent is going okay when the comm hails us. "Vessel 1910-SZ4, please come in."

Jorden gives me a puzzled look and presses the call button.

"This is vessel 1910-SZ4."

"This is Earth Space Command. Your trajectory indicates you are off course and headed to an unidentified location. Please confirm your trajectory."

We exchange glances. Jorden whispers to me, "Do you have the coordinates we used?"

I shake my head.

"Negative ESC, we're on our planned course," he responds.

"Your instruments must be malfunctioning. Don't worry, we'll override and guide you in."

"Can they do that?" I whisper.

Apparently, they can. Our computer screen changes and the course trajectory shifts slightly. Jorden gets up and starts fumbling beneath the control panel.

"What are you doing?" I hiss at him.

"I'm going to disconnect the computer and reboot it. Maybe we can break free."

"Are you insane? Everything will go offline."

"Well, I just want to disconnect the flight-control software that manages entry and landing."

"Wait. According to the flight plan, we still have at least twenty minutes to reach our destination. Don't kill the computer until we're much lower. Then, even if you can't reboot, we have a chance to glide down manually."

He gives me a nervous nod.

We watch the computer as the clock ticks down. When there are five minutes left to go, I nod to Jorden.

"Take the controls."

Fumbling underneath the control panel, I yank the cables we think are the right ones. Everything goes dark and the sound of engines disappears. For a moment, it's like we're suspended on air, before the craft tilts sideways and we plummet. I grab for the console as I'm knocked away, lunging for the cables I unplugged in the dark. Luckily, there's daylight coming through the windshield.

"Haley? Have you got it?" Jorden's voice crackles with tension.

Lying under the control panel to reconnect the cables, I grope frantically, hoping I don't electrocute myself, and eventually find the empty socket. Nothing happens. The ship's list is more pronounced now, and gravity reaches up to snatch us and smash us into the ground. I push the socket harder and, with a *bop*, the computer's power returns. The computer is restarting itself. It's been less than a minute, but it feels longer.

The lights are still off. Jorden yells, "Haley, sit down and put your harness on."

I dash to the closest chair and fumble with my harness, trying to close it before we hit the ground.

The systems are rebooting, but we're out of time. The craft skims low over the trees, but we're losing altitude as we careen towards the side of a mountain. Jorden tries to pull up, slowing our descent and straightening the craft, but the steering is stiff and unresponsive. The front window fills with green and brown. There's nothing we can do; we're going to hit.

The computer blares, "Proximity alert, proximity alert," as if we're blind and can't see the ginormous hill right in front of us.

We're out of time.

The front of the craft collides with the ground and the rear end rises. We're both thrown forward in our seats. The harnesses should hold us in place, but I haven't done mine up properly and it flies open. I tumble out with a scream, just barely grabbing the edge of the harness.

If I let go, I'll fly across the cabin into the imploding glass from the shattered windows. The fabric is slipping through my hand, rubbing it raw as I struggle to hold on. My other hand is flailing. I'm going to fall.

There's movement on my right as Jorden hurtles out of his seat, grabbing me before I fall. His momentum, combined with the movement of the craft, rolls us both to the side of the cabin. Grabbing the cargo webbing, he pins me to the wall and covers me, his elbows on each side of my head, protecting me with his body as loose objects fly around us. A piece of metal hits him like a projectile, leaving a bloody gash on his forearm and cheek. He gasps, but holds on. If we make it through this, we'll need to find something to stop the bleeding.

I can't see what's happening from my position between him and the wall, but I feel the impact. Something is burning. Meanwhile, the craft is crumpling as it rolls, smashing into the ground repeatedly. Jorden struggles to hang on, his muscles contracting. So, I grab hold of his shirt, pulling him closer, lending him support with all the strength I can muster.

It feels like we're being shaken to bits as the craft rolls down the mountainside, bouncing off trees and rocks, until I can't feel anything but vibrations.

The craft slows and finally comes to a stop. The deafening sound fading to an ominous creaking.

We're alive. Unbelievably.

The craft is on its side at an angle, and Jorden

is lying on top of me. His head hangs down over my shoulder, his breath ghosting over my neck, the warmth of his body on mine. I'm shaking, still trembling from the impact.

I can't breathe. I'm not sure if it's because of having my lungs rattled out of my chest, the dust and smoke in the air, because he's crushing me, or just because he's so close.

After he's sure we've stopped moving, he exhales and pushes up on his elbows. Some of the pressure releases and I can breathe easier.

I draw in a deep lungful, but my breath catches when I look up and see Jorden hovering above me, his eyes seeking mine. His face is so near that if I just push up...

It would be so easy to stop fighting the way I feel. Just allow the fragments of my heart straining towards him to take control.

Locked in his gaze, I stare at his lips for far too long. Imagining wrapping my hand around the back of his neck, pulling him down to me and kissing him. Forgiving everything he's done, forgetting everything he is.

I place my palm on his chest, feeling his heart hammer furiously.

If I think about it any longer, I'll do it, but I can't.

I *mustn't*.

Instead, I push up, pushing him away.

"Get off me," I snap in a fit of sudden annoyance,

as fear and adrenaline from the crash wash over me. Brimming over with annoyance at myself, at all the things I want but can't have. And annoyed at him for the same reasons.

He rolls off me at once, looking surprised by my reaction. "I was just trying to protect you."

"Well, I wouldn't need protection if you hadn't kidnapped me," I add.

It's a bitchy thing to say, especially since he just risked himself to save my life. As soon as I say the words, I regret them. Jorden looks as if I kicked him in the gut. He shakes his head and turns away from me.

I should say, "I'm sorry," or, "Thank you for saving me." Instead, I stare at him silently as he picks his way out of the ruined ship.

As he leaves, he stops to pull something from the ruined control panel and smash it. It's the ship's tracker. If they didn't ping us as we went down, they won't be able to use it to trace us now.

There goes my chance for rescue.

Chapter 6

Dangerous Paths

Jorden

I pick my way out of the wreckage of the craft and look around to get my bearings. We're on the side of a mountain somewhere. The crash cut a swath down the hillside; hopefully, it will be at least partly obscured by the trees, but it will be dark soon and then the burning wreckage will be visible from afar.

Haley emerges from the ship, dusting herself off. She's holding a rag that used to be one of my shirts.

"Let me see to your arm," she orders.

I hiss as she touches my forearm, surprised to see an ugly, bleeding scratch. When did that happen? Then she pats my cheek with the cloth and it comes away bloody. I take the cloth from her.

"It's okay," I mutter. "Let me do it."

I don't know how to act around her after she

pushed me away moments after landing. Everything was fine the past few days and now she's suddenly mad at me again. Whatever reminded her of my past actions will probably stand between us forever.

"Don't be stupid," she frowns, staring at the cloth instead of me. "I'll go get a first aid kit, or at least some water, to wash the wound." She returns to the ship, but everything is busted up and ruined. Bending, she lifts something.

"Do you want your scalpel back?" she calls, her tone deadpan.

A minute ago, I saved her, and now she's so angry. It's almost as if she's angry *because* I saved her. I try to catch her eye.

"Why are you being like this?" I ask.

Without looking at me, she keeps on rummaging and replies in a singsong rhythm, "You know why. I can't trust you. You kidnapped me..."

I throw my palms up in frustration. My hands itch to grab her and make her listen or, preferably, kiss her until she remembers how good we were together.

Instead, I take a deep breath and walk back to the ship to help. There's no sign of a first aid kit, but I find a small bubble of water and hand it to her.

Haley nods at me. "Sit down."

I obey and perch on a rock jutting out of the hillside next to the wreck. She wets the cloth, squeezing lightly on the side of the bubble to extract the moisture, and dabs at my cheek. It hurts a bit, but I don't move. She exhales, so close that her breath glides softly on my cheek. I'm dying to reach out and pull her to me, but I hold still.

Not looking me in the eye, she mutters, "Thank you. For grabbing me when we crashed."

I peek at her out of the corner of my eye, stifling a smile, but my mouth quirks up on one side despite my effort. She punches me on the uninjured arm, scolding, "Stop looking so pleased with yourself."

I can't help it. This is progress. She gives me a tiny smile and cleans out the wound on my arm, dressing it by wrapping it with a sleeve torn off one of my shirts. When she's done, she nods. "That's as good as I can do right now."

"Thanks."

She pushes her hair back behind her ear. "We should find something to disinfect it. Are we going into the city?" Ha. Sneaky. She's trying to get more information.

"We need to get out of these woods first and find transportation. I need to figure out which side of the city we're on." To be honest, I'm not sure exactly where we are. There are no landmarks. "Come on, we should go downhill."

I lead and Haley follows as we push through the trees, heading downhill. It's moderately cold, so it's probably late March or early April. I try to wrap my brain about the fact it's been three years since I last set foot on Earth.

We emerge onto a crag overlooking the forest where we can see for miles. An amazing vista spreads out before us. A valley stretches out below, a river winding through it dwindling into a lake in the distance. The sun has begun its descent and the mountains are lit by a fiery blaze, reflected in the clouds and in the lake, coating them all with a dusting of gold. Farther away, snowy peaks tower over the valley, while wildflowers dot the lower slopes amid vibrant, green grass.

I couldn't have chosen a more perfect spot for Haley's first view of Earth.

She clutches my arm, her eyes widening.

Stopping, I take a deep breath. My first fresh air since I left. The air up here is untainted by the pollution from the cities. It's marvelous, fragrant, and fresh.

"What's wrong with the sky?" Haley asks, gripping my arm. "It looks like it's burning."

"It's the sunset."

Her eyes widen. "Oh. I've never seen one before." I cover her hand in mine, watching with her as her eyes widen in wonder. I'm so lucky to be by her side for these firsts. "It's like my sim on the station..." she adds, "but it's real and all those flowers."

"In the past they'd bloom around May, but their seasons changed as the earth warmed."

She shrugs. "It's still beautiful."

The last glimmers of sunlight shine on the grass, which is peppered with tiny yellow flowers. Gently, I slip my arm around her waist. She glances at me but doesn't object. It just feels right as we stand there, watching the perfect sunset. I breathe it all in, enjoying the mountain air, having Haley in my arms, and knowing I'm finally home.

We make our way down the steep mountain in the fading light. I offer Haley my hand as we descend at a sharp angle, bracing our heels to avoid sliding down the incline. We slither from tree to tree, supporting ourselves on the trunks jutting up out of the hillside.

Haley's breathing in big gulps. It's the first sign of altitude sickness. Eventually she'll get dizzy and suffer headaches. I've lived here most of my life, but she's used to the controlled environment of the space station.

We need to get lower, fast.

I stop and turn, planting my back to a tree, and Haley slides from the tree above into my arms. She exhales, looking up at me, her cheeks flushed.

"How are you doing?" I ask.

She bobs her head. "I'm okay, why?"

"The air pressure at this altitude is different. Your

body gets less oxygen with each lungful."

"Maybe t-that's why I'm having t-trouble... catching my b-breath." She leans against me. I feel her heartbeat racing.

"Let me know if you need a rest, okay?"

"Shouldn't we try to g-get... as far as p-possible... from the crash site... before they c-come... to investigate?" She has a point, but I don't want her to overdo it. It took her four breaths to finish the sentence.

"We can spare a minute."

She nods and takes another big breath, her cheek resting against my chest. I focus on breathing slowly, wishing I could synchronize her breathing with mine. After a minute, she pushes herself upright again. "Okay. Let's go."

We continue our descent in the gloaming. The warmth in the air evaporates, along with the sunlight. Visibility narrows to a few feet. I grasp Haley's hand, afraid of losing her in the dark. After what seems like ages of stumbling in the dark, the hillside flattens and we stumble out onto a road.

Haley looks up at the sky and smiles. "Hey. Stars. I missed them."

Under the trees I could barely see her but, here, she's wrapped in starlight, the depth of space reflected in the depth of her eyes. Her lips are bluish in the moonlight.

"Are you cold?" I don't wait for her answer. Taking

off my shirt, I wrap it around her and she gives me the most beautiful smile. Left in only a t-shirt, my skin erupts in goosebumps as the night air hits it, but I'm warmed by her smile. She touches my arm.

"What about you?"

I'm cold, but I'd rather know she's warm.

"I'll survive. Once I spent the entire night outside, shirtless."

"What? Didn't you freeze?"

"I did. But there's a point where you can't feel it anymore."

Her eyes crinkle with concern. What would she think if she heard the whole story? Then I see car lights picking their way down the hill towards us. I freeze.

"Someone's coming," I say.

"What do we do?" Haley is looking at me as if I'm in charge.

"We need to get down the mountains and some-where warm, but they may be the people who are looking for us." I don't have a good explanation for our presence here. Improperly dressed, with no equipment. But we need help.

Before I can stop her, Haley walks into the middle of the road, holding her hands up to the oncoming vehicle. Luckily, it slows and stops close by, its head-lights blinding me momentarily. A window hums open, but I can't see the speaker.

"What y'all doing up here, darlin'?" a male voice

calls out.

"Um..." Haley glances back at me, unsure what to say, "my friend and I are lost. Could we get a ride with you?"

The car is a fantastically expensive luxury vehicle, low riding with huge side rims. Equipped with both auto drive and self-drive modes. Not surprising, as most people who can afford to live in the mountains are filthy rich and eccentric.

The driver seems to be in his forties, balding, with expensive clothes and a hungry look in his eyes. The type of guy who stops for a girl by herself on the road, but not for a couple. He eyes me with distaste. He couldn't see me in the shadows of the trees before he stopped.

"You look kind of familiar, son," he drawls.

Yep. Hard to be incognito with your father's face plastered all over the news.

Haley laughs. "He gets that all the time. He just has one of those faces."

The man hesitates, but then he smiles. It's not a very nice smile. The back door swings upwards with a hiss.

"Sure thing. You and your boyfriend can get in the back. Sorry, if it's tight. These cars don't have much in the way of a back seat." He sounds smug, not sorry in the least.

Haley blurts, "Oh, he's not—" I raise my eyebrows at her in warning, because we shouldn't explain our relationship to this guy on a dark, abandoned road. Her voice trails off, but it's too late. He heard her. "Um, thanks," she mumbles and moves towards the back.

He grins, his teeth glinting unnaturally white in the moonlight, obviously implants. "Oh, well, if he's not your boyfriend, why don't you come sit here by me then, sugar?" He pats the seat next to him.

Haley has zero street smarts, growing up on the station, but even she can tell a creep when she sees one.

Haley freezes like a doe in the headlights but I take her arm, guiding her into the back seat and sliding in next to her. The guy turns around in his seat, glaring at me.

"It's fine, mister. She's fine back here." I speak softly, gearing myself for action if this turns into a problem. He hasn't closed the door yet. What is he waiting for? What have we gotten ourselves into?

"Why don't you let the little lady speak for herself, pal?" He almost spits out the last word.

Haley's eyes widen, aware she made a mistake. The back seat is tiny. I barely have room for my legs but, instead of trying to get further away from me, she curls into me, putting her head on my shoulder. Ignoring the driver, she murmurs, "I'm still cold," in a pampered baby voice. *Clever girl.* I put my arm around her, cuddling her to me.

Turbo megabucks guy makes a disgusted sound

and faces the front again, pressing the door button. As soon as the door slides closed, he picks up speed, zipping down the mountain in sullen silence.

Haley peeks up at me. I laugh silently in relief and wrap my other arm around her, too.

We wind down the mountain. The GPS screen indicates we're nearing a town, but Turbo stops before we reach it, next to a lonely cottage on the side of the hill. I'm just warming up and I don't feel like getting out into the cold again, but it looks like this is all the ride we're getting. The back door slides up and cold air pours in, making my skin prickle.

Haley lifts her head, blinking at our surroundings. "Where are we?"

The guy barely looks around, all his attempts at charm gone.

"This is the park ranger station. If you're lost, they can radio your folks and get you back to your camp-site."

That makes sense. No point in protesting, so we scoot out of the back seat.

"Thanks," Haley says as she gets out, but he scowls.

"Not your boyfriend, huh?"

She shrugs, "It's complicated."

I can't keep the grin off my face as I say, "Thanks for the ride."

He ignores me and peels out of there, tires raising dust in the road.

"Well, he was nice," Haley says as we both laugh.

"We're near a town," I say, pointing at the lights on the hill below us. She turns to the lighted cabin behind her.

"Why not go into the ranger station?"

"And say what?"

Her smile fades. "Jorden, what are we doing? You're back on Earth. Let me go. I need to go home. I don't belong here."

I shake my head. "Sorry, but I can't let you go. You know too much. You could tell them everything they need to catch me before I get back."

"No, I won't. I promise. I won't." Her voice drops to a whisper. "I didn't tell them any of the things you told me on the station. About your home and your dad. They don't know who you are. I'm not sure why, but I didn't."

I believe her, but I can't let her go yet.

Shaking my head again, I say, "I'm sorry."

Her fists clench and she turns her back on me. I'm the monster again. The night just got colder.

"We've got to go." Moving to her side, I take her hand. She doesn't pull away, but her hand in mine is stiff, unyielding.

The clump of houses below us is only a short walk away. Lights are on in the homes, but the streets are empty. Haley's face is dark and her silence is grating. I hope she doesn't run. She must have assumed I'd let her go as soon as we landed.

I don't have a plan. I just know I can't let her go till I'm home safe.

My arms are going numb by the time we're between the houses. If I can't find a self-drive car, I'll steal something, but I'd rather not. City dwellers don't have cars, but there must be people here staying in vacation units. To my relief, we soon find a transit station with four self-drive cars charging in the sockets. We have self-drive cars on the Farm, so this is familiar territory for me.

I press my wrist to the door panel on the nearest one. The panel glows green and the doors slide open. Haley glares at me as I walk her around to the passenger seat, watching her closely. If she's going to run, it will be now. But she's quiet as she slides into the passenger seat, hugging herself, shivering with cold, and turns away from me. I slide down her door before entering the driver's side.

The car has GPS, so it's easy to program a route to the city. We'll have to drive most of the night to reach the outskirts. I'm cold, hungry and beginning to feel feverish, but the thing that cuts me like a knife is the coldness that's crept back into her eyes.

Chapter 7

The Blue Penguin

Haley

Jorden's head is drooping.

We've been driving most of the night. He pulls it up once more with a start, moments before we veer off the road, and turns to me.

"I have to rest."

A blue sign flashes at the side of the road and Jorden pulls into a large, flat, paved expanse. Two cars sit at the far end of a tall, narrow building, three levels high. The long structure spans the length of the lot, with stairways at the end and walkways along the front. On the side, a flashing sign proclaims, "Blue Penguin Auto Sleep Booths," with a happy blue penguin waddling side to side next to the words.

The way he's wobbling when he gets out his side and walks around the car, Jorden reminds me of a penguin. A big, blond penguin. He opens my door and takes my arm, firmly.

"Come on," he's swaying on his feet, eyes trying to shut, but he's keeping them open by sheer force of will. A good shove would probably knock him over, but then where would I go? We're in the middle of nowhere. I don't know how to operate the car. He started it with a touch of his wrist, so I'd need an implant to use it.

I don't know who to call, or how to operate surface comms. Do they even have comms here? My station comm bracelet is now a useless decoration.

Grudgingly, I let him guide me out of the car and over to a compartment on the ground level. They're all lit up green, except for one at the very far end and one in the middle of the top level. If I scream, will the occupants hear me? Will they come to my aid?

As if sensing my thoughts, Jorden leans close to me, wobbling with fatigue and whispers, "Quiet."

I'm quiet.

He presses his wrist to the panel on the compartment door and codes in a number on the dial pad.

"What's that?" I ask.

"My chip, it holds my information and credits."

I wonder what kind of world makes you pay someone for a place to sleep. The door whooshes open and he guides me inside, locking it with another touch of his wrist. Inside, the cramped room is about the size of my bedroom on the station. The compartment has three steep steps down to a tiny lavatory and wash area. Thankfully, it looks clean. The top of the compartment is a wall-to-wall bed, about four feet wide. Jorden guides me up a short ladder to a wide pallet that can sleep two, as long as they don't mind being crammed together. I mind, but I'm not being given a choice.

The pallet is soft and well padded. I sit on the edge and slip my shoes off, dropping them to the floor beside the entrance, and slide in feet forward. There isn't much space above the bed, barely enough to sit up, so I lie on my stomach, my head on my arms, watching him.

Jorden discards his shoes, leaving on his pants and the plain gray t-shirt. He must be cold. I'm still wearing his shirt. I'm being selfish, but I'm mad at him and he can freeze for all I care. He brushes against me as he slides in to the bed but, instead of cold, his body radiates heat. I think he might be feverish.

The situation triggers a memory of the night we slept together in his bed after I taught him to fly the cargo pod. When I couldn't bear being parted from him. Before he slashed out my heart with an ice pick.

I keep my eyes on him in case he gets any ideas, but his head drops to the pallet at once and soon his breathing slows, his chest rising and falling. For a few moments, I watch him sleep. Then I test my theory of a fever by touching his forehead with the back of my hand, then my lips.

The wound he got when we crashed is probably infected, because he's burning up. I'd get him medicine, but I have no idea where or how. Can I even open the compartment door by myself? There's nothing I can do right now, except hope he survives the night.

I turn my back to him, cradling my head on my arm. It's not as cold as it is outside, but I'm still not warm enough. Then an arm creeps over me in the dark, pressing me into his warm body, as he snuggles close. I tense, but his even breaths tell me he's asleep, hugging me to him as if it's the most natural thing in the world.

The plus side is that I'm not cold anymore. Delicious warmth envelopes me, and I allow myself to enjoy it for a minute before I push him away.

Meanwhile, I drift off to sleep.

Chapter 8

BURNING UP

Jorden

I wake up holding her. She's fast asleep under my arm, curled into me like she belongs there and, for a few minutes, I don't move. I just lie there, breathing in the scent of her hair, holding her with my heart quivering like a bird that could take flight at any moment. Running my fingers down the side of her neck, barely touching, she stirs, leaning back sleepily into my shoulder.

"Good morning," I whisper.

It takes another minute before her eyelids flutter open. The change as she realizes where she is, and who she's with, is heart-wrenching. One moment she's leaning against me, the next she stiffens and rolls away, back to the wall, as far away as she can get in the cramped space. Facing me, her eyes are wide and fearful, as if she just realized her mistake.

I sigh, dragging my fingers through my hair. There's nothing to be done. She's here against her will, and she knows who I am and what I did. It's my own stupid fault for confessing the truth when I thought I was going to die. I hate treating her like my prisoner, but refusing to let her go last night shattered the tiny acorn of trust that had grown back between us.

"Good morning," I try again.

Haley takes a breath and relaxes, releasing some of her apparent tension by stretching and running her fingers through the tangles in her hair. She gives me a tiny smile.

"Good morning," she answers. Leaning forward, she touches my forehead with the back of her hand. "How do you feel? I think you have a fever."

I lean into her cool palm. It feels so good against my scorching forehead.

"I'm still woozy. I thought it was an after effect of my head injury. Maybe it's both?" I say.

"We should get you something."

I nod. "Yup. Medicine we can do. I'd also planned to get us some food and some warmer clothes."

She smiles, but she still looks freezing.

"Let me see your arm." She gently unwraps the cloth wrapped around the wound. The scratch on my arm is reddish and tender. I hiss in pain and flinch as her finger touches my wound. "Sorry. I don't like the look of it." Her eyes linger on mine. "I wanted to ask you last night. You said you were using the credits on your chip." I nod. "Don't they know who you are by reading your chip?"

"Well, they don't know who I really am. It connects to a false profile. My *fake* information says I'm Dawn's older brother. Father deceased. No current home address since I left the planet."

"Yes, but if you use it now, on Earth, won't it lead them to you? To where we are, or at least where you used the chip? If it's the same identity you used on the station, they'd have notified the ESC after the explosion, when they took you into custody."

Shit. I didn't think of that. I bolt upright and smack my head on the low ceiling.

"Ow." I rub my head. "Of course, you're right." I was so out of it last night; I wasn't thinking. They're probably looking for us. How long will it take to figure out who could have stolen and crashed a ranger ship? If they're looking for me on Earth, I just planted a big target on my back. Hopefully, it will take them time to process the information and longer to find us in the middle of nowhere. "We need to go. Right now!"

I leap down from the bed, hopping on one foot, then the other, to drag my shoes on. Despite the good night's sleep I had, I'm still light-headed. Something is definitely wrong with me.

Haley crosses her arms. "Then I guess this is

where we part ways. Leave me here. I'll stay and wait for the authorities."

Her stubborn expression is achingly familiar.

I don't have time for this and she knows it.

"Don't do this." Picking up her shoes I hand them to her. She takes her shoes, sitting on the edge of the bed to pull them on.

I hold out my hand, "Please, come with me." She shakes her head.

Opening the compartment door, I peek outside. There's no one in sight. Dawn is breaking over the tops of the faraway trees. I wonder if she's ever seen a sunrise.

Haley sits on the bed, arms crossed, jaw set, staring at me defiantly. Ignoring my urgency.

"I won't come, and you can't make me. What are you going to do, threaten to stab me with the scalpel again?" she challenges.

"No, I'm going to do this." She gasps as I grab her wrist, yanking her off the bed and over my shoulder into a firefighter's hold. It takes a second to secure my grip and maintain my balance. I'm not at full strength and she's not the lightest girl I've ever picked up, but I manage. Hopefully, she won't start kicking. If she does, I'll probably drop her.

I can't see her face, which is good because she's probably about to go ballistic.

Instead, she starts to laugh.

Shaking with relief, I carry her to the car and

swing the door open. Bending carefully at the knees, I cradle her legs, swinging her down into my arms. She grabs my neck, afraid I'm going to drop her. Her breath gusts over on my cheek as I place her in the car seat, bending close, my face next to hers. My heart thumps painfully as she slowly releases her arms and I pull back, gazing into her eyes, before shutting and locking the car door.

"We need to go." I hop into the driver's seat and shoot out of there as fast as I can. If they track my implant, they'll also have the car information. We need to switch rides or get other transportation.

Haley studies me as I drive. "So, we can no longer use your credits, right? Is there another kind of currency? Does it have to be your chip?"

My mind is fuzzy as I search my brain. "Some places still accept currency, but I'm not sure where I'd get it and who I could give it to." I punch the steering wheel in frustration. Damn. "Now I can't risk paying for anything. We'll have to drive straight through till we're past the city, or maybe I can scrounge up something. Somehow."

Or I risk reaching out to the Farm. I'd been hoping to avoid that.

Keeping my eyes on the road gets harder, as my vision is blurry. I'm swerving a bit.

"Can you even see straight with that fever?" Haley places her cool hand on my forehead again. "Pull over."

"Not here." I continue till I spot a dirt road leading into a grove of trees to the side of the road. I drive until we're hidden from the road and kill the engine. "This might be a good place to dump the car. We can hike till we find another ride," I say.

Haley turns to face me. "How are you feeling?"

The smart thing would be to hide how vulnerable I am right now, but I'm sick of lying to her. "I'm feeling rather woozy," I admit.

"Yeah. I noticed you had trouble standing up straight before," she says. She rolls her eyes as I grin, and adds, "even before you were carrying me." My grin widens, and she punches me in the arm. "I didn't ask you to carry me to the car, so if I'm heavy that's your problem, pal." I shrug and she continues. "Balance problems, dizziness, fuzzy or blurry vision, and sleeping more than usual are all symptoms of your concussion. They can appear days or months after the injury, or when the person resumes their everyday life. Which in your case means kidnapping girls, stealing spaceships, and running off to Earth."

"Okay," I rub my neck, "we know I'm not okay, but there's nothing I can do about it right now."

"And the wound infection is the reason for your fever."

I cross my arms. "Where are you going with this?"

"Rest is very important after a concussion be-cause it helps the brain to heal. You shouldn't be driving; you should be taking it easy."

"I agree, but walking would be even more activity. We're nowhere near a place with public transportation."

She glances at me sideways. "Maybe I could drive."

I shake my head firmly, which only worsens my dizziness. "Oh, no."

"Why not?" she pouts, looking so cute.

I count out the reasons on my fingers. "You don't know how to drive, you don't have a license, and you could kill us both."

"Well, that didn't stop you from flying us to Earth."

Touché. I shake my head again, but my resolve is cracking. We need to get moving and the way I feel, I'm likely to drive us into a wall.

"Ok."

"Really?" She looks surprised. "Yay." Then flings her arms around me. If I'd known it would make her happy, I'd have agreed sooner. She catches herself after a moment and releases me. In my defense, I'm not thinking straight because of the fever and the concussion. Or maybe it's the way she's looking at me with those honey-toned eyes.

We run through the basics of operating the vehicle. Haley quickly finds similarities to the cargo pod she flew on the station. We do a few practice loops through the trees until I allow her to return to the road.

I hope we don't get killed.

Chapter 9

Snake Bite

Haley

We crest a hill and come face to face with an immense city. It lurks in the valley below us like a dark monster with a million eyes. I stop the car, shrinking closer to Jorden. On the outskirts, smoke billows from chimneys sprouting out of enormous buildings that must be factories. The dark curls make my throat itchy. In the center there's an almost solid wall of high-rises connected by a spider-web of walkways. Flying craft flit between them like buzzing insects. One of those buildings could house more people than I've met in my entire life.

Jorden was dozing, but now he lifts his head. He's groggy and his eyes are unfocused, groaning when he spots the city. Obviously, he doesn't want to enter it, but we have no choice. The city spans the horizon, barring our way to our destination in the mountains on the other side.

This is my chance to escape. With all those people, I can ask for help. Despite wanting my freedom, I'm terrified of this dense gathering of humanity. Jorden is the only person I know in this world.

Meanwhile, Jorden shakes violently in the seat next to me. I turn up the heat, but what he really needs is medicine.

"You have to take something to bring down this fever," I insist.

He grumbles in protest, but I speak over him. "If you won't do it for your sake, then do it for mine. I don't know how to cope here, or who is safe to contact. If you pass out, I'm completely on my own, so stop being stubborn."

"Okay. Stop being so bossy," he mumbles, wrapping his arms around his shoulders and hunching lower as he programs a route to a pharmacy into the GPS. I wonder if I can ask the pharmacist for help when we get there. Will Jorden leave me in the car or drag me inside? But when we arrive, I discover it's a machine that dispenses drugs, positioned behind an iron grate. So much for my escape plans.

If the world is overpopulated, where are all the people? Everything we've seen is automatic. It's eerie, as if the whole world is deserted but for the two of us. The street looks abandoned.

There's a panel on the front of the vending machine, which Jorden reluctantly taps with his wrist, giving away our location again. I wait in the car while Jorden describes his symptoms to the machine AI; fever, shaking, blurry vision, cut on his arm. The machine beeps, speaks in a soothing female tone, and dispenses a small box of painkiller tablets, a spray can of disinfectant for his wound, liquid bandage to close the gash, and a small bottle of water. He quickly downs two tablets while I remove his bandage and use the rest of the water to clean the red, swollen wound, then I disinfect it and apply the liquid bandage.

He nods gratefully and I feel worse about what I'm about to do.

The medicine makes him even more drowsy, and Jorden leans back in his seat. I continue driving, keeping an eye on him as his eyelids droop. I'm glad there are no other cars around. Once we reach the bottom of the hill, amongst the buildings, I stop the vehicle at a crossroads.

This is my chance. Slipping out of the door I run as fast as I can, not looking where I'm going.

It takes Jorden a moment to realize what's going on. He shouts, "Haley," then there's a crash. I don't turn around, putting all my focus into running on the littered street. Usually, Jorden could run me down easily with his long legs and athletic build but, currently, he's almost too sick to move.

Footsteps pound behind me, but he doesn't sound

close. I turn a corner, then slip into an alley while he runs by, missing me.

Heading further away, I keep running, not knowing where I'm going. When I'm sure I've lost him, I slow to a walk and keep going till the alley lets out into another street like the first. There's still nobody in sight. We're so close to a population center, why aren't there any people?

The surrounding buildings are covered in fading posters, with warning signs on the doors. Most include the words "Hazard" and "Condemned" in big red letters. Some buildings have colorful writing on them in intricate designs. I'm drawn closer to study the art.

Several tags say, "The New Kings," "Yellow Tide," and "Black Death." The messages scrawled below are more disturbing. "Death to Earthers," and further down, "#@*k this planet. I'm leaving."

Other places bear the Earther sign. Only Earth. An O and an E joined and surrounded by a circle. The words "Earth or heaven, nowhere else," scrawled beneath it.

Even though we're out of the mountains, I still find it hard to breathe. The air tastes foul, making me cough intermittently. Since I don't know where I'm going, I keep walking, unsure which way to turn. I've lost track of where I was originally. It feels like I've been turning corners and weaving down alleys for hours. Then I round a corner and see Jorden in front of me. He's not looking my way, though. I duck back into the alley and hide, peeking out as I watch him search for me.

I'm surprised he hasn't given up yet. How long will it take before he drives off and leaves me? He tried to chase me but, by the way he's weaving, he can barely stand.

"Haley, come back, please." His voice trembles, then his legs wobble and he sits down hard on the curb and lowers his head to his hands.

Even as I hide from him, I feel torn. The whole point was to escape him, but seeing him so upset makes me want to comfort him.

"*Stop it*," I scold myself. "He's a liar, and a terrorist. He kidnapped me, he destroyed Nano." I say it like a mantra, as if I need convincing. Which I do because my heart and my mind are at war.

I should be afraid of him. *But I'm not.*

I should hate him. *But I don't.*

Despite being mad at him, the thought of never seeing him again tears me up. All I know for sure is that I can't think straight when I'm around him. I need to get away, because I'm not equipped to deal with these unreasonable feelings.

Creeping back into the last road I came from, I head towards a point in the distance where the lights are brightest. The light is fading, and it's getting colder. The foul smell in the air makes my throat feel as if it's coated in something thick and sticky, making it hard to breathe. As the light fades, street-lights come on, but many are broken or malfunc-tioning, providing pools of light separated by long stretches of darkness.

I'm so hungry. I've never been hungry like this in all my life. My teeth chatter from the cold. My thin station clothes aren't suitable for these tem-peratures. When we left at dawn, I still had Jorden's shirt, but I returned it when he started trembling. Shivering, I pull the edge of my sleeves down, trying to cover my hands.

I'm on the brink of exhaustion.

I walk, teetering from side to side, trying not to fall over. In the distance, I hear a sound like glass rolling, shattering. Harsh laughter. Are there people here? But what kind of people live in this place? Do I really want to meet them?

At the end of the street, something gray moves out of the shadows into the light, lingering close to the ground. I draw closer, wary but curious. It's a dog, but it's nothing like the happy furry dogs in the vids I've seen. Its tail is tucked between its legs, its ribs are poking through its thin coat. Whining, it licks its lips and takes a few steps in my direction. I crouch lower, holding out a hand and call out, "Here, boy."

I don't know if it's a boy dog or a girl dog, but I hope my tone will convince it I'm friendly. Wag-ging its tail hesitantly, it approaches. I'm so amazed at seeing a real, live dog I don't register the steps approaching till they're almost upon us. A hail of stones sails by me and the dog flees, whimpering.

A rough laugh erupts behind me, echoed by two more.

"Whaddo we 'ave 'ere?" The man's voice is rough and raspy.

I whirl and find myself face-to-face with three men. At least I think they're men. I've never met people who look like this before.

The one immediately in front of me is tall and thin, almost stretched out. Papery skin that looks strained, as though covering his frame is too much for it. Scaly cheeks with flaking dry skin that is pock-marked with tufts of untrimmed beard, sprouting in untidy clumps. His hair is an unnaturally bright red, shaved at the sides but swept up in the middle into a greasy wave, stiff with gel. His black clothes are in tatters. I can't tell if it's a fashion statement or disrepair.

He grabs my arm, pulling me closer and sniffing me like an animal. He stinks of sweat and disease and chemicals. The smell hits me like a blow, making me want to puke.

One of his companions draws in, staring at my comm bracelet.

"What's that? Never seen one o' those before."

The speaker is a large, black man, his hair caught up in dozens of tiny coils, each decorated with a metal ring. He has a tattoo of a blue snake crawling up his arm and, when I peer at it, it moves. His pants and boots are black, but he has a red tank top with a skull on it. As he draws closer and grabs my arm, the skull looms into the center of my vision, its eyes staring at me.

"Looks expensive," he rasps.

"She looks expensive," the first one adds, eying me up and down, licking his thin lips like I'm a piece of meat, not a person. "Bet ya fifty creds, some upper city folk will pay us mucho coin to get her back."

The scaly man runs a finger down my cheek.

"Don' mean we can' 'ave a bit 'o fun with 'er first..." He laughs, his laughter grating at my ears like nails scraping on metal.

Snake man laughs too, sending shivers down my spine.

"Bet they'll pay for 'er mostly intact too...."

"No," I cry and try to break away from Scaly's grasp. He snaps me back and hits me across the cheek so hard my head rings. My cheek feels on fire. I reel back from the force of the blow and he lets go, dropping me on the ground, in the filthy black scum that fills the streets. For a moment, I lie there, dazed.

No one has ever hit me. Ever in all my life. I've had scuffles with kids on the station when we were much younger, but no one has ever slapped me. I can't catch my breath.

From my position on the ground, I watch a third man step forward. He looks younger than the other two, barely out of his teens. His hair is long and platinum blond. His face has an angelic quality to it, with deep blue eyes emphasized in black eyeliner.

He reaches down and grabs my forearm, pulling me to my feet. His voice is soft, hypnotizing, and more refined than the others. "Don't do that, Viper," he purrs, "you'll damage the merchandise."

He sniffs me, too. *What on Earth is wrong with these people?* Then he continues in that soft, singsong voice, "She looks good enough to eat. Smells tasty, too." He grins widely, so I can see he's filed his teeth into points.

I scream, and he laughs again.

"Get away from me!" I yell as loudly as I can, and try to push him away. The men exchange glances, smirking as if I've told a joke. My heart sinks. There's no one around to hear, no one who can come to my aid. I'm completely alone. They can do whatever they want to me.

Demon boy shoves me back, hard, into the wall, banging my head till I see stars. Then he crowds me as the other two chuckle. His hand winds its way into my hair.

"What lovely curls you have." He speaks in undertones now. I try to slap his hand away and he grabs both my wrists, pulling up, pinning my hands above my head.

Sniffing my skin, he hovers inches away. His nose travels across my face to just below my ear. Then he licks the length of my neck, tasting me, like a person sampling a savory dish. "Hmmm."

"No. Please," I beg. Tears stream down my cheeks, but he isn't deterred. Quite the opposite. He seems encouraged.

Leaning forward, he presses himself against me. He's heavy, and I feel like I'm being crushed out of existence.

"Make sure you leave some for us now, boy," one of the others grunts from behind.

Demon boy smiles and looks over his shoulder, without letting go of my arms. "Don't worry. Looks like there's enough of her to go around."

All three of them chuckle.

I don't want to be here for what's going to happen.

He turns back to me, shifting his grasp so that he's pinning both my hands with one of his, freeing his other hand. His grip is iron, holding me in place as he runs the free hand down my body. I'm sickened by the touch, but frozen in terror. I twist my face to the side, away from him, and notice a blur of movement coming in from the right.

The men are caught off guard when Jorden tackles Demon boy, ripping him away from me and crushing him to the ground. Jorden straddles him and starts punching him repeatedly. Demon boy squeals as he tries to block the blows.

At first his companions are stunned, allowing Jorden to get some good shots in. Demon boy's face isn't so angelic anymore. Blood spurts from his lips and nose and big purple bruises erupt under his eyes. Then the others advance, dragging Jorden off. Demon boy remains on the ground, dazed and bleeding, grasping his stomach. Jorden twists out of their hold, and steps in front of me, putting me between his back and the wall.

I want to help, but I'm petrified. Jorden is sick, he has a fever and the after effects of a concussion. How can he possibly take on three healthy guys? Hours ago, he could barely stand.

Scales and Viper flank us. They know he can't deal with them both at once. Scales lunges towards me from the right. Jorden turns to block him and Viper grabs Jorden from behind in a choke hold, as his scaly friend pummels him in the gut.

I scream, "No!"

Jorden's jaw clenches and a moment later he squats, pulling down on Viper's arm while turning his face to the side as he breaks free. Settling into a crouch, he sweeps his left foot behind Viper's leg, yanking it out from under him and dropping him onto his back. Viper hits the ground hard, grunting in surprise and rolling as pain shoots up his back.

Jorden keeps moving. From his crouched position, he lunges into Scales, tackling him around the waist, throwing him down and landing on top of him.

Blows rain down on Scales this time.

Both men seem stunned at meeting their match.

Finally, I find the ability to move. Viper looks like he's about to get up, so I pick up a wooden board from the street and whack his head. Once, twice, till he looks dazed. Then I pivot towards Demon boy, who's still on the ground, hitting him hard in the chest.

Hysterically I swing again, and again, hitting him in the face, the shoulders, anywhere I can reach. Until there's a touch on my shoulder. I turn, raising the board to strike, but it's Jorden. I stop just in time.

To my surprise, all three guys are on the ground.

Jorden grabs my wrist and takes off at a run, almost pulling me off my feet. We run blindly through the dark streets. Our only purpose is to get as far away as possible. My breath saws in and out of my lungs. Jorden's hand on my wrist is my only anchor.

There are no sounds of pursuit. They aren't chasing us.

When we finally stop, we're alone. I'm still holding the board, and he's still holding my wrist. I can't believe we survived.

Our eyes meet, and we stare at each other for three heartbeats. Then I drop the board, my eyes welling over. Jorden pulls me into his arms, enfolding me tightly as I sob into his chest.

"It's all right. It's okay. I'm here. I've got you," Jorden murmurs into my hair and I cling to him like a life raft in a storm. Right now, I don't care what he's done or where we are because of his decisions and mine. I'm safe in his arms where I belong. All I want is for him to keep holding me.

He holds me until my crying abates. It feels like he's content to hold me for as long as I need but, now that the adrenaline has dissipated and the medicine has worn off, he's swaying with exhaustion. Drained and over-exerted by the fight and escape. We aren't safe here.

I wipe my eyes. "We've got to go." Jorden nods his agreement.

Slipping under his arm, I hold on to his torso to keep him upright. His skin is so warm, driving home the point that, despite his exhaustion and fever, he didn't leave me; he kept looking for me and saved me when he could have driven away.

As we stumble along, I ask, "Where did you learn to move like that?"

He snickers. "Terrorist school."

I can't help laughing too.

We hurry before the men regroup and return with their friends, or we encounter some other lawless gang. Thinking of Demon boy's tongue running down my neck makes me shudder. Escaping here was a terrible mistake. I almost got Jorden killed. I almost got myself killed, and worse...

Jorden looks down, hugging me close. "It's alright, we're almost there."

He seems to know where we're going as he steers us around street corners that all look the same to me, until we finally reach the car. I've never been so happy to see a vehicle in my whole life, including the first time I flew a cargo pod. Easing him gently into the passenger seat, I help him fasten the seatbelt and then run around to the driver's door.

As I buckle up and glance in the rear-view mirror, I notice a large group of people coming out of the alleys behind us, appearing like ghouls in the darkness. Advancing towards us, they carry long sticks and other makeshift weapons that I don't recognize. I can't tell if our three assailants are among them, but I wouldn't be surprised.

Jorden taps his wrist to the ignition. Before I can share the frightening sight with him, his head drops back, and he's out cold. I'm on my own, but I can't be mad at him. Despite his exhaustion and injuries, he held on as long as he could, pushing himself way beyond the limits of his condition. Now it's my turn to save him.

I press 'Drive' and the people behind us break into a run, shouting as they charge at the car. A few are close enough to bang on the rear of the car as I accelerate. Thankfully, I soon leave them behind, going as fast as I can without a clear destination.

Driving towards the city lights seems the safest solution. I'm searching for a road to take me where
there are people. Normal people who can offer us
shelter. Jorden needs food, warmth, and lots of rest.
Somewhere safe to hide that doesn't require using
his chip. There must be decent people somewhere.
Those men can't be all that's left of Earth.

After a few wrong turns, I find a wide boulevard
that runs towards the lights. Finally, lights are on
in the buildings we pass. There are a few people
here and there on the streets. I'm too spooked to
stop till I feel safer. The road climbs and I pass
through a huge gateway spanned by a wall of giant
fans, blowing outwards. It reminds me of an airlock.
Up close, it's apparent there's a transparent dome
covering the city. Inside, the road climbs, winding
between tall buildings. The streets are clean and
maintained. I spot well-dressed couples strolling
hand in hand and families out for a walk. Trees line
the next street, accentuating a few small houses
wedged amongst the skyscrapers, as if the high rises
grew around them like beanstalks.

It feels safe and homey here. My eyes are sliding
shut, so I stop the car, thinking I might sleep here.
Across the street, warm yellow light spills from the

window of a small house, where a black and white cat sits on the windowsill. A real-life cat, like the cats in my vids. Beside the cat, a gray-haired woman sits, stroking it gently. She reminds me of my Nana.

I didn't really know my Nana. We met when I was a baby, but I was only two when we left Earth. She'd send presents and vid recordings on birthdays and holidays. The red quilt on my bed at home was from her. She died when I was twelve and, six months later, the transport delivered my Bat Mitzvah present, an enamel fish pendant on a gold chain.

The woman in the window meets my eyes and smiles kindly. It's silly, but I feel like I can trust her. It might be the exhaustion talking, but I'm cold, scared, and I can't run anymore. Not like this. I don't know enough about Earth, but there must be some decent people I can trust.

My eye catches a glint above her head. A tiny globe, suspended from a golden thread, spins in the window. Just like Jorden had in his bedroom on the station. It might be a coincidence, but I take it as a sign. I have to try.

Jorden is asleep, breathing evenly. I kill the engine and slip out of the car. The woman watches as I cross the street and climb three steps to the front door. There isn't a call button on the door, which is made of lovely reddish-brown wood carved with intricate lines. I run my fingers along the smooth surface and knock.

The door opens at once and light spills onto my face. Up close, she seems curious but pleasant. The cat twirls around her legs.

"Yes," she smiles, and I can't help smiling back.

Suddenly I don't know what to say. This is such a strange situation. How do I explain our situation? Embarrassed, I take a step back, lip quivering, prepared to flee. Her smile falls, and she steps towards me, taking me gently by the shoulders. The cat runs forward, brushing against my legs, and I flinch at the unfamiliar sensation.

"What is it, child?" she asks in a warm, soothing voice. "You look freezing. Come in, have some tea."

I let her guide me into the living room and sit me down on a soft yellow couch with green throw pillows. Her home is colorful and warm. Everything looks like it came out of an old vid. She bustles into another room for a minute while I contemplate escaping, but her couch is too soft for me to want to leave. When she returns, she sits beside me and takes my hands, enfolding them in her cool, creased palms.

"Tell me what's wrong," she says.

I hesitate, afraid to say the wrong thing. Pointing to the tiny globe in the window, I say, "I was wondering... about your globe."

If I'm mistaken, this may be nonsense to her.

"Yes." She nods, lowering her voice, even though it's just us. "Earth or Heaven. Nowhere else."

I can't believe my luck. If she's an Earther sympathizer, then this place is safe for Jorden. My eyes tear up.

"Sorry if this is strange, but I need help. I'm lost and my friend is sick. Can you help us?" I babble.

"I'll do my best," she says, glancing towards the car on the other side of the street. Jorden's face is visible in the passenger seat. "That's your friend?" she asks, and I nod. "Can you bring him here?"

"Well, I don't think I can lift him by myself, but hopefully I can wake him enough to walk in." I get up. "Let me try," I say as she walks me back to the door, waiting in the doorway as I cross the street, open the passenger door, and crouch beside Jorden.

Heat radiates off him as I bend to release his seat belt. He stirs as I brush past him, opening his eyes blearily.

"Hey," he says.

I crouch back down. "Hey."

He smiles sleepily. "Where are we?"

Honestly, I have no idea. "Somewhere safe." I hope that's the truth. "Can you get up?"

He nods, grasping the car door for balance. I slip under his arm to help him wobble his way up the stairs. At least he can walk. As I guide him into the house, the woman moves out of the way and points me towards a bedroom. Inside is a wide double bed made of wood, covered in a flowery, white duvet. I help him to the bed, sit him down, and kneel to help him take off his shoes.

"I can do it," he protests, bending down. The forward motion almost topples him headfirst off the bed. So, I press a hand to his chest, shoving him back, and he collapses onto the bed. "No, you're right. I can't," he admits.

I giggle and yank off his heavy shoes. The woman has disappeared into the kitchen. I hear the clink of cups and cupboard doors opening and closing.

Getting up is hard because I'm so tired. I feel drained, and the bed looks so inviting. Jorden is lying with his eyes closed. Has he fallen asleep again? If he's feverish, I should ask the old woman for a thermometer and some medicine.

Kneeling on the bed, I rummage in his shirt pocket for the pain tablets, hoping they weren't lost during the fight but, before I find them, he takes my wrist and pulls me towards him. I fall half on the soft covers, half onto him. Too tired to protest, I nestle into his shoulder, soaking up his warmth for just a moment. It's so pleasant I don't want to move.

I'm almost dozing off when he stirs. I'd assumed he couldn't move, but apparently his condition is better than it seemed. He raises himself on one elbow and rolls toward me, rolling me onto my back.

"Jorden?" I ask. With my back on the bed, he's looking down at me, his mouth so close to mine. His breath caresses my face. Is he going to kiss me? Do I want him to?

The first time he kissed me, he didn't wait for permission, but now he is. This is our second first kiss. I nod, almost imperceptibly, but it's enough.

He bends and kisses me softly, deeply. His lips are warm, probably because of the fever, but they feel so good. His fingers caress my cheek. After the kiss, he pulls back and smiles gently at me. I reach up and touch his face.

My heart is exploding or reassembling.

It hurts. It's *perfect*.

For a moment we don't speak, just gaze into each other's eyes, smiling. Then I push up, pressing him back down into the bed.

"You need to rest."

He takes a deep breath and nods, collapsing back into the soft covers. I get up and draw a blanket over him, then I take off my shoes and go into the kitchen.

The last time he kissed me, I tried to kill him. Literally.

I almost succeeded.

Where will this kiss leave us?

Chapter 10

Haven

Jorden

When I wake up, it's morning. My head feels clear again after the fuzziness last night. Unsure how long I slept, I peek at the window. The sun is bright and high in the sky. There's a vague memory of someone feeding me soup and tablets to lower my temperature.

I remember kissing Haley. It feels like a wish come true. Hopefully, it wasn't a dream, but if it was, it was the best dream.

Rising gingerly in case the dizziness returns, I stretch, feeling for bruises or cracks from the fight yesterday. My side is tender and my knuckles are sore from pounding the guy who pinned Haley to the wall. I don't care about my bruises. He deserved what he got and more.

Walking into the hall in my socks, I look around, listening for voices. The house is real old school, like a museum of traditional furnishings and old-fashioned materials. Full of wood and leather and wool. Who lives here?

There's an old woman setting the breakfast table in the dining room. She nods at me and smiles. "I take it you're feeling better?"

Her smile is friendly, making me feel at ease.

"Yes, thanks."

Thanks doesn't really cover what she did by taking us in.

A black and white cat is purring and sunning herself on the window. I notice a little globe spinning above her. The Earther sign. Ahhhh. Clever Haley. That's how she knew it was safe here.

Turning around, I stop in my tracks. Haley has emerged from the kitchen carrying a bowl of vegetables. The sight of her takes my breath away. She's wearing a long, white cotton dress cut low in the front, with a soft, white cardigan over it for warmth. It looks like she's showered and brushed the tangles from her curls.

The old woman follows my gaze and smiles.

Haley blushes furiously, and it makes her look even more beautiful. Pushing her hair back behind her ear, she says, "I didn't have a change of clothes."

The old woman beams at us both. "It's my grand-daughter's. Luckily, she left it here the last time she visited." She takes the bowl from Haley and places it on the table. "Haley's clothes are in the wash. You're welcome to have a shower and I'll do yours too." She eyes me up and down. "Sorry, but I can't offer you anything to wear in the meantime. My Frank, God rest his soul, was nowhere near your size. Can you make do with a towel for the time being?"

I'm not usually self-conscious, but the way she says it next to Haley makes me blush, too. We stand there, smiling and flushed as the woman keeps on talking, ignoring our awkwardness.

"Well, sit down already. Let's eat first. Then you can shower and, after, we can talk."

I pull out a chair for her, then realize I don't know her name.

"Thank you so much—" I pause, and she fills in: "Judith."

"Nice to meet you. I'm Jorden and I guess you already met Haley."

"Yes, we had a long conversation this morning before you woke up."

How much did Haley tell her? Judith is so relaxed. It can't be everything. I pull out a chair for Haley too, and, as she steps past me, I catch a whiff of her hair, clean and moist. Her smell is intoxicating. The way she brushes my shoulder as she passes sends a shiver down my spine.

Does Judith have a food printer in the kitchen? I'm sure she can afford it. Despite the simple décor, houses like this cost a fortune. Or maybe she's really old school and cooks. *Whatever*. I'm ravenous. I can't remember the last time I ate. Probably on the ship to Earth. The food smells wonderful and tastes even better. Sitting next to Haley, our knees touch under the table, our arms brushing against each other as we reach for toast and eggs, cheese and orange juice. When Judith rises and goes into the kitchen to get more coffee, I take Haley's hand and brush it to my lips. She beams at me. When Judith returns, I drop it hastily and we both giggle.

Yesterday was terrifying, and now everything is so perfect it seems unreal. When we polish off every last bite of food, Judith guides me up the stairs to a white, tile bathroom.

Despite the antique décor, the bathroom has a modern auto shower and clothes-cleaning units. Before she leaves, Judith programs the auto wash for a quick cycle and hands me a large, white towel.

"Just pop your clothes in the machine and close the door," she tells me, before removing Haley's clean, fragrant clothes from the auto folder. Hopefully, Haley won't change back too quickly. I loved seeing her in that white dress.

Judith pauses outside the door. "When you're done, go back to the bedroom. I'll bring you your clothes when they're ready."

The shower is bliss. Warm water washes over me, removing the grime and sweat of the past few days and massaging the pain out of my muscles. I bask in the warmth till I'm well and truly relaxed.

When I'm done, I check the bathroom cabinet and find a shaving machine. I'm glad she kept it.

Clean shaven, I wrap the towel around myself and creep down the stairs. No matter how old she is, I don't want to run into Judith wearing only a towel. I make it into the bedroom without incident and, ten minutes later, there's a knock on the door. Peeking out, I find Haley, still in the white dress, holding my folded clothes.

Opening the door only as much as necessary, I pull her inside by the wrist and shut the door, trapping her against it.

Gazing down, she notices the towel and looks up fast, cheeks flushing.

"Oh, hell no. You're only wearing a towel."

I grin. "Well, you have my clothes."

"Yeah, fine, here they are," she says, shoving them at my chest.

I take them, tossing them onto the bed, then lean in till we're an inch apart. Haley leans back, but she has nowhere to go. Her smile is timid, but then she straightens her shoulders in defiance. "I don't know what you think is happening right now, but I assure you it is NOT happening."

I laugh, then take a deep breath. "The only thing happening right now is this."

Leaning forward, I close the gap between us and

kiss her, drinking in her scent, cupping her face. Running my fingers down her shoulder and around her waist. She kisses me back, and it's so electrifying I have a hard time pulling away. But I do. Haley is breathing fast, a little smile dancing on her lips. Then she opens the door and slips out.

Taking a few breaths to calm myself, I then get dressed.

When I reach the living room, Haley is curled up in a corner of the couch. Judith sits beside her, so I opt for the armchair beside Haley. Though I'm giddy about being back together, I need to get my head in the game. We still have a long way to go. It isn't safe out there and I need to focus.

Judith turns toward me. "This is the part where we talk," she says.

I nod. "Do you know who I am? Who we are?" I ask carefully.

"Your friend was very discreet," she smiles at Haley, "but yes. I know who you are. It was obvious the minute you walked into the house."

I raise my eyebrows.

"You're the spitting image of your father," she elaborates. I rub my jaw. That damn resemblance. No matter how far I go, I can't escape it.

Judith continues. "I knew him years ago, before he moved to the Farm. Both him and your mother. I was your mother's friend before they married. Did you know she founded the Earther movement?"

I shake my head. "No. I always thought Father started it."

Judith tsks. "He does that. Takes credit for other people's ideas. In her time, it was more peaceful. Then Peter got involved and advocated a more militant approach. His motto was, '*If they won't listen, we'll make them listen.*' His stance drove many of the early supporters away, especially after your poor mother—"

Her voice trails off, her words opening a wound that's never fully healed. My shoulders hunch. Haley reaches for my hand. I take hers gratefully, trying to force a smile.

Judith pauses, her eyes full of sympathy, staring into the past. "Sorry. The last time I saw her was at a rally near Cape Canaveral 11 years ago. You must have been six or seven."

I shake my head. "No, you're mistaken. She died when I was five."

"Oh." She seems surprised. "Well, you'd know. I'm getting on in years, and I get confused sometimes. Anyway, we were all much younger and idealistic. I would have been more involved, but my Frank, God rest his soul, didn't like the direction the movement was going. He made me keep away from the rallies and the protests, but I still wanted to help. To do my part."

I know the upkeep of the Farm is expensive, but I never thought too hard about where the money came from. As I listen to Judith, I realize my father must have many supporters who bankroll his cause.

"Now don't be alarmed, but the networks have shot info-blasts about Haley every hour since the news reached Earth. They're looking for both of you. But they don't know who you really are, Jorden, not yet. All they have is a false identity. But anybody who knows you or your father—" She pauses. "It won't take them long to figure it out. Have you talked to your father yet?"

"No."

She frowns. "I'm sure he's worried."

"I didn't want to lead the authorities back to the Farm." My blood runs cold as realization sinks in. "We didn't prepare for this situation. Nobody believed I'd survive, let alone make it back home to Earth." *I can't believe it myself.*

"Do you want me to contact him and tell him to expect you?"

Refusing would seem strange, so I nod even though I'd rather she didn't. Fear fills my throat, cutting off my airway. I failed my mission and now I'm running home, trailing a girl I kidnapped from space, with the whole world in pursuit. How can I face my father again? Will he even let me back in?

Judith's gaze shifts from me to Haley. "You need to go soon, try to blend into the crowd and maybe," she points to Haley's hair, "do something about your blue hair. It's too distinctive."

Haley sits up, her hands going to her head. "Change my hair?" she cries.

"You can always dye it blue again when you go home."

Haley opens her mouth, closes it again, then she looks Judith defiantly in the eye.

"Forgive me for saying this. It sounds awful, after you helped us and all, but you seem like such a sweet lady. How are *you* an Earther sympathizer?"

Judith laughs, then she leans forward and takes Haley's hand.

"Earther views weren't always associated with terrorism, my dear. It's not a violent cause. Earthers believe in saving the people left on Earth, as opposed to fleeing to a colony. You must understand how important that is." Haley nods. "At first, Jorden's parents tried other ways to get people to listen. But the corporations refused to put the Earth before their profits. It was only after the police started raiding Earther rallies that Earthers began fighting back and became more militant. That's when the leaders went into hiding."

"How can you live on a farm so close to the city? Don't the authorities know you're there?" Haley asks me.

"The Farm is hidden," I explain. "You can't reach it by accident, and we've had help keeping us off surveillance cameras. Still, we stay off the grid as much as possible," I add. "Most city dwellers have an embedded identity chip. But I didn't get mine until I started prep for my mission and it's not in my skin. Father commissioned skin tight bracelets to embed the chip in." I show her my wrist. "So, we can switch the chip out as necessary." Haley examines my wrist closely but, unless you know what you're looking for, it's impossible to tell. The thin layer is indistinguishable from skin. "My friend Aaron and I went into the city once without them. Big mistake. We didn't know you need them for everything, including transportation, communication, and shopping."

"I don't have one. Won't I need it?" Haley asks. "Could I get a bracelet like that?"

Judith nods at me. "It's probably best, and you should switch yours too, Jorden. Give me a few hours. I know somebody who can help."

As the discussion continues, Haley draws away from me again, raising her walls. After getting a stark reminder of who I am, I'm not surprised. Even if she wants me as badly as I want her, she can't reconcile her feelings for me with my background and past actions. While Judith goes upstairs to arrange our new chips, I lead Haley to the steps outside the house. Talking in the bedroom is too private and there's too much potential for distraction.

Haley leans on the side of the doorway, breathing in the aroma of the trees, enjoying the fresh air and the warm sun on her face. I shift from one foot to the other, debating how to ask my question. Leaning forward, she halts my nervous movement with a hand on my arm.

"What is it?" she asks.

I let out a breath. "We're about to head into the city center, but we can't use the car to drive through. That means continuing on foot or public conveyance."

"All right. What's your point?"

"Once we're in the inner city, I can't prevent you from turning me in or running away from me again." My heart aches as I replay yesterday's events after I thought I'd lost her. The terror of my desperate search. Hearing her scream in the darkness. The relief of finding her. Only a few hours have passed, but it feels like a lifetime ago, so much has changed. At least I hope it has. I take another deep breath. "I won't threaten you again. Coming with me has to be your choice. If you decide you won't, I'll leave you here with Judith and she'll help you contact the authorities. They'll get you home."

Haley stares at me silently, and I'm afraid that's her answer. Obviously, she's going to leave me and I'll never see her again.

But I won't coerce her any more.

When she speaks, her voice is as soft as the breeze caressing my cheeks.

"I'll have to go home, eventually. I can't stay here forever."

That's not a 'No'. The knot in my stomach releases

a fraction as I take her hand. "I know, but I was hoping you'd stay with me a bit longer. Come home to the Farm with me. Not because I'm forcing you, but because you want to."

She lets me reel her in as I draw her towards me and nestle her under my chin. *There, perfect.* I take a few deep breaths, inhaling her scent, trying not to think that these may be our last moments together. I only just got her back. Losing her all over again will crush me. Leaning back, I tilt her head up to look at me. Her big brown eyes undo me.

"Will you come with me, Haley?"

My heart is pounding so hard I can barely hear her answer. She says just one word.

"Yes."

Before we leave, Haley changes back into her clean station clothes. Judith presents us with a couple of skin-colored bracelets embedded with identity chips.

"These are preloaded with currency to use at your discretion," Judith explains. "If facial-recognition software tags you, the new identities should override any system alerts. But there's nothing to do if security personnel recognize you. So, blend in, and keep your heads down."

Judith gives Haley a black, hooded jacket, which she wraps around herself, putting up the hood and shielding her face from me. Staring out the passenger window, she crosses her arms. Is she tense because we're returning to the dangers of the road, or is she frightened to be alone with me again? Does she regret coming with me?

I squeeze her hand. "It'll be alright," I promise.

Haley nods.

We bid Judith's haven goodbye and head into the heart of the beast.

Chapter 11

TRANSFORMATION

Haley

We leave the car in an immense car park beneath the buildings, continuing on foot. Hopefully, we can lose any pursuit in the inner city. As we join the throng of people, Jorden takes my hand. His tension is obvious in his hunched shoulders and moist palm.

Jorden isn't a city kid; he grew up on the Farm. Though it's the headquarters for a protest movement/ terrorist organization, *whatever you choose to believe*, it was still an actual farm. Remote, outdoors and close to nature. Surrounded by a small community of people he knew his whole life. Our opinions may differ, but we have that in common. We both shy away from the writhing masses of people and draw together for support. I hang on to his hand to avoid getting separated; I'd never find him again in this crowd.

I hate the throngs of people, but I find the city fascinating.

"Have you been here before?" I ask.

Jorden seems embarrassed. "Once, with Aaron, when I was sixteen. We were woefully unprepared and didn't get very far. And then for a week or so just before I left Earth, as we arranged my cover story."

Huge, smooth blocks of concrete pave the footpath. Everything is shiny and sleek. Walkways cross the sky above us. There are vehicles on rails, and giant displays broadcasting commercials and announcements. I soak in the sights hungrily.

The people swerve around us like schools of brightly colored fish wearing tailored, sleek outfits. Some dress in amazing splashes of color, while others don lustrous black suits. There seem to be several types of acceptable clothing here, but I feel too casual. Jorden's outfit and mine look kind of scruffy.

"We don't exactly blend in," I whisper in Jorden's ear.

"Yeah." He pauses thoughtfully. "We should do some shopping."

I raise my eyebrows. "I've never been shopping."

On the station, we dressed practically for comfort. When we needed new clothes, the quartermaster printed them for us from a fixed catalogue. If I wanted to get whimsical, I could ask for a design or print on the fabric.

Jorden laughs, admitting, "Neither have I."

He tugs on my hand, dragging me onto a moving staircase that seems to go up and up into the sky till the height makes me dizzy. When we finally reach the top, we're on an open terrace high above the plaza. The wind whips my hair into my eyes. Grasping the transparent railing at the edge of the terrace, I look down. The tiny people below are rushing in every direction. A human tide.

"We're so high up, it's almost like flying," I gasp. As if to punctuate my words, a gray bird lands on the railing next to us, cooing softly and ruffling its feathers. I've never seen a bird up close like this. "Look. A bird." I nudge Jorden excitedly.

He grins and kisses me on the cheek. "You're the only person in the world to get excited over a pigeon." He pulls my hand. "Come on."

The terrace surrounds a building made entirely of glass. Every window is full of objects. So many they make my head spin. Hissing transparent doors part to admit us and we're engulfed by low-level music playing on the edge of my consciousness and the buzz of conversation. Dozens of people crowd the mall and amazing smells waft towards us as we pass the food court.

The first clothes shop we enter is enormous. I have no idea where to start. A sales clerk approaches, eyes flicking up and down as she silently judges our clothes.

"Would you like assistance?" she asks. I nod, hesitantly. "Human or auto shop?"

Jorden and I exchange glances and answer without hesitation, "Auto shop." We don't want to interact any more than necessary.

Leading us to a row of booths, she opens the door, gesturing to me to step inside. Though I don't know what's about to happen, it doesn't look dangerous, so I enter. I'm surrounded by screens reflecting my image back from every angle. *Ugh,* TMI.

Once the door closes, the booth activates. Text scrolls across the surfaces, read out by an automated voice. REMOVE CLOTHING. I double check the locked door, then strip. Hanging my clothing on a hook. I press the READY button flashing in front of me. "SCANNING," the booth says, then a minute later, "PROCESSING".

Dozens of pictures of me appear on the screen. I'm wearing a different outfit in each image. When I tap an image, it expands, displaying on the surrounding screens, each from the angle it should reflect.

There are so many options it makes me dizzy. Finally, I choose a burgundy, velvet dress. It has a deep V neckline and long, flute-shaped sleeves. There's black trim around the cuffs and a knee-length, A-line skirt. It even comes with matching black undergarments.

I press SELECT. A machine whirrs and then a hatch pops open, revealing the garments I chose, suspended on a hanger. To my surprise, they all fit perfectly. The dress looks exactly the way it did in the generated images. The fabric shimmers and is smooth and luxuriously warm against my skin.

The screen prompts. ACCESSORIZE?

I giggle. This is fun.

The booth suggests little black dangle earrings, a black sparkly necklace, and short, black boots over sheer, black tights. I've never worn heels and we might have to run, so I sift through the boot options, selecting one that barely has a heel.

After I've finished dressing, I scoop up my station clothes, depositing them in an elegant, black bag. The mirror has returned to its original reflective state, but I barely recognize myself. I look different, older, and more sophisticated. Like I belong here in this complex world.

Taking a deep breath, I exit the booth, and stop in my tracks.

Jorden is right outside, leaning against the side of the booth. I gulp. He looks so handsome. He's wearing a tailored suit that showcases his body, highlighting every feature. A white, buttoned shirt emphasizes his strong shoulders. The silky, black jacket hugs his physique and the matching pants and shiny shoes accentuate his height.

He looks up and his eyes widen, the green

sparkling at me. Stepping forward, he takes my hand, twirling me around as if we're dancing. I twirl and laugh. Feeling giddy.

"How do I look?" I ask.

Instead of answering, he pulls me towards him and kisses me. When we break apart, I joke, "That bad, huh?"

His eyes are soft as he replies, "You look breath-taking."

I blush and notice the way he's fussing with his jacket. "Is everything okay?" I ask.

He grins self-consciously. "If my friends at the farm could see me now, they'd die laughing. The fanciest clothes I ever owned were new combat boots. Before I got my disguise for the mission, I'd never even worn flexi-fabric."

"Well, I think you look amazing." Slipping my hands around his waist, I tug him towards me, drawing his head down for another kiss. After I've shown my appreciation, we pay with Judith's credits and leave hand in hand.

There's a hair salon booth across the building. Recalling Judith's advice that my hair is too distinctive, I park Jorden beside the booth.

"Give me a minute."

Stepping inside, I eye the wide variety of colors. I need to blend into the crowd so I can't choose a fun color, like green or pink or purple. Scrolling through the options, I see the perfect choice.

When I step from the booth, I have auburn hair. Just like my mother's.

Jorden's eyes go wide. He runs his fingers through my hair like he can't believe it.

"Nice?" I ask.

"Wow." He breathes me in, pulling me close to whisper in my ear. Leaving me tingling all over. Glimpsing myself in a display window, I barely recognize myself. Is that me? The girl in the window looks like she belongs here with Jorden and all the beautiful people.

After we exit the building, we board a moving walkway heading east, towards our destination.

Suddenly Jorden tenses. There's a checkpoint at the end of the walkway. People disembarking press their wrists to a scanner before progressing into the building ahead. A guard sits at the terminal, watching the screen.

We haven't passed any check points yet. They might recognize us if the guard looks too closely or if there's something wrong with the information on our identity chips.

The walkway is high up in the air, and we're effectively boxed in. People crowd the walkway behind us. We try retreating. Weaving in and out of the crowd, stepping on people's toes and pushing past them, but it's so dense. People grumble and stare as we try to shove our way back. We only get a short way before the solid wall of people is impassable.

"It's useless," Jorden whispers. "We're drawing too much attention". He squeezes my hand, whispering, "If the alarm sounds, leave me. Step away and then tell someone who you are."

I shake my head fiercely, gazing up at him in despair, and tighten my hold on his hand. A few hours ago, he asked me to come with him of my free will, and I agreed; I won't abandon him now. We need more time together. I'm not ready for this to end.

Turning back towards the checkpoint, we trundle inexorably closer to our impending doom. I scan the building behind the checkpoint, plotting an escape route, if we can run when the alarm sounds.

As we reach the scanners, Jorden halts and kisses me like he's saying goodbye, holding up the flow. The guard scowls as people pile up behind us, grumbling impatiently.

"Come on." Jorden takes my hand, approaching the scanner like a condemned man stepping up to the gallows.

It beeps green. No alarms sound.

Jorden passes, pulling me with him. I press my wrist to the scanner and the gate stays open till we're both through. The guard is already looking at the next passenger, focusing on the crush of people behind the gate caused by our delay.

It worked. We exchange relieved glances and hurry into the building before the guard looks up again.

Chapter 12

BOUNTY HUNTERS

Haley

The building in front of us houses the city's main thoroughfare. Walkways cross it at varying speeds, disappearing into a tunnel that fades into the distance as far as I can see.

Stepping onto the closest walkway, I gasp as the moving path jolts under my feet. It's not going much faster than a walk. To get onto faster paths, we have to cross the five lanes. Further in, the conveyors zip past with people hanging onto poles or sitting in a single line of seats.

"We'll need a faster means of transportation to get to the other side of the city," I say. "Even the fastest walkway looks like it'll take forever."

Jorden points up, musing, "We should take the train."

Through the large windows in the roof, I can see a track high in the sky, looping through a series of circles. As we watch, something long and white flashes through it, going so fast I almost can't make it out.

"Are you sure that's a train??" I huff. "It's going so fast."

Jorden laughs. "*Blue*, we just flew to Earth at near light speed."

"Blue?" I lift an eyebrow at him.

He wraps a finger around one of my curls, smiling. "I like the red, but you'll always be my blue-haired girl."

"Oh," I gulp, flustered, my heart galloping as fast as the train. "Anyway," I finish my point, "regarding trains. We flew to Earth and crashed. Remember?"

He takes my hand again. "Well, I'm not driving the train, so you can relax. Come on."

We stay on the walkway, following the signs leading towards the train station but, before we reach the correct exit, Jorden tenses. A woman in black is heading towards us on the walkway, going against the traffic.

"What is it? Who is that?"

"Bad news." He frowns, looking for a way off the walkway we're on.

A transparent wall, high as my waist, divides the walkway from the rest of the thoroughfare. Jorden places his hands on it and vaults over easily.

Planting my hands on my hips, I pin him with a frustrated look. "I can't do that."

He reaches out to me, keeping up with the moving walkway. "Come on."

Placing my hands on the barrier, I jump, boosting myself as high as I can. Jorden grabs me around the waist and pulls me over. Setting me on my feet, he takes my hand and we run in the opposite direction, away from the woman who snarls and chases us. Running parallel to us on the walkway, she shoves people aside, drawing a long, black weapon from underneath her coat.

I yelp in surprise and stumble into Jorden as he skids to a halt.

"What...?" I ask.

Jorden's gaze is on a hulking man with mottled skin like white marble, standing in the center of the path like an impassable barrier.

Looking around frantically, Jorden launches into motion again, veering off into a side corridor that ends in an elevator. We slam through the doors just as they're closing, startling the occupants. Jorden jabs the number 68 button. Then jabs a few more above it, "in case they're following".

How tall is this building? Sixty-eight isn't even the top floor. My whole life I've lived in a structure with only eight levels.

As soon as the door opens, we rush out into a long hall filled with identical numbered doors. Signs glowing on some doors. DO NOT DISTURB and PLEASE MAKE UP MY ROOM.

A couple pass us, heading for the elevator. Jorden squeezes my hand.

"It's a hotel. Let's find an empty room that's being cleaned."

The hallway seems endless. We turn a corner, then another, as we search for an open room. The elevator pings, the sound reverberating in the empty hallway. Turning another corner, we finally find several open rooms.

"What about the cleaning staff?" I whisper.

As if in answer, a squat, gray, metal unit with numerous arms rolls out of the room just in front of us. *Turboclean* 3000 is stamped across its side.

Jorden grins at me. "Don't worry. They won't tell."

We dart into the nearest open room, closing the door behind us.

The room is luxurious, nothing like the blue penguin self-serve motel. A wide bed that could sleep at least three people dominates the center of the room, covered in a fluffy duvet and piled high with pillows. Floor-to-ceiling windows provide a mesmerizing view of the city. Opening the balcony door, I step out onto the small terrace. Wind hits me like a slap, throwing me backwards. Jorden catches me as I stumble into him.

"Whoa, careful."

He threads his arms around my waist, supporting

me as I peek over the side of the glass balustrade. The height is dizzying. People on the ground are barely visible specks. Other buildings are so close by it seems possible to jump from one to the other; I wonder if anyone has tried it. Covered bridges connect the buildings, and small air crafts flit between them like colorful insects. One passes by us at eye level and I can see the people inside.

There's a soft knock on the door. Then louder. Jorden tugs at my hand.

"Come on. We need to hide. We're too exposed standing out here."

Pulling me back into the room, Jorden closes the balcony door and flips a switch by the bed. The doors fade from transparent to black, leaving the room in semi-darkness. The only light is a strip of faint LEDs along the wall. Enough to allow a sleepy occupant to find their way to the bathroom in the dark.

The only places to hide are a closet by the door and the bathroom. Jorden flips his gaze between them, deliberating.

"If we hide in the closet and they check it first, we're done for. On the other hand, if they check the rest of the room first, we're closer to the door. We can make a dash for it as they check the bathroom or balcony," he says.

"They'd trap us in the bathroom. We'd have to fight our way past them," I add.

Jorden took down the three men in the alley, but they weren't armed and he took them by surprise. They probably had no training, either. I have a feeling whoever's after us is armed and ready.

"Over there." Jorden slides open the closet door.

There are three shelves on one side and a narrow hanging area on the other side. Along the top, a shelf holds blankets and pillows.

"It's not big enough for both of us," I say.

The rattling of the door gets louder. They're going to break in here any moment. *How did they know we're in here?*

Jorden shakes his head. "It's cramped, but it will do. There's no time."

Jorden sits on the floor of the hanging space, taking up practically all the room.

I put my hands on my hips. "What am I going to do?"

He takes my hand, pulling me towards him. "Sit on me."

My cheeks heat up. "I'll crush you."

"Don't be silly." His expression is the same as when he grabbed me off the bed in the motel. Combined with the deafening bangs on the door, there's no point in arguing.

"It's your funeral," I say as I turn and lower myself into his lap. Pulling my legs up, I hug my knees, so they fit into the closet space. Jorden slides the door shut, his muscles rippling against my back.

"You, okay?" I whisper.

"I'll survive." He chuckles, his breath hot on my neck. I lean into his chest and he puts his arms around me.

The noise outside stops for a moment, then the door slams open with a crash. If they open the closet now, we have no way out. Footsteps pass us by, muffled by the carpeting. It sounds like three different people entering the room. If one of them guards the door, we can't escape. Jorden holds me tighter, then opens the door a crack to see what's going on.

They line up, one facing the bathroom, one facing the balcony, and one must be by the door.

Jorden breathes into my ear. "When I open the door, get up and get out of the way. As soon as the doorway is clear, run. Nod if you understand."

I nod.

There's a crash inside the room as they kick the bathroom door in. Jorden slides the cupboard door open. Grabbing the bar above his head for leverage, he slides forward and kicks out his legs so I'm propelled up and out. I glimpse a man in a sleeveless black tunic with dark hair and a mustache standing in the doorway. Turning to my right, I move further into the room as Jorden turns left towards the door. I scoot into the gap between the dresser and the closet wall, sliding down to the floor to get out of the way.

I can't see Jorden, but I hear grunts and thuds.

The mirror opposite the closet shatters, spraying the room with bloody shards. Hopefully, the blood isn't Jorden's.

The woman from the walkway emerges from the bathroom, pointing a gun at eye level. Across the room, her companion shoots out the balcony doors: the floor-to-ceiling windows and the glass balustrade separating the balcony from the sixty-floor drop shatter. The wind whips into the room, tearing at my hair and clothes. In a smooth move, they turn towards us.

Jorden is getting up off the floor. Thankfully, the blood on the glass isn't his, but he's taken a beating. Unfortunately, his opponent is still on his feet in front of the door. Blood is dripping down his arm, but his grip is steady as he points his weapon at Jorden.

Jorden backs away from his adversary into the room, placing himself between me and the gang.

Peeking around Jorden, I see the woman stalking towards us like a leopard, hunting her prey. The wind blows her shoulder-length black hair around her face, strands catching on her full red lips. Tight black leather pants, paired with high black boots, hug her body. Her top leaves her midriff bare, showing off taut olive skin and toned abs. She sweeps a calculating gaze over us, as if we're ripe fruit waiting to be picked. Then she gestures at me with her gun.

"Up."

Jorden steps forward. "Leave her alone. She has nothing to do with this. It's me you want."

"Au contraire, my dear," she answers in a sultry voice, "we need both of you." She raises her other wrist, and an image appears in the air before her. Jorden's face and mine, side by side. Data streams across the bottom of the picture. "It doesn't specify that I have to bring *you* in alive." She emphasizes the '*you*' with a pointed look at Jorden. *Oh.* Then I should protect him, not the other way around. They won't shoot me.

I grab his hand and rise to my feet, moving to his side. The wind whips at my hair and my dress like a fourth assailant. I raise a hand. "Don't shoot."

"Haley," Jorden mumbles out of the corner of his mouth, trying to push me back behind him, but I don't budge.

The giant who blocked our path downstairs is the same man who destroyed the balcony. My head tips back as he approaches us. He's at least 6'5" and covered in rippling muscle. Silvery hair surrounds his face in a halo of spiky tips and his skin glints like polished marble. Crossing the room in three strides, he grabs my arm, dragging me away from Jorden and closer to the window. Then he aims his gun at Jorden.

"I say we shoot him now. He's too much trouble to take alive," he rasps in a casual tone, as if he's discussing a business decision, not murder.

My heart plunges, afraid he'll shoot Jorden in front of me unless I do something. Twisting in Goliath's grasp, I lunge for his gun arm, which is oddly smooth and slippery, barely budging it enough to mess up his aim. Luckily, he misses. The shot goes wide, the bullet hitting the wall inches from Jorden's head. Jorden flinches and pales as we're sprayed with plaster.

The woman snarls. "No. I want them both alive. They're more valuable."

As they argue, I pull all the way out of Goliath's grasp and fall against the wall beside the broken balcony doors. Jorden's gaze moves between our three assailants. We aren't armed and they're blocking the door. The woman pulls a contraption from her belt that looks like a long, black, thick figure eight with a thin rod in the middle. She holds it towards Jorden.

"Okay," she says to Jorden. "Slip your wrists into one end."

Jorden glares at her. "What if I don't?"

She advances and presses her gun to his forehead. "Then we do it the hard way."

"No," I cry.

Jorden darts a glance at me and his shoulders droop, some of the fight going out of him. He places his hands in the noose and she presses a button on the device. The loop contracts, pinning his wrists together.

She drags him towards me and gestures with her

gun. "Now you."

I want to resist, be as defiant and brave as Jorden was, but he shakes his head slightly. "Just do it, Haley."

Trembling, I push to my feet and place my hands in the contraption.

The woman presses the button and the end contracts, pressing my wrists tightly together, trapping us facing each other. Jorden's eyes crinkle, as if he's trying to convey a message.

With us restrained, the other two goons relax their stances and grin. The woman turns to them, smiling. With a swift movement, she raises her gun and shoots the surveillance camera above the door. Then, to my surprise, she shoots Goliath and the dark-haired man in quick succession.

As she turns towards us again, Jorden springs into motion, dragging me by our connected hands towards the ruined balcony.

"Run," he shouts, but the only thing in front of us is open air and a long, long drop.

"What? No!" I barely have time to shout.

Glancing over my shoulder, I'm faced with the barrel of the bounty hunter's gun. I stop resisting the madness and run.

Chapter 13

Airborne

Haley

Running at full speed, Jorden flings himself out from the balcony as far as he can jump, dragging me after him. We spiral out and down, rotating around each other, connected by our hands. The wind rips away my scream.

The fierce wind between the buildings pushes us sideways. We might have been lucky enough to make it to the closest building, but then we hit something hard enough to knock the breath out of me.

A flying car.

My momentum carries me over the roof and down the other side. At first, I think I'm going to fall right off and carry Jorden with me, but my movement halts abruptly, almost pulling my arms from their sockets. Our restraints catch, wedging tightly across the top of the car. Jorden is on the other side of the vehicle.

Scrabbling for purchase, my feet find a step outside the door, a tiny ledge large enough to support my weight. I scoot up till I see Jorden's face.

"Find the step," I shout, hoping the wind doesn't snatch my words. He nods and, a moment later, rises higher. The tension in our arms abates. Looking down through the window I'm pressed against, I notice an elderly couple staring back in amazement from inside the vehicle.

Their incredulous gazes make me smile and, when I look over at Jorden, he smiles back. Shaking my head, I shout, "You're insane!"

He laughs. "You only just noticed?"

There's nothing we can do except hold on as the car rises, gaining altitude, skimming towards the center of the city. Landing on one of the tallest buildings, it glides to a stop on the topmost floor. The external car port doors close, shutting out the freezing wind. We're still in trouble, straddled over the craft. The car doors open, and the shaken couple emerge.

Jorden has the audacity to smile at them.

"I don't suppose we could trouble you for help with these?" He lifts his wrists, displaying the cuffs.

Doors on the other side of the room swish open and a group of armed men in dark blue combat gear, but with no insignia, storm in, pointing their weapons at us. *Why does everyone want to shoot us today?*

One of them approaches the older woman. "Are you alright, governor?"

She nods. "Quite alright, but we seem to have acquired passengers."

A guard vaults onto the roof of the craft and examines our restraints, pressing a button on the side. The loops stretch wide, enabling us to pull our hands out. As soon as my hands are free, my knees buckle and I sit down hard on the step I was standing on. Most of the guards lower their weapons, but one keeps his firearm trained on Jorden.

Another guard approaches me. "Are you alright, miss?"

I shake my head. "I need a minute." Jumping out of buildings isn't something I can just walk off.

"What should we do with them, ma'am?"

The governor looks bemused. "I don't know. At the very least, we should question them. Take them to the conference room and watch them."

The guard behind Jorden gestures with his gun. "Walk."

Jorden turns slowly towards him. *Please, don't let him do anything drastic right now.* "Can I help her up?" he asks in a placating tone.

The guard nods and steps back, leaving Jorden enough space to walk around the craft to my side, while keeping the gun on him. Jorden crouches and takes my freezing hand.

"Why doesn't anyone ever assume I'm the dangerous one?" I mumble.

He grins. "You look too sweet to be dangerous." I wasn't fishing for compliments but I blush, nevertheless. He pulls me up and looks me over. "You okay?"

I nod. The near-death experience has my knees shaking, but I don't want to antagonize the men with the guns.

Jorden stays between me and the armed guard. With his arm around my waist, he guides me out the door, following the guards. We march down a lavish hallway, paneled in wood and decorated with expensive-looking artwork. At the end, there's a conference room filled with an enormous table and large, plush office chairs. An enormous screen covers one wall, while floor-to-ceiling windows provide an astounding view of the city on the other side. Just when I thought we couldn't get any higher up.

Jorden steers me towards the windows, but I dig my heels in and shake my head. I'd rather keep my distance from the drop. The guards stay outside the door, giving us a moment alone.

Sitting in a plush chair, with the table between me and the windows, feels the safest.

"I'd love to know what you were thinking when

you jumped out the window," I hiss in an undertone, glaring at Jorden.

The wind has ruffled his hair, making him look more dangerous, but it suits him. He runs his hand through the tangle and plops into a chair opposite me.

"I was thinking she was going to shoot us, and I'd rather take my chances getting to the other building."

"We were sixty storeys up," I hiss.

He shrugs. "So, lots of time to figure it out."

I shake my head. "You're crazy."

"So you've said, yet here we are, not dead."

"Yet," I point out. "And, as a bonus, in a new and exciting type of trouble."

I fall silent as the door opens and two men march in, taking up positions beside the table. The governor enters, followed by a younger man. He remains standing while she takes a seat, clasping her hands in front of her on the table.

"My security detail thinks you two were trying to assassinate me." I sputter an objection, but she holds up her hand. "Trying to kill me by jumping onto my vehicle, with your hands tied together, 60 floors in the air, seems very ineffective. At best, you are extremely incompetent assassins. But I'll give you the opportunity to explain. Hold out your wrists, please."

Jorden looks at me and shrugs. There's no way to

get out of this. The false identities Judith supplied worked at the checkpoint. Though I'm not sure how the bounty hunters found us. The governor's assistant approaches me, running a scanner over my wrist. It beeps and my false identity flashes on the screen. Then he approaches Jorden and does the same.

Instead of resisting, Jorden grins as if he has a plausible explanation for our actions. The scanner beeps again and the screen fills with data. The young man walks back to the governor's side, showing her the screen. They converse in low voices.

"According to our scan, your name is Jorden Peters. Resident of Boulder, Colorado. Would you care to explain why you and this young lady were skydiving without a parachute?" The governor asks.

He leans back. "Are you going to let us go?"

The governor frowns. "First, provide me with a satisfactory explanation."

Jorden stalls, looking at me. *I wish I knew what he's thinking.*

The door of the room opens abruptly, revealing a woman dressed in a blue business suit. "I apologize for the interruption, Governor. You have an urgent phone call," she says.

Frowning at the interruption, the governor leaves the room, trailing her assistants and the armed guards.

Jorden waits till we're alone and then rises, walking around the table as if searching for a way out. I watch his actions with growing apprehension.

"If you suggest jumping out a window again, I'll push you out and surrender," I say, only half joking.

He smiles. "I don't think that'll be necessary."

Feet in heavy boots pound on the carpet in the hallway, accompanied by the whine of charging grav weapons. I've only heard them in movies before. Is this really happening?

"They're coming for us. She turned us in," Jorden pants, wide eyed. "I thought she'd at least listen to what we had to say."

Pulling me out of my seat, Jorden presses me into the corner closest to the door. His knuckles are white around my hand. Staring down the length of the conference room, his eyes move as if he's calculating our chances of fighting our way out. The immense oval table and the boardroom chairs fill the room, leaving almost no room to maneuver. His gaze drifts to the windows overlooking the city.

I shake my head. "No. Jorden, please, not that way. Not again."

Jorden deflates slightly, then pushes up his sleeves, preparing for a fight. My feet are numb and I'm shaking. *Not another life-and-death fight.* I don't want to see him get hurt. We were unbelievably lucky last time, but we can't count on luck twice in a row.

"Maybe we should surrender," I suggest. "She's a

governor. They probably won't shoot us."

"That's not an option," Jorden growls. His jaw is set and his expression is stubborn, reminding me of the day he tried to blow up the jump ship. Even if it costs him his life, he's determined to fight.

I need to get through to him.

"Jorden, look at me." Placing my hands on his cheeks, I turn his face to mine. "I'm scared. There must be at least a dozen guards with guns... You can't fight our way out of this."

Confusion crosses his face, as if for an instant he was so wrapped up in his own mind he forgot that I'm here and this affects me too. Then he nods.

I sigh with relief and wrap my arms around his neck, press my cheek to his, and hold him tightly, forcing him into inaction. Pressed against me, his hand trembles on my back and his muscles shake with tension. His instinct is to fight, but following his instincts puts him in danger.

I hope this isn't a mistake. That I can save his life.

The door crashes inward and men storm into the room, aiming their weapons at us. I cling to Jorden till they pull him roughly away and place silvery cuffs on him. They cuff me too.

I guess someone finally thinks I'm dangerous, too.

When we're both cuffed, the soldiers turn us towards the door.

"I hope you're happy," Jorden grumbles under his breath. His reaction stings, but I don't regret preventing the fight.

"You're not dead. So yes. I'm happy," I whisper back. His glare softens as my words sink in.

The guards maneuver us into two chairs on the further side of the table beside the windows, covering us with their weapons as the governor takes a seat opposite us.

"I'm sorry about the harsh response," she says when everyone is seated again, "but your identities triggered an alert." We exchange glances. The only people who know our new identities are Judith and whoever programmed them. "Jorden?" she asks, and he nods. I'm hoping she's referring to our cover identities. "...and Haley, I presume? Welcome back to Earth."

My heart sinks.

She knows who we are.

Chapter 14

Message from the Past

Jorden

"How do you know who we are?" Haley asks.

I shake my head, trying to warn her from giving out more information. We should say as little as possible. Maybe she's fishing for information. We don't know how much she knows about us.

"A mutual friend asked me to keep an eye out for you."

Haley and I exchange glances. *My father? Judith?*

"A friend?" Haley asks.

"I had my suspicions when your data popped up on the system, but the scan as you walked into this room confirmed it. After all, your comm bracelet is our technology."

Haley's eyes widen. "Your technology?

"Conglomerate," she says simply.

I want to slap my forehead. We never even thought about Haley's comm bracelet being read, since I'd assumed it wasn't compatible with anything here on Earth.

Haley moves to remove her comm, but the governor smiles.

"Don't bother. We've already read it, and you'll need it, for when you return." Haley drops her hand and stops fumbling with the clasp. "It's an ingenious piece of technology if I say so myself. For example—" the screen behind her fills with Haley's picture, with her blue hair, and columns of data. "We know your system received several doses of nanobots while still on the station. Which is curious, isn't it, since you weren't scheduled for departure to New Horizons." Lifting her eyebrows, she waits for us to explain. She doesn't seem annoyed, only curious.

Keeping quiet about things she already knows is pointless, but the truth could work in our favor, make us seem more cooperative. I clasp Haley's hand to my heart, pulling her closer.

"Haley was leaving for New Horizons with me. We wanted to stay together." Haley looks at me, following my lead, and her eyes soften as we gaze into each other's eyes. *We were so in love when we decided to run away together.* Regret surges through my chest like a lightning bolt as I think of how I hurt her. Before I pushed her away, she trusted me implicitly. I'll never have that again. I broke something we can never mend. Now, there'll always be fear and doubt. I'd give anything to fix it, but I know I can't.

"I'm sorry," I mouth. Haley caresses my cheek. She's trying so hard to forgive me, but I can't forgive myself.

"Ah, young love," the governor muses. Haley blushes and drops her hand. "But then something went wrong... the accident? In the pod bay."

Haley stiffens by my side. Accident?

The governor apparently has excellent information sources. She knows a lot, but she doesn't know everything. Don't they know I planned to sabotage the jump ship? That I'm an Earther? Is that possible?

"Yes," I answer carefully, peeking at Haley, who comes to my aid.

"I was going to fly the pod ship over to the jump ship. The plan was to hide and wait for Jorden, but when we got to the pod deck, we discovered somebody had rigged the pod to blow. We couldn't call for help with the comms array down. Jorden locked me into the control room to protect me before the pod exploded."

We both hold our breath. The governor's eyes narrow.

"That's an interesting explanation of events. There's evidence of sabotage around the station. How do you explain the destruction of the comm array, the mass food poisoning, or the fire in the training center?"

Haley doesn't waver. "There were obviously Earthers on the station. We stumbled into their plans."

The governor leans forward. "And who were they?"

We shake our heads. "No idea."

The governor's shoulders slump slightly. She consults her handheld again and her assistant whispers something in her ear.

"You were traveling with your family, Jorden, your mother and a sister. Strange that they left while you were in the infirmary. Was your mother not concerned enough to stay on the station with her injured son?" The governor raises her eyebrows.

"You'd have to ask her that, since I was unconscious. The station was in an uproar. Maybe she didn't realize I wasn't on the jump ship?" I don't hide the bitterness in my voice. "But it's not my job to excuse her behavior. It's not the first time she abandoned me."

"So, if you were planning to continue to New Horizons, why come here, to Earth?" The governor's trying to sound casual but her eyes darken as the silence extends.

Haley replies. "We just wanted to get away. It's not like we could reach New Horizons on our own. Without the jump ship, it would take years."

"All right. Since you are both under ESC jurisdiction, Jorden as a traveler and Haley as the daughter of station employees, I've alerted the ESC to come get you. They will return you to where you belong. I assume you both want to be reunited with your families?"

Haley nods. I can't object now. I'm just relieved they don't know I'm an Earther. We begin to get up, but the governor adds, "Before you leave, could I see the object you have in your pocket, Jorden?"

How does she know I have the pendant? But she obviously does.

We were so close to getting away. I hold out the spinning disk of Earth. She doesn't react. Does she know it's an Earther symbol?

"Ah," she says, "lovely, and the recording on it is so touching."

"Recording?" I ask.

"You didn't know? The scan picked up a message on the data chip inside it."

Data chip?

"Would you like to hear it?" she asks.

My mouth is dry as I nod. It might incriminate me, but I can't refuse. She swipes the screen and a message from the past plays, the sound scratchy.

"Jorden, if you're listening to this, I just wanted to say I'm sorry. I never chose to leave you. I love you."

It's my mother's voice. My real mother, Elanor. *Even though she's been gone for years, since I returned to Earth, I keep getting closer to her.* Plunging my fingers through my hair, my heart beats wildly.

Haley notices my turmoil and leans closer.

"I see your mother left you a message after all," the governor says.

For a moment, I'm confused. Then I realize she thinks this is a message from Nancy, explaining why she abandoned me, unconscious, on the space station. So, I nod, still at a loss for words.

"That concludes our business here." The governor motions to the guards. "Deliver them to the ESC headquarters. They will see them safely home."

We get up and the guard march us over to the opposite wall. Invisible panels slide open to reveal an elevator. The guards flank us as the doors slide closed. I haven't let go of Haley's hand, letting her touch ground me as my thoughts race, replaying the message. Of course, my mother didn't choose to leave me. She died in an attack.

As if reading my mind, Haley whispers, "How did your mother die?"

"In an explosion, at Earther headquarters in Chicago. After her death, my father moved our base of operations to the Farm."

Haley rubs my arm. "I'm sorry. I miss my mom, too."

"It isn't the same. Your mom isn't dead," I say bitterly before I can stop myself.

Haley drops her hand. "She may as well be. I don't know if I'll ever see her again."

We glare at each other, hurt, and each wrapped

up in our own misery. Logically, I know it's my fault she's here and has lost years of her parents' company and will lose more before she ever sees them again. But the topic is too raw for me to be rational. Still, I exhale, struggling to control my emotions. I don't want to fight with her.

Haley wraps her fingers around my clenched fist. "I'm sorry," she whispers. "It's not a competition who misses their mom more."

Relaxing my hand, I let her thread her fingers through mine, bending my forehead to hers. "Sorry. It's just—" I trail off, not finding the words.

"I understand. Hearing from her is hard for you."

"Yes." I nod. "I'm sorry I took you away from your parents."

Her strained smile is tight-lipped, biting back pain, but she exhales and pushes up on her toes, planting her hands on my shoulders. As she brushes her lips against mine, my heart skips a beat. We lock eyes, her hand caressing the back of my neck.

"We're together again," she whispers. "It makes all of this worthwhile."

"OK. Cool it, lovebirds," a guard snaps, and we reluctantly break apart.

The elevator opens into a huge, marbled lobby at street level. Our guards remove our cuffs before starting across the marble expanse, where a group of agents in ESC jackets await. As our guards march us towards them, the front doors slide open and my breath catches: the female bounty hunter we'd escaped in the hotel strides into the lobby, a terrifying glowing weapon with a wide muzzle clutched in each arm. Before anyone can react, she aims a gun at us and fires, blowing us back into the wall with a powerful sonic wave. The blast tears Haley's hand from my grasp as we fly through the air. Our guards hit the wall. I land hard, dazed for a moment, as my ears ring and my vision blurs, but I force myself up. Using a sound gun means she wants us alive.

As we stumble to our feet, she turns towards the ESC agents and lets loose with the other blaster. Bullets rip through the lobby, shattering the floor-to-ceiling windows behind them. *This chick really hates windows.* A few agents make it to the cover of the reception desk, firing back at her. Others are down, dead or bleeding out.

Someone touches my arm. Tearing my gaze away from the agents, I find Haley next to me, gripping my arm hard.

"Come on," she whispers, or maybe she's shouting and my ears are still ringing from that blast. Pushing to my feet, I grab her hand. My shoulder aches, but I ignore it as I pull Haley towards the stairwell at the back of the lobby. It's separated from the open space by a massive, black door.

We're close when bullets thud into the wall beside it, spraying us with granite chips. Haley gasps as a piece slices her chin, and blood erupts. I clamp my hand over the cut and pull her through the doorway, letting it slam shut behind us. Bullets hit the door a moment later, but it's thick enough to stop them. *So much for not wanting to kill us.*

The stairwell muffles the sound from the entrance hall. My world contracts to the sound of our breathing, my heart thudding in my chest, our feet pounding on the stairs as we race up the darkened stairwell. Haley's face is wet and sticky underneath my hand. Her breathing sounds like sobbing.

At the top of the first flight of stairs, we burst through the door into an empty cafeteria. Ribbons of light filter through the window blinds.

The room has two levels, separated by three steps and a railing. A row of food printers and dispensers for utensils fill one wall. I can't see another exit besides the elevator. We dash towards the raised area as the elevator doors slide open and a band of light spills into the room.

I duck behind a table, pulling Haley down with me as our pursuer stalks into the room. We crouch face to face. Haley is pale but determined, her chin smeared with blood, lips pressed tightly together. I squeeze her hand and point towards the exit. If the hunter gets any closer, we'll make a run for it.

Footsteps draw steadily closer as the hunter prowls the room. We watch under the table as her boots approach, getting closer and closer.

Until she stops.

Chapter 15

Destiny

Haley

Jorden tenses when the hunter stops, preparing to run. He points toward the door, signaling we should run around the table, on the side farther from her. He opens his hand, showing me five fingers, then four, three, two, one. I push to my feet but, as soon as we move, the hunter whirls and dives in our direction.

"Keep going," Jorden yells and turns to face her.

Before I can take a step towards the door, she vaults over the tables and tackles Jorden with a flying leap, sending him crashing to the ground. His head bangs into the marble floor. It's the second hit to his head in ten minutes, and he's still recovering from a concussion. Grabbing him by his shirt, she lifts him easily and slams him into a chair. Then she pulls out a silvery magnetic tie and secures his hands to the backrest.

The hunter prowls forward and grabs me. I struggle, but she raises her fist menacingly. She looks like the type who would punch me. I stop struggling; I've already been hit and shot at enough for a lifetime. I allow her to tie my hands to the nearest railing. When I'm secure, she turns back to Jorden, circling him, as if she's assessing him from every angle.

"You look just like your father." She trails her fingers lightly across his shoulders and up his neck. Scowling, he moves his head away from her, but she chuckles and runs her fingers down his arm. My hackles rise possessively. I want her to stop touching him RIGHT NOW.

"Do you know who I am?" she purrs. Jorden's blank stare is her only answer. "I guess you were too young to remember me, but I remember you. I'm Destiny. Your daddy and I were very close friends, if you know what I mean." She trails her fingers down his cheek and straddles him, sliding into his lap. "We could be good friends as well. If you like..."

Threading her hands into his hair, she kisses him full on the mouth. He tries to pull back, but her hands lock him in place. My mouth drops open in shock. I feel sick. *What is wrong with these people?*

Releasing Jorden, she smacks her lips. "Delicious."

"Get off me!" Jorden pulls out of her grasp, looking her dead in the eye.

"Have it your way," she chuckles, rising slowly, as if she owns him and can do whatever she wants.

I'm going to kill her. I don't care if she can put me down with one hand behind her back. Straining against the ties on my wrists, I discover one is slightly loose. Wriggling my hand, I work it out bit by bit while Destiny focuses on Jorden. She sits facing him and puts her feet up on the table.

Swallowing my fury, I ask, "What are you going to do with us?"

Holding up a datapad, she taps the screen.

"I'm having a little auction. You two are mega popular. Your spacer ass is worth thousands of credits and Earther boy here—" she chuckles. "Let's just say there are several interested parties. I'll hand you over to the highest bidder. Don't want the authorities getting to you first."

Jorden glares at her. "If you want the bounty, why shoot us in the hotel?"

"I wasn't going to. I took out the competition before *they* shot you. And I hate sharing. Then you two idiots dove off the building. My clients want both of you alive. But I don't think you are going to stay alive." She leans forward, lowering her voice conspiratorially. "At least one contender wants to kill you themselves. Slowly. To send a message."

My mouth dries up. "Why? What did we do to them?"

"Your little space station adventure. Until now,

they considered Earthers a bunch of crackpots not worth taking seriously. But causing an explosion on the space station made things very real."

"We didn't—" I protest, but Destiny raises her palm.

"Save it. You're messing with an immense financial power with endless resources and you've made them look weak and vulnerable. They are really, really mad and they're coming for you. Probably won't stop until all the Earthers are dead." Her head whips back to me. "You too, honey. I presume they'll claim you were caught in the crossfire. You're liabilities."

Jorden is staring at her in disbelief. "They can't just kill us."

She snorts. "They can do whatever they want, since they control the media. They care about public opinion, but it won't stop them from doing whatever they like. I can see the headlines: *Doomsday cult commits mass suicide... Attack on compound causes massive casualties...* they'll spin it to suit their needs."

Jorden gasps. "I need to get back and warn them."

Taking her feet off the table, our captor leans forward. "You aren't going anywhere." She raises the datapad. "Done. I just need to make the call."

I finally pull my hand out of the restraint. Now it's easy to free my other hand from the loose tie. But in order to free Jorden, I'll need to distract her.

Leaving my hands hidden, I start to cough. The

hunter frowns.

"Can I get some water?" I ask. "I'm really parched from all that running."

She sniffs with disdain. "Only water? Maybe you'd like some iced tea or a few biscuits too?"

I smile at her. "Iced tea would be lovely, actually."

"Yeah? Well, tough. I'm not your server."

Jorden lifts his eyebrows, silently asking what I'm doing. Destiny scans the room, her eyes sweeping from Jorden to me to the doors, waiting for her clients to arrive. What can I do? I don't have any weapons, nor a chance of taking her on in a fight.

"I'm not feeling so well," I mumble, crumpling to the floor. Now it's obvious my ties are gone.

"What the—" the hunter rasps as she jumps to her feet, stalking over to inspect me, leaving her gun on the table. It's my best chance to even the odds.

As she bends and grabs my shirt, I snap up as fast as I can and grab her shoulders, tugging her off balance, and kick up. She struggles, but crashes to the floor behind me, tucking and rolling like a professional. Running on sheer terror, I jump up and tackle her. I'm well aware she's going to rearrange my face any minute now. In the struggle, I yank on her top and see a moving tattoo on her left shoulder, like snake guy had, of a small, blue and green spinning globe.

"You're an Earther?" I pant, sitting on top of her.

She pauses, grinning at me. "Sorry, kids. I really

sympathize, and I love Earth, but—"

Jorden looks furious. "What about supporting the cause?"

"My loyalty lies where the money is. Earthers haven't done anything for me lately." She takes a breath, squirming under me. I'm using my weight to my advantage, but she'll shove me off in a second.

Jorden is still tied up. I have to do this myself.

I grab her head. She twists her hips up and bucks enough to throw me off. I scream as I fly towards the row of food dispensers. My outstretched arm lands on the metal tray holder on the closest dispenser. Using it to pull myself to my feet shifts the entire machine off balance, toppling it towards me. I roll out of the way at the last moment, but Destiny isn't so lucky. The heavy appliance lands on her upper torso with a sickening crunch.

I don't want to look, but I need to assess the threat. Thankfully, I can't see her head or upper body. Her legs jerk from under the machine as a trickle of blood seeps towards me. *Ugh.* Even though I know she was going to hurt us, I feel sick to my stomach. Hopefully, I haven't killed her, but she's definitely injured. Scooting back, I rush to Jorden.

"Hey," Jorden searches my eyes, taking in my pale complexion and somber expression. "You had to do it, *Blue*. I know you didn't want to hurt her."

I gulp again and run my fingers down his arms to release his restraints. Jorden gets to his feet, swaying slightly and wincing in pain, rubbing his wrists to restore the circulation. He snags an arm around my waist, pulling me close to comfort me. I lean into his chest, trying to calm my heart, still beating wildly from the fight with the hunter. An awful screech startles us apart. There's a groan behind us and the squeal of dragging metal.

Twisting in Jorden's grasp to look behind me, I can't believe my eyes. The heavy machine is moving.

His fingers tighten on mine. "What's it going to take to get rid of her?" he pants, pulling me into a run again.

The elevator and the stairs are the only ways out of here. The relentless hunter is between us and the elevator, filling the space between the wall and the closest tables. As we edge around the machine, a bloody hand snaps out, almost latching on to my foot. I squeal in terror, and Jorden snatches me away from the grasping hand and positions me behind his back.

Destiny is slowly extracting herself from under the machine. I glimpse her bloodied face, hair matted to her forehead, her eyes glinting in feral determination. We lock eyes and she snarls at me.

"Stairs it is," Jorden gasps and we turn and run.

Slamming open the door, we dash into the darkened stairwell. Heavy boots stomp up the stairs. Jorden grabs the railing, starting up the flight of stairs to the next level. The door behind us slams open and it feels as if the hunter's breath washes over my neck.

The thump of boots in the stairwell increases, coming from both above and below. We're stuck between the agents on the stairs and the hunter at our back.

Luckily, the injured hunter flees back into the empty cafeteria. Several agents thud through the door in pursuit. I hope they catch her: one less thing to worry about.

There's nowhere left to run. We pull up short as multiple red dots dance on Jorden's forehead and chest. Thankfully, he doesn't resist as the agents force us to our knees on the cold marble of the staircase.

The ESC wants us just as bad as the Conglomerate. At least they won't kill us.

At least I hope they won't.

Chapter 16

Breathless

Haley

I've been sitting for hours in an interrogation room at ESC headquarters. Seated at a black info-desk, staring at an empty metal chair in front of a gray concrete wall. They even have a swinging light fixture to aim into the suspect's eyes. Very clichéd. Surprising that Earth Space Control has this setup ready.

My butt is numb from sitting on the cold, metal chair for so long. Checking my reflection in the shiny surface of the one-way observation window, I groan at how awful I look. A medic patched up my bleeding chin, spraying on a flesh-colored adhesive, but my new dress is in tatters and smeared with blood. My hair is a rat's nest.

It feels like I've been awake for days.

The surveillance camera in the corner blinks at me with a baleful red glare. I'd lay my head on the table and try to sleep, but I can't relax until I know what they've done with Jorden. I haven't seen him since we got here.

Everyone we talk to seems to know our true identities. *And we actually thought we'd get through the city undetected.*

I jump in my seat as the door slides open and a short, brown-haired man with a mustache enters. He sits opposite me with the self-satisfied air of a person who can feel his promotion being granted as we speak. He looks the same height, sitting down and standing up. A moment later, he's joined by a familiar face that I take a moment to place: *Humpty Dumpty.* The ranger we stranded on the station.

How did he get here so fast? He must have hitched a ride back on the colony transport that arrived after we left.

He looks around for a chair but, finding none available, he leans against the wall by the door.

I just glare at them both. Mr. Mustache taps the info desk and my file appears on the desktop between us.

"Miss Haley Shavit. Sixteen years old, resident of VOR space station," he reads.

I don't answer. He doesn't need me to confirm what he already knows. Unbothered by my silence, he continues, "I'm inspector Rogers with the ESC

THE GIRL FROM THE SKY   153

Crimes Unit."

"Crimes unit? Am I being charged with something?"

"Of course not, Miss Shavit. You're an innocent bystander caught up in this situation. Ranger Davis was an eyewitness to your kidnapping. He confirms your story."

Humpty Dumpty grunts. The inspector taps the info-table again and an image pops into the air between us. I assume it's real-time footage. Jorden is in a stark, white cell, pacing back and forth. He looks frantic, his muscles tense, as if he's going to explode at any minute. I hate seeing Jorden caged up.

"My sources tell me you thwarted this miscreant's plan aboard the station. That was very brave. I imagine he took you as payback for your actions."

I almost reach out to touch the image. The inspector raises his eyebrows at my expression.

"Ah, you have feelings for this boy. Even though he kidnapped you and brought you here against your will?"

I roll my eyes and clench my fists. *Why insist on discussing my feelings, trying to make them sound so trivial and childish?*

He lowers his voice. "Don't be upset. You're not the first to experience feelings in this situation. It's called Stockholm syndrome, falling in love with your kidnapper. You're young, emotionally vulnerable, and alone on an unfamiliar planet with a handsome boy." The inspector leans back and crosses his arms, his expression smug. I want to punch him in the face.

Of course I have feelings for Jorden, but it's not as simple as he thinks; I fell in love with Jorden long before the trip to Earth. The past few weeks added layers to feelings that were already there. But I refuse to explain myself to the inspector. Instead, I mimic his position, crossing my arms and glaring at him.

He smirks. "If you want to help him, help us and we can make a deal. Get him to turn in the ringleaders of his organization. If he does, we'll grant him a full pardon. He can have a life after this."

"That is—" I pause. It's a good offer, if I can trust this guy. Jorden might escape the consequences of his actions. Finally, some hope. "What about the events on the station?"

This time the ranger answers. "There's no footage from the space station of Jorden. It's like he wasn't even there. Not a single camera picked him up. Can you explain that?"

"I can't," *but that means...* "So, you have no proof of the crimes he's accused of...?"

"None. Except the items Dawn Fowler turned over to command, and your testimony."

Why is he telling me this? Whose side does he think I'm on? Come to think of it, whose side am I on?

"So," I say slowly, "just so I understand... you need

me to make the case against him? And if I don't testify?

"That may be the reason he kidnapped you," Davis says.

His words hit me like a slap; I never considered that possibility. Davis looks pleased at my reaction. They're trying to undermine my faith in Jorden.

"No," I say, shake my head, and shove the thought away. Jorden cares about me. He risked his life for me, over and over. *That isn't why he took me.* "How would he know you don't have any footage?" I challenge.

"There's technology to scrub all digital evidence of a person. Even his station data-strip info has disappeared." He points to my wrist. "Why are you still wearing your data-strip? It's useless here."

Glancing down, I realize he's right. It's such a part of me I never considered removing it. I shrug. "Well, it's useless *now*, but I'll need it when I go home."

He smiles as if I got the right answer.

"Indeed, you will. And very soon. But before you do, I'm sure you want the people responsible for endangering your home brought to justice."

Ah. I sit up straighter. "I'm not testifying against Jorden." When I opened the airlocks, I almost killed him. I'm not sending him to prison.

Davis and Rogers exchange glances.

Rogers smirks. "I'm not asking you to. I'll level with you. We don't care about Jorden. He's just a kid.

Luckily, he hasn't killed anyone yet. Since he was a minor when he left for the station and was in his father's custody, we'll hold his father responsible for his actions. Since Jorden was only following his father's orders, I can offer him a deal if he testifies against the Earther ringleaders."

I shake my head. "No. Jorden won't turn on his father. He'd never do that."

The condescending smile turns into a frown. He thought I'd be eager to cooperate. "If you agree to this, I'll make sure you both leave this place today. If not, well..."

They exchange a glance. Davis nods and leaves the room.

On the screen, a guard approaches the cell and activates the cuffs on Jorden's hands. The two bluish bracelets on his wrists spring together, dragging his arms in front of him. Opening the cell door, another guard grabs him by the arm and guides him along a long, bleak passage, ending in an ominous elevator.

Jorden doesn't resist until they reach the elevator. The doors slide open and Davis stands inside, grinning. As soon as Jorden spots Davis, he bucks, but the guards push him relentlessly into the elevator. The doors close as if they were waiting to swallow him and take him down into the bowels of the building.

The screen goes blank.

Meanwhile, Inspector Rogers peers at me, gauging my reaction. My hands are sweaty. I grip the edge of the table, my knuckles whitening as I wait to see Jorden again.

"Where are they taking him?" I ask.

The image reappears, displaying a room arranged like an operating theater with a metal gurney. Numerous displays with various readouts line the walls. The elevator opens and the guards guide Jorden out of the elevator and towards the table. Davis follows.

"Do you remember what I told you on the space station?" he hisses over Jorden's shoulder. Jorden ducks, twisting out of the guard's grasp and away across the room, falling into a fighting pose. The guard grins and presses a remote. Jorden drops at once, his whole body spasming.

"No." I leap to my feet. "What is that? What are you doing to him?"

When the guard releases the button, Jorden lies still. His head rolls forward as the guards pick up his limp body. They place him on the table, strapping down his arms and legs and head. I can't tell if he's alive, but at least the medical readouts come to life, proof that he's still breathing.

"What are you doing to him?" I ask.

"This is a technique we call suggestive therapy."

My skin feels clammy. "Do you mean torture?"

"Oh, no, no. That implies we'd physically harm him. We aren't barbarians." Rogers scoffs.

"This can't be legal," I protest.

"You'd be surprised how specific court definitions of torture are nowadays. I wouldn't dream of breaking the law. We're merely... jogging his memory." He smiles as if he expects me to agree this is a brilliant idea.

A man in a lab coat enters the room carrying a tray of instruments. He places electrodes on Jorden's temples, rips open his shirt and places more electrodes on his chest above his heart. Lifting a data pad, the technician faces Davis.

"We're ready," he says in a bland tone.

Rogers speaks in an informative tone, as if he's narrating a documentary, waiting for my reaction. "Suggestive therapy makes the body think it's going through an unpleasant experience. It's most powerful if you choose something significant for the individual." He gives me a meaningful look. "I understand this young man had a traumatic experience with asphyxiation lately. An explosion draining all the air from the landing deck he was on?"

My fists clench so tightly my nails dig pits into my palms.

"You're a monster," I grit between closed teeth.

His smile recedes. "Not at all. To be fair, I'm not actually depriving his body of oxygen. I'm making him remember what another person in this room did to him in the recent past."

I want to lunge at him, but I can't tear my gaze

away from Jorden.

Davis nods, and Jorden writhes on the table, struggling to draw breath. Gulping for air, his face contorts. The monitor shows his heartbeat racing.

The camera view zooms in. I couldn't see him on the pod deck, but now I have an up-close view of what he went through. *What I put him through.* I take a deep, shuddering breath, as if I could somehow help Jorden breathe.

"Stop," I beg him. "Stop it now."

The inspector examines my face. The bastard knew exactly what buttons to push. "Will you help me bring the Earthers to justice?"

"I can't make him testify against his father," I insist.

"Will you do as I ask?"

My heart pounds so hard I can't breathe. Every time Jorden gasps, it's as if the air is sucked out of my lungs. For a second, I'm back on the pod deck, watching him die. Hating myself for what I did. Needing to look away, but I don't. I deserve this punishment, seeing what I did. So, I force myself to watch despite the tears streaming down my face, blurring my vision.

"Yes, yes. I'll do whatever you ask. Just stop hurting him," I cry.

The inspector presses the comms. "That's enough," he says.

I gasp in relief.

Davis looks disappointed. The man in the lab coat

swipes his data pad and Jorden's body collapses onto the table. His breathing resumes, but his eyes stare straight up, as though he can't process what happened.

"Is he okay?" I ask.

"He will be in a few minutes. Prepare for transit."

Rogers gives me a few moments to compose myself. I wipe my eyes, examining the crescent-shaped wounds on my palm.

"What do you need me to do?" I ask.

Rogers steeples his fingers in front of his face. "Don't worry. I'll let you know when the time comes."

Chapter 17

IN THE AIR

Jorden

When I come to, I'm looking up into a bright, white light. The men moving around me cast dark shadows. My mind buzzes like a thousand flies. I can't think straight. The steel table underneath me is freezing, the cold seeping through my clothes, but I can't sit up.

A guard bends over me, untying my restraints, and I flinch. The guard grins at my reaction. "Not so brave now, ha? You scared? You should be."

They lift me by my arms and lead me out of the room, practically dragging me into the elevator. My feet are numb.

"Where are we going?" I ask.

They don't answer. Behind them there's a familiar face that I can't place. He scowls when we make eye contact.

My brain is fuzzy, and my stomach is tied in knots. I'm not sure what happened, but my whole body is shaking in panic.

The elevator rises. I'm having trouble catching my breath, buzzing with weird sensations. My returning memory doesn't make any sense. A minute ago I was back on the pod deck on the space station, as the air escaped into space. I couldn't breathe. It was so vivid. I shudder and take a big breath, filling my lungs. Trying to breathe normally. It must have been a nightmare. Another memory hits me: Haley. We were together, but she's gone.

What if they already sent her back to the station and I never even get to say goodbye?

"Where's Haley?" I ask, but they ignore me.

The elevator climbs, suddenly breaking out of the building as the left wall falls away. We're outside, scaling the exterior of the building. I flinch and press back against the wall. The guards chuckle. The sudden shift of perspective makes my stomach rise uncontrollably. Before I can stop myself, I hurl on the third guy's feet.

Groans and grimaces fill the elevator.

"Damn it," the guy yells.

"Sorry," I mumble, focusing on the view to overcome my vertigo and trying to ignore the smell.

The city spreads out below us. It's light outside. *How long were we cooped up here?* When the elevator stops, we exit onto a launch pad. There's a small copter and my body floods with relief as I see Haley beside it: she's here, I haven't lost her yet.

I look her up and down, searching for signs of abuse. She's crying and, as we draw near, she flings herself at me, hugging me tightly.

"Are you okay? Did they hurt you?" I stammer in her ear.

"No. I'm fine. Sorry," she cries. "I'm so sorry they hurt you. It's all my fault." She's trembling.

I want to touch her, but my hands are tied, literally. All I can do is kiss her hair and murmur, "No. I'm okay. It's not your fault."

One of my guards steps away and returns with a bottle of water. He lets me rinse my mouth out and take a few sips.

"Where are they taking us?" I ask.

"Inspector Rogers said they're sending us to the spaceport. Ranger Davis is our escort." *Oh, so that's who that guy is.* "They want to interrogate you about what happened on the station and—" she pauses, "they're sending me home."

My heart almost stops. So, this isn't the end, but soon we'll be separated for good.

Haley's guard pulls her away and shoves her into the craft. My guard guides me into the seat opposite Haley and straps me in. He hasn't released the cuffs yet.

"What about these?" I raise my wrists. "What am I

going to do? Jump out a moving copter?"

The guard looks unsure. Davis takes the remote, sitting down beside Haley. His shoes are wet and he looks even more pissed than before. He gives me a hard look.

"Do you think I'm stupid? I uncuff you when we get there and hand you over. Not a minute before."

Haley is buckled in, but she isn't cuffed. She isn't exactly a prisoner, but they're treating her like my accomplice. They must wonder whose side she's on. Maybe I should wonder about that myself, but I trust her. She peeks at Davis out of the corner of her eye, then leans forward and grasps my hand. I squeeze her hand before Davis pulls her away again.

We take off, flying over the never-ending city. Davis' presence dampens any conversation we might make. The only thing passing between us are looks, looks that need to say all there is to say. Every mile we travel brings us closer to being parted forever. I can't bear to say goodbye.

Finally, we put the city behind us. The city outskirts are a deserted no man's land: nobody lives in the area outside the scrubbers, from the lowlands till high in the mountains, above the pollution. We clear the outskirts, climbing into the wooded mountains. These are familiar surroundings. We're drawing closer to the Farm. To be so near but so far from my destination is agonizing.

Davis leans his head on the bulkhead behind him,

his eyelids drooping. His head lolls sideways, revealing his neck tattoo, with his service number just beneath the buzz cut. Tough guy. He'd have to be, to become a ranger. He jerks upright one or twice, fighting the drowsiness, but then he doesn't stir for a long while and begins to snore.

Haley and I exchange amused glances.

Then it hits me. This is our chance to escape.

I nod to Haley, lifting my cuffs to draw her attention to them. I tap my chest, point to Davis and mouth, "Find the remote." She nods back.

Where did Davis put the remote to my restraints? Must be in a pocket on his combat gear, but which one? The vest alone has six pockets, three on each side. He's wearing a harness strapping him in to the aircraft, fastened around the waist with two shoulder straps. It partially covers the pockets. Haley will have to work around it.

She's wearing a similar harness. If she swivels towards him, she can reach into his right-hand pockets, but not the left-hand ones. We hold our breath as her fingers start a fleeting search, patting them lightly from the outside. Davis shifts and we both recoil.

We wait a few breaths till Davis settles again before Haley's fingers creep back. She's using both hands to feel the pockets, but the remote isn't on the right side. To search the left side, she has to release her harness and get up. There's no other way. The craft is flying smoothly on auto pilot. If we don't hit turbulence or shift suddenly to avoid something, the craft should stay level.

Still, I don't like her being unprotected. I almost tell her not to do it, but she unbuckles her harness and slides out of her seat before I can speak.

She squeezes my hand, then she turns to Davis.

Crouching on his other side, she pats the vest pockets. I pray he didn't put it in his pants pocket. I'd hate to watch her feeling around there. But we're in luck. She smiles triumphantly, lifting the flap and reaching into the second vest pocket on the left. Moving at a glacial pace, she lifts the remote between her finger and thumb.

I hold my breath. My muscles tense. The remote is almost clear of his pocket when Davis snaps up and grabs Haley's wrist.

"What do you think you're doing?" he snarls.

She gasps, trying to pull away, but he holds on tightly. Before he can take back the remote, she presses it, and my cuffs disengage. Lucky she didn't hit the electrocution button.

That's all I need.

Scrambling, I release my harness. Davis is roaring, with Haley in his grasp. I need her out of the way and safe before I can make a move.

Shedding my harness, I rise. Haley and I are both standing. Davis is at a disadvantage because he's still pinned to his seat, holding Haley's wrist. He can use her as a shield, but then he only has one free hand to release his harness, a tough act one-handed.

Hand-to-hand combat in a small, closed space is complicated. I need to incapacitate him without hurting Haley. While I'm wondering how to get her out of the way, she stomps down hard on his foot with the heel of her boot. Davis yelps and releases her wrist.

I grab her and pull her towards me.

"Good girl," I praise, and she smiles. I give her a peck on the cheek and push her to the other side of the aisle. Davis is on the far left. I'm in the middle, so I direct Haley to my right.

"Get down. Stay low," I say.

She nods, getting behind me. Now I have a clear path to the guard but, with both hands free, he opens the front of his harness.

Grabbing the harness with one hand, I punch him with the other. He grunts, but the guy is tough. All I did was piss him off.

Davis seizes my hand on the harness, locking it down and shedding the other side of his harness. He swings out and into me with his shoulder, pinning my arm; I have to let go before he breaks it. His momentum carries me over to the other side of the aisle, colliding with the seats. I twist, trying to break free, but I lose my balance and fall to the floor.

Davis lands heavily on top of me and goes for my neck.

It's the worst position I could be in. I need to get up fast, but first I need to get him off me. Lifting my legs, I wrap them around his back and pull him off balance towards me. Then I grip his arm, lock it down, and swivel my hips, bringing my right leg up over his neck. Keeping my knee tight around his neck, I shove him away and down to the ground. I bring his elbow above my waistline and extend my hips up from there as I pull his arm down. Bone snaps and Davis cries out. As I'm pulling away, I add a kick with my heel.

I'm up, but Davis rolls over, grunting and favoring his broken arm, but he's high on the adrenaline rush and still fighting. I aim a kick at his face and he goes back down. He's not out cold, but he's dazed.

Haley is standing on the seats, out of the way. We exchange glances. We don't have a lot of time.

I can't reach the controls; the copter will fly to its destination without human intervention. We can use that to our advantage. I open the emergency latch on the door. Wind whips through the cabin, the temperature dropping immediately.

We're flying low over the woods. Skimming over the tree line.

I pull up Davis and say, "Sorry."

Haley raises her eyebrows at my apology, then cries out in surprise a moment later when I drop him unceremoniously out the door.

"He'll survive. We're not that high up. Worst case,

he has a few more broken bones, but I don't want him reporting us."

She looks rather scared of me, but she nods as I sit on the seat beside her. This part is hard. "We're next," I say.

"What?"

"We can't stop this copter till it gets to its destination, but we can jump."

Her eyes go wide. "Oh no. No way."

I sigh. I didn't think she'd agree to jump out of a moving aircraft. But it would be easier if she had. "I'm not thrilled with the idea, but it's the only plan I've got."

"No, no way." She grabs the harness behind her. "I won't let you throw me out." Her statement is like a tiny stab to the heart. I thought she trusted me.

"*Blue*, I'd never throw you out." I take her hand in mine. "We'll do it together." The copter rises and I point to a lake up ahead. "You see that lake? That's our best chance. But we need to go soon."

Haley shuts her eyes, shaking her head. I try prying her hand out of the harness, but she just holds on tighter. We don't have time for this and I'm holding on to my own nerves by a thread. I'm trying to keep my cool and stay focused on her, shoving my fears aside.

"Haley. Look at me, please." She opens her eyes, irises expanded so wide in terror that her brown eyes look almost black. "I need you to trust me. Will you trust me?" She doesn't answer, but she nods. "We'll do it step by step. First, let go of the harness and give me your hands." Her hands tremble as she releases the strap and places her hand in mine. "Now we're going to stand up." I pull her up with me, backing towards the door. The wind whips her hair wildly around her face. I smooth it back with both hands. Her steps falter as we approach the opening.

The lake is coming up.

The copter's programing keeps it a constant distance from the terrain. As we emerge from the trees and hover over the lake, it descends, skimming over the dark water that rushes below us. I brush her lips with mine and disentangle her fingers from the side.

"We have to go. Now. Haley, let go."

Despite her whimper, I wrap my arms around her waist, and jump, flinging us away from the copter and into the air.

Chapter 18

Cocoon

Haley

I'm falling, the wind whistling past my ears like a scream. *Or is that me screaming?*

Jorden held me as we jumped, but after a moment we splash into freezing water. Plunging down, down, deeper and deeper into the murky depths. Greenish-black water surrounds me. I can't hear a sound or see Jorden. For an instant, his hand grasps mine, but then he's gone.

My descent slows. I'm floating beneath the surface with my hair waving about me. I need to breathe. I've never been in deep water before. There are no swimming pools on the space station. Fighting the urge to fill my lungs, I force myself to hold my breath.

Find the light. I read that somewhere. One direction is mildly lighter than the others. Bubbles escape my lips and float up. *Follow the bubbles.* Kicking towards the surface helps, but I can't swim. Losing direction in the murky water, I start sinking again. Then a hand grasps mine.

Jorden pulls me upwards, dragging me towards air, towards life. Finally, we break the surface. I gasp for air, coughing as he helps me to the shore. Falling flat on my stomach, I run my fingers through the dirt, marveling at every grain of sand, every inch of solid dirt supporting me.

Jorden crawls to my side, brushing back the strands of wet hair plastered to my face. He takes my cheeks in his hands, concern in his eyes.

"Are you alright?"

His hands are so warm. I touch his palm with mine, watching my shaking hands, covered in sandy specks. The only warmth is where Jorden is touching my face. My new dress molds against my skin, wrapping me in an icy hug, as if I'm floating in the subzero temperatures of space.

"You're freezing," he gasps and pulls me up, gathering me into his arms, trying to warm me with his body heat, but we're both drenched. His teeth chatter between blue lips. "We need to dry off as soon as possible. Before we both freeze. There are houses along the shore. We can warm up there. Come on."

Taking my hand, we stumble along the shore toward the lights. Walking is good. It warms us up a bit, but I'm so cold. My breath steams before me in a cloud of white. I marvel at it while everything turns numb. I can't feel my fingers or my lips, though I can feel Jorden's hand holding mine.

The light is fading.

The last rays of sun strain over a distant hill. Once they disappear, the warmth drains from the air. It's almost fully dark by the time we reach the first house. The house's doors and windows are shuttered and unlit. There's no car in the driveway. Nobody to help us.

Further along the shore, the other houses are small, distant lights. But they seem so far away.

"I c-can't walk anymore," I say. My whole body wants to curl up into a little ball and shiver.

Despite the echoing emptiness of the house, Jorden approaches the door and knocks. There's no answer. He pounds on the door, shouting, "Hello, is anyone home? Please, we need help."

"We should go. There's n-nobody home." I stammer. My teeth chatter, as cold rivulets from my hair stream down my neck. Water drips from my dress, making tiny puddles around me on the porch.Jorden bounds off the porch and wraps his arms around me again. His breath against my forehead is a tiny dot of warmth in the arctic of my face. He shakes his head.

"We can't wait. We have to get inside, even if it means breaking in."

I'd protest, but I'm rapidly becoming a girl-shaped block of ice.

Jorden circles around back, looking for an open window, and returns shaking his head. "Everything is locked," he says.

I walk away from the porch and then notice a balcony on the second floor with a slightly open sliding glass door.

"Can you get up there?"

Jorden grins. Though he's shaking with cold, he climbs the wooden supports surrounding the porch, grabs the edge of the balcony and swings himself upwards. I could never pull that move. I'm not even sure I could climb the railing.

While I'm busy being impressed, Jorden hops over the banister on to the balcony and enters the house. Waiting for an alarm to sound, or floodlights to go on, I hold my breath and pray there's no sophisticated security alarm. Though getting caught again is less lethal than hypothermia.

But nothing happens.

Moments later, Jorden appears at the front door, and peeks out, smiling.

I step inside, closing the door behind me. The house is cold and dark.

"Come on." Jorden takes my hand and leads me up to the second floor. "I saw a warm blanket in the room upstairs."

"Should we turn the lights on?" I whisper, even

though the house is obviously empty.

"We shouldn't. They'll be looking for us soon."

Upstairs is a large bedroom. Jorden has closed the window and the flowery curtains, but moonlight filters through the gauzy fabric, illuminating the room. It glints off a wooden queen-size bed, an armchair and a dresser with a vanity mirror. There's a crocheted rug by the bed. It looks so homey and romantic, like something out of a brochure.

This is probably somebody's vacation cottage. I'd enjoy it more if my whole body didn't ache from cold.

Jorden lifts the blanket from the bed, turning towards me. "It doesn't make much sense putting the blanket on wet clothes. It'll just soak everything through."

Returning the blanket to the bed, he turns his back. "Take your clothes off and get into the bed. I promise I won't look."

My brain is misfiring. I want to argue; my sense of propriety is going wild at the thought of stripping down next to him, but I'm too cold to argue.

"D-don't turn around," I try to say, but my teeth are chattering too badly.

Peeling off the sodden dress, I remove my boots and tights and lay the clothes over a wooden chair in the corner, wincing as they drip onto the floor. I leave on my underwear: no way I'm getting naked. The sheets will survive a wet spot. Jumping into the bed, I pull up the duvet. The bed is soft, but the covers are cold and I'm still shaking.

"Okay, you can turn around," I say with only my face peeking out.

Jorden shivers violently. His lips are blue but he smiles, rubbing his arms futilely and searching the room for another blanket. But there isn't anything else.

I bite my lip. Then say in a stern voice.

"Don't get any ideas. I can't have you dying of cold. You understand?"

Jorden lifts an eyebrow, checking that I'm saying what he thinks I'm saying. A crooked smile buds on his lips as I scoot to one side of the bed.

"Get in. So you don't freeze."

I don't have to tell him twice. Peeling off his dripping shirt, he pulls down his pants and I look away. I'm relieved when he leaves his underwear. Then he slips under the covers. I want to cocoon myself, to prevent the cold from getting at me from any angle, but it isn't a very wide blanket. There's no way to do it properly with us on different sides of the bed.

My teeth are still chattering and I can't stop shaking.

"We need to get closer. For warmth. You've lost too much body heat. So, I'm going to move nearer," Jorden whispers, as if trying not to spook me. My cocoon shifts, letting in cold air, and my shiver intensifies. Then he slides towards me, his arm creeping around my waist, drawing me to him so that we're pressed together in the center of the bed. He tucks the covers back around us, pulling them over our heads, so we're nestled in a dark, warm cocoon.

His skin feels clammy, but his body is deliciously warm. The small space soon fills with heat. He rubs my arms to encourage circulation. Lying face to face, he touches my cheek, then drags his fingers over my nose.

"You're freezing. Your nose is so cold. Here, let me heat it up."

He breathes warm air onto my nose, and I giggle.

His mouth shifts lower and his lips brush mine.

"I see your lips need warming, too."

I lick my lips, and he kisses me. His lips are so warm; I savor his heat. Running his hands down my arms, he warms me with his touch. When his hands find my waist, he pulls me closer again. *And um. Okay.*

The sensation of his skin on mine has my body tingling, but I place my palm over his. "That's as low as you go," I warn, but it comes out breathless.

Even though it's hard for me to talk with him so close, I force myself to sound stern. I don't want to stop just yet, but I'm not going to let the circumstances dictate the outcome. Yes, we're practically naked in a bed together, but that doesn't mean I have to do anything more.

I'm calling the shots.

"You're the boss." He chuckles, his voice husky.

I don't feel like the boss of anything right now. Even my body is sending me signals I don't want to ignore, while my mind objects. While I find my words, Jorden rubs my nose with his, drawing little circles on my face, his lips playing with mine, then flitting away, driving me wild.

I need to disengage, because in a minute I won't be able to.

Raising my hands, I grab his face, forcing him to look me in the eye.

"Jorden. Stop," I gasp. "I can't do this."

"We won't do anything you don't want to do," he says in that husky tone.

My face is burning up. "I may want to, but I'm not going to. Do you understand me?"

I hope he's listening, because he's staring at my lips again, and... there's a certain pressure on my leg.

"Jorden?!" I repeat.

He gives himself a little shake as my words finally get his attention. "Yeah, okay." He doesn't sound too happy, but that's fine as long as we're clear.

"Can I trust you?" I ask. He nods. "Will you be good?" He gives me a wry smile, wrinkling his nose. "Okay, then."

If I can trust him to be good, I can be a little bad.

Grinning, I grasp his hands to keep them under control. Entwining my fingers in his, I press them down to his sides, pinning his hands to the bed. Then I kiss him gently, starting on his lips but continuing along his jawline. As I kiss under his ear, he strains against my hands.

"Nah-ah." I hold him prisoner, kissing down his neck, across his shoulder to the base of his throat, then back to his lips again. I release his hands, allowing him to grasp the back of my neck and pull me towards him with a hungry sound, but he keeps his promise.

He's good, so good that I almost regret making him promise.

In the end, we fall asleep, our bodies warm and intertwined.

Chapter 19

JAGUAR

Jorden

I'm woken by sunlight streaming through a crack in the curtains, painting a golden line across the floorboards. I feel so rested. So peaceful.

Stretching, I turn to look at Haley. She's breathing deeply, her hair strewn around her face like a strawberry field. I kiss her full, pink lips and she stirs, opens her eyes, and a smile brightens her face.

"Good morning," I whisper.

"Good morning." She caresses my cheek, taking a deep breath.

"How are you feeling?"

She stretches, grinning at me, "Warm."

"Good." I peek out from under the covers. Our clothes are cold and damp on the floor. Haley follows my gaze and frowns.

"We should look in the dresser," she suggests.

I didn't even think of it last night. To be fair, I was thinking about other things. Sacrificing my warmth for the common good, I slip out from under the covers. My skin erupts in goosebumps as the cold hits me. Running on tiptoe on the cold floor over to the dresser, I pull open the drawers.

Jackpot. In the top drawer there's a long-sleeved white t-shirt, about my size. It's a little snug, but thank God for flexi-fabric. No jeans, but there's a pair of lovely, warm fleece pajama pants in a black-and-red plaid design. Pulling them on, I continue searching for clothes for Haley.

The second drawer has women's clothing. Haley nods happily when I hold up a pale-yellow oversized sweater and a pair of stretchy black leggings.

"Perfect."

I toss them to her and she ducks back under the covers to put them on, suddenly shy. She's adorable. I may not have seen her last night, but I felt her, which was so much better.

My hair is a mess, so I run my hands through the strands to make it more presentable. Haley stands up on the bed in her borrowed clothes, trying to see herself in the mirror on the dresser.

"How do I look?" she asks with a shy smile. As if I'd think she was anything but beautiful.

Instead of answering, I cross the room and grab her around the waist, picking her up and twirling around with her. She screams as I lift her off the bed, then laughs, wrapping her arms around my neck. I lower her gently to the ground and kiss her as her feet touch the floor boards.

"Shall we go see if they have something to eat?"

Hand in hand, we explore the first floor of the house. It seems nobody has been here in a while. The pantry is bare. There's a food printer, but the cartridge is low and it only displays 2-3 options. We choose cookies and hot chocolate and have a picnic in the living room, sinking into the soft leather of a caramel-colored two-seater sofa facing the lake.

Haley leans on the armrest and puts her feet in my lap. I stroke them and tickle her a bit. We need to go soon, but I don't want to move. I wish we could stay here together forever in this perfect little hideaway.

"I wish we didn't have to go." Haley echoes my thoughts. She leans her arm on the back of the sofa and rests her cheek on her hand. "Do you think they're looking for us?"

"I'm sure they are."

She sighs. Kneeling on the sofa, she places her hands on my shoulders and kisses me. Before I can get too excited, she sits back and says in a practical tone, "Then we should dry our shoes and get going."

"Sadly, I have to agree. It feels safe here, but the woods could be teeming with ESC agents."

There's a cleaning unit beside the kitchen. We wash and dry our clothes and shoes. "Should we change back?" Haley asks.

"The pretty clothes won't be comfortable if we have to walk a long way," I point out.

"Are you wearing that?" Haley glances at my ensemble.

Huffing a laugh, I admit, "I'd rather arrive at the Farm in pajamas than in a suit. I'll feel less out of place."

"My new dress is ruined anyway," she sighs, surveying the damage to her velvet dress. Despite its rips, Haley folds her dress carefully, placing it and my suit in a backpack we find in a closet.

"I'll get you another one," I promise, even though I don't know how I'll accomplish it. I just want to see her smile, which she does, then kisses me.

Before we leave, we tidy up to hide our presence in the cabin and I check the info screen in the kitchen to see where we are. The ESC did us a favor, taking us a long way in the right direction. We're out of the city, but we have no transportation and no navigation tools. It will probably take several days to walk out of the woods and back to the Farm, but I'll follow the roads and get a ride somehow. Even if I have to steal it.

"Do you know this area?" Haley asks.

"Sort of. We're close to the Farm, but it's not like we were popping out to visit the neighbors very often."

We set out on foot, following the road leading

away from the lake and over the hills. It's a pleasant walk. The sun is up; the air is brisk and clear but not too cold. We carry the peaceful bliss of the cabin with us. It feels like we're on vacation, enjoying the forest and the fresh air. I keep having to remind myself we're on the run., because... where is the pursuit? The ESC must know we escaped the transport by now, but maybe they don't know exactly where.

There are very few cars out here in the woods, mostly auto drives. Their occupants peer curiously at us as they pass. Hopefully, nobody reports us.

Another concern is Haley's breathing, now that we're in the mountains again and headed to the Farm that is even higher up. I keep checking on her and taking small breaks but, so far, she's okay. The night we spent here helped her adjust and we're progressing slowly.

We circle the lake to reach the mountains. At first, we follow the shore. The only sounds are water lapping the beach, bird cries in the sky, and the occasional snap of a twig as we tread between the trees. Eventually, the coastline recedes, making us return to the road. The problem is that, as the road climbs, it hugs a steep cliff overlooking the water, forcing us to walk along the narrow shoulder. What will we do if a car comes barreling around a bend without seeing us?

The roar of a motor answers my question. Pulling

Haley over to the side, we hug the cliff wall on our left as the most beautiful vehicle I've ever seen pulls up beside us.

The sleek, black motorbike gives the impression that the rider is straddling an actual Jaguar. Eight feet long, featuring ebony lacquered fibro-plastic over stainless steel, the creators shaped the machine like a snarling black cat with bared fangs. The undercarriage features gold-plated supports and footrests, and I can't help a low whistle.

"I think I'm in love," I whisper as I squeeze Haley's hand.

Haley laughs with me, but her smile turns to fear as a familiar voice speaks up from under the driver's shiny, black helmet. "Well, I'll be damned."

Chapter 20

HOME STRETCH

Haley

Not this guy again.

The driver pops his helmet off, clutching it under an arm and flashing his too-white teeth at us. His smile is wide, but his eyes sparkle with malice. Obviously, he remembers us.

"What are the odds of meeting you two again?" he drawls.

Jorden and I exchange a dismayed glance. Apparently higher than we'd like. It's the guy who picked us up the night we reached Earth, on another of his high-priced toys. Doesn't he have a job, or anything else to do, but ride up and down the mountains all day picking up hitchhikers?

"Imagine my surprise when I learned you two were famous?" he smirks. "You're on the news. Miss

Former Blue-Hair and her junior terrorist accomplice."

He hasn't powered down his bike. It continues to purr underneath him, emphasizing his words. "Did ya' know you two are worth a veery nice reward? I don't really need the money, but I can't neglect my civic duty, now, can I?"

If you ask me, civic duty couldn't be farther from his mind. He enjoys the power rush. Noting the way Jorden stands protectively in front of me, he adds, "Still not your boyfriend, right?"

Silver starlight. He's still sore about it.

Megadouche swipes a hand across the screen between the handlebars.

"Emergency services. How can I direct your call?" a computerized voice intones. He shoots a toothy grin at us.

"Get me the police."

This guy is an idiot. How can he detain us till the police get here? Does he expect us to wait patiently? Not to mention, we're standing in a dangerous spot in the middle of the road. A car could come around the corner any minute. Preparing to run, I glance at Jorden, waiting for his signal.

As if summoned by my thoughts, brakes squeal and a motor revs as a car hurtles round the bend.

Megabucks tenses, sucking in his breath and snapping up his head to gaze wide-eyed at the car swerving wildly around us. Jorden takes advantage of the distraction to punch him in the face, so hard the jerk flies right off the bike and onto the gravelly surface of the road. I gasp but, before I can blink, the bike lunges forward. I grab the handlebars before it falls on me, just as a voice comes through the speaker.

"This is Denver PD. What is your emergency?" I clap a hand to my mouth. Jorden darts towards me, bending over the screen.

"There's been an accident," he says. "A cyclist went over a cliff. I'm sending his coordinates."

He presses a button on the screen and disconnects the call. Dragging Megabucks up from the road so he doesn't get hit by a car, Jorden slams him into the cliff wall we were hugging moments ago. The guy slumps to a seated position, head lolling to the side, a small trickle of blood dripping from his lip.

"Thanks for the ride, pal," Jorden says as he swipes the guy's helmet and hands it to me, hopping on the bike. I stand for a moment, staring at him in shock, till Jorden's voice penetrates my haze. "Snap out of it, *Blue*. We have to go. Now!"

I've never been on a motorbike, but I know they go fast and Jorden needs to keep the wind out of his eyes to see.

"It's a sweet gesture, giving me the only helmet, Jorden, but it doesn't make sense." Placing the helmet on his head, I pop the visor down. "You need it more."

The custom leather seat behind Jorden is warm and smooth. Sliding my arms around his waist, I hop on and scoot close, blushing as his stomach muscles contract under my arms. It's incredibly intimate, but I don't have any other choice.

"Hold on," he says as the engine's purr rises to a roar.

He doesn't need to tell me twice. Moments later, the chilly wind snatches my embarrassment, leaving only my desire to live. I hug him as tight as I can, pressing my chest to his back. We need to disappear before the police arrive. We couldn't have chosen a more outlandish ride. It's probably the most beautiful vehicle either of us has ever seen, but it's also the most conspicuous. Designed to draw attention, it screams, "Look at me."

Hopefully, by the time the police arrive, we'll be long gone.

But we're out of luck.

A blue-and-white ESC drone pops up right in front of us. Jorden swerves to avoid it, skidding perilously close to the edge. I hold on tighter, my arms around Jorden's waist, probably cutting off his circulation. The wind whips my hair around my face as I press my cheek to his back.

The land drops away as the narrow road climbs further into the mountains. On one side, we race past the tops of fir trees growing on the slanting hill below us. A dark cliff rises into the sky on the other. The sharp turns force us to slow down or risk colliding into the cliff or careening off into the abyss.

The motorbike is loud, but it can't drown out the roar of the three cars closing in behind us. Two dark vehicles and a much larger truck bringing up the rear, close on our position. I tap Jorden's shoulder and shout in his ear, fighting the wind that whips my words away.

"We have company."

He glances in the mirrors. "Damn. How did they get here so fast?"

"They were probably already in the area, looking for us. They must have intercepted the call."

Jorden swears again softly and puts on another burst of speed, cresting a rise and almost launching us into the air. I let out a small scream as we touch down.

"Sorry," he says over his shoulder.

We're forced to slow again as the road climbs. Luckily, the cars pursuing us are slowing as well. The heavy truck struggles the most up the steep hill, but the cars grow closer.

"Almost there," Jorden pants.

Approaching a narrow mountain pass, we whip into the dark mouth of a tunnel. Swallowed by the darkness inside, Jorden slows almost to a stop, making a sharp left turn into a side tunnel. If you didn't know it was there, you'd surely miss it. He stalls for a moment inside the opening, waiting till we hear the three cars barrel past. I hold my breath, as if that will make a difference.

As soon as the sound of pursuit fades, he guns the motor and we're flying upwards through the dark. The winding path cuts through the rock, lit only by the motorcycle's headlights. When it feels like we've climbed forever, we emerge from the mountain. A short stretch of winding road leads downhill to a valley nestled between two peaks. Massive iron gates barricade the mouth of the valley. Higher up, past the gates, log cabins of various sizes peek out between the trees. Jorden always referred to this place as "the Farm" but, from where I'm sitting, it looks more like a fortress.

Jorden drives full speed towards the gates, confident they'll open for us. We're approaching the gates fast, the bike skidding on the sharp turns. Jorden flicks the headlights in a fixed pattern, a signal of some sort, to show he belongs. The heavy gates trundle sideways, like a giant's jaws, sliding into concrete walls on both sides. Armed guards sitting in raised towers on both sides of the gate train their guns at us. I tighten my arms around Jorden, as if I could protect him somehow. *Is this how we die? Shot down by Jorden's Earther buddies?*

A guard walks into the center of the road, sighting through his weapon at Jorden's head. The red laser dot from the weapon flicks from Jorden to me and then back to Jorden. *Will the guard shoot first and ask questions later?*

Finally, Jorden lifts his visor and slows, letting the guard see his face. The light flicks away as the guard lowers his weapon. Jorden races past him and into the compound. Behind us, the gate trundles closed again, the two sides meeting in the middle with a resounding snap, a row of clasps connecting and locking on both sides.

Just past the gate, Jorden stops the bike and turns around, smiling, and huffs out a sigh of relief. "We made it."

This is supposed to be safety, but it feels like we drove into a prison.

The man, who'd pointed a gun at us a minute ago, approaches, his eyes wide in disbelief. "Jorden?! We thought you were dead, or in a deep, dark hole awaiting trial. Even though I'm seeing you with my own eyes, I can't believe it's you."

Jorden smiles, clapping the man on the back. "Geordi. Good to see you. I can barely believe it myself."

Jorden dismounts and helps me off, but my knees are shaking, and I almost fall. He pulls me up, holding me tightly to his chest with an arm around my waist.

"That was intense," I say breathlessly.

Geordi eyes me, and the way Jorden is holding me.

"Who's your friend?"

"This is Haley. She's going to be visiting us for a while."

"Nice to meet you, Haley." His smile is strained as his eyes travel from Jorden to me and back again. "Jorden, your dad will want to hear your report ASAP. Nice to see you back."

Patting Geordi's shoulder, Jorden takes my hand and together we walk up the hill through the Farm. Now that we're past the main gates, I can see where the place gets its name. The place has an old-timey feel to it.

Nestled in the cleft between two mountain peaks, wooden buildings straddle both sides of the path in even rows. We climb slowly. There aren't many people around and I'm grateful for a few moments to pull ourselves together before meeting the Earthers.

At the top of the hill, the path winds down again, opening into a green valley encasing fields and an orchard, a large barn, and horses in a paddock. Surrounding hills create a natural fortress protecting the Farm from attack, while the trees hide most of the buildings. The whole compound is visible from the top of the hill.

We stop to catch our breath at the apex of the path and I clutch Jorden's hand. "It's so green here. It's beautiful," I tell him.

He nods, smiling a wide-open smile I've never

seen on him before. It makes him look younger, as if a weight has lifted from his shoulders.

Jorden turns to a small cabin that sits on the highest point of the path, just before it curves down into the valley, and squeezes my hand.

"Can you wait for me for a few minutes? I have to talk to my father alone, first."

"Sure."

There's a comfy porch swing outside the cabin, so I sit there to wait. Taking a deep breath of fresh, mountain air, I let it out slowly. I'm so ready for some peace and quiet.

I hope we are finally safe.

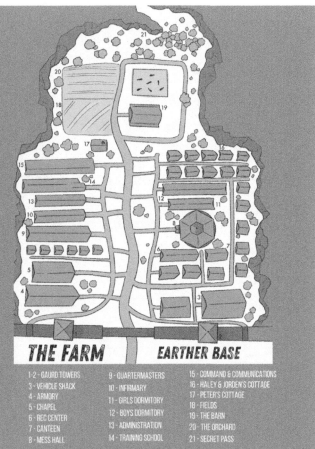

THE FARM

EARTHER BASE

1-2 - GAURD TOWERS
3 - VEHICLE SHACK
4 - ARMORY
5 - CHAPEL
6 - REC CENTER
7 - CANTEEN
8 - MESS HALL

9 - QUARTERMASTERS
10 - INFIRMARY
11 - GIRLS DORMITORY
12 - BOYS DORMITORY
13 - ADMINISTRATION
14 - TRAINING SCHOOL

15 - COMMAND & COMMUNICATIONS
16 - HALEY & JORDEN'S COTTAGE
17 - PETER'S COTTAGE
18 - FIELDS
19 - THE BARN
20 - THE ORCHARD
21 - SECRET PASS

Chapter 21

Homecoming

Jorden

The door handle is so familiar in my hand. I've gone through this door thousands of times but, right now, pressing the handle seems an impossible feat. I glance back at Haley. She's curled up, feet under her on the swing, breathing in the fresh, mountain air. If only she could be by my side, giving me strength, but I must do this on my own. Taking a deep breath, I knock on the door.

"Come in," my father's voice calls from inside.

He's on his feet, standing by his desk. They probably notified him the minute we got to the gate. He stands there for a minute, taking me in, looking me up and down, whether checking for injury or looking for weaknesses, I can't say. For me it's only been six months; for him it's been over three years. He doesn't look much older. Same steely eyes.

"My boy," his voice wavers. It's not like him to be overcome by emotion.

I'm surprised when he strides towards me and even more when he hugs me. The last time he'd hugged me was when I left for my mission, but it felt like a formality for the audience. I can't remember the time before that. But there's no audience here, so I hug him back, uncertain what to say as he steps back.

I don't know how to start, so I say, "I'm sorry. "

His forehead creases, deep lines he's accumulated from years of frowning. "What are you sorry for?"

"Can we sit down?" I take a seat on the sofa near the window.

He nods and sits across from me. My palms are sweating and I wipe them on my pants as I say, "I'm sorry I failed you, and my mission. Sorry for getting caught. They almost arrested me—" I peter off at his silence and unfathomable expression. *Should I continue?*

Because he doesn't answer and just stares at me, I keep talking even though I should probably shut up. Forgetting that anything I say can and will be used against me. Continuing to blabber nervously.

"I'm sorry I didn't contact you as soon as we landed. I didn't know how much the authorities knew. That my chip was a false identity, or that we'd infiltrated their system. If they'd be waiting for me..." I pause, correcting, "waiting for us."

"Us?" Father places both hands on his thighs and leans in, very close to me. His voice is low and menacing. "Is she here?"

I nod, watching the muscles twitch in his cheek, the reddening of his face as the cords pop out on his neck. He's going to blow. I know the signs. He stands abruptly, and I flinch. Though I'm only two inches shorter than him, when he gets that look, I'm five years old again, scrambling for safety.

"YOU STUPID, STUPID BOY!" he roars and I cringe. Haley can probably hear the shouts from outside. "Obviously, I've been monitoring the news feeds. I understand you taking a hostage in order to escape. It's not the best plan and it would have been better to dispose of her after boarding. But there is no excuse to keep her with you after you landed. NONE! Do you realize what you've done? Bringing her here? You've forced their hand. We might have had months or even years before they reacted to your actions. Now you've brought them right to our doorstep. The whole situation is too visible. They can't let this slide. They will attack us to free her."

I don't have an answer. They'll eventually retrace every inch between where we disappeared and the Farm and find us if they are desperate enough. Even Destiny said they'll kill us all. It is my fault, letting my feelings for Haley guide my actions. A good soldier would have seen Haley as nothing more than a tool to use and discard to complete my mission.

But I didn't; I don't.

He stops with his back to me, leaning on the desk, stating, "We need to return her; show we're cooperating with the authorities. Any other way is madness. It will get us all killed." His tone is final.

I stand, my fists clenched. "We can't."

He turns, takes three steps towards me, and grabs me by my shirt, pulling me within an inch of his red face. "We can, and we will, and I won't hear any lip from you about it." Then he drops me like I'm a piece of trash and I fall back onto the sofa. "This has to be done delicately," he continues, talking more to himself than to me. "I'll reach out and negotiate her return. Before they realize we have her here, before they turn up in force."

"Jorden!" Haley's worried voice drifts in from outside.

I open the door and rush out, followed closely by my father.

A blue-and-white drone hovers in the air just in front of her, where she still sits on the swing. Its colors clearly mark it as ESC surveillance tech. It's scanning her, broadcasting back to its headquarters. My father reaches inside the door and pulls out a blast gun. Without hesitation, he shoots the drone right out of the sky. It falls to the ground, blackened and smoking, way too close to Haley.

He turns to me, jaw clenched with rage. "So much

for hoping they don't know we have her."

Stomping back inside, he slams the cottage door so hard the windows rattle in their frames.

Chapter 22

A HERO'S WELCOME

Haley

So that's Jorden's dad? I see what Judith meant about the similarity.

It's stunning how much the angry man who slammed out of his cabin, shot the drone, and slammed back in again, is like an older version of Jorden, but so different. He seems harder, like a man who's solidified into rock over the years. His steely green eyes are the same color as Jorden's, but they lack the warmth and golden glint. As his eyes dragged over me, assessing my worth, evaluating how dangerous or how useful I could be, the cold, calculating intelligence made me shiver.

Jorden seems shaken. All the joy of his homecoming has drained from his face, leaving me stunned and heartsick for him. My parents have never shouted at me like that. I can't believe a parent raining such fury down on their own child. After being gone for three years, he's practically returned from the dead. What kind of man treats his son that way?

Taking my hand, Jorden starts walking, leading me down the hill and into one of the larger cabins. We pass by a common area with sofas, a sink, and bookshelves. I've never seen actual books before and I'd like to examine them, but Jorden doesn't stop, leading me to one of the last rooms in a long hallway. The sparse room contains two narrow beds pushed against the walls, with a window and a desk between them. The left side looks occupied. Bed messily made up, clothes strewn over the side of a chair, with various items filling the shelves above the bed.

On the right, the bed is bare. There are a few things on the shelves, but everything has a thin coating of dust.

"Where are we?" I ask.

Jorden's tone is subdued. "My old room, mine and Aaron's. I guess he hasn't gotten another roommate. Probably enjoying having the room all to himself. It's not every day your roommate goes off to get killed and you get a room alone." He doesn't sound like himself.

Dragging his fingers through his hair, making it stand up in spiky strands, he kicks off his shoes before sitting on the bed. Leaning into the corner beside the desk with his back to the wall, he pulls up his knees, hugging them to his chest. "I don't know what I expected. What was I thinking? That he'd be happy to see me? He's right. I'm stupid," Jorden moans as he lowers his head to his arms so I can't see his face.

"No." I kick off my boots and kneel on the bed next to him, pulling him closer, and he leans into me, shoulders shaking. "You're not stupid. Don't listen to him. You're amazing, and brave, and you got us here. You're home." I rub his back, running my hands along his arms. Holding him till the shaking subsides, murmuring, "It's okay, everything will be okay."

I plant little kisses on his neck as the tension pours out with the tears. It must have taken such strength to carry this tension since the day he left for the station. Returning home, against all odds, must be such a relief. To be safe in his own bed. And after enduring all that... the way his father greeted him makes me want to cry for him too, but I don't. It's my turn to be strong.

At last, he lifts his head and smiles at me, back to his old self again.

"Better now?" I ask, and he nods, sniffing and wiping his eyes.

"I'm sorry you had to see that," he mutters.

Does he mean his father yelling at him? Or him crying? Or both? I put my hands on his moist cheeks, looking him in the eyes.

"I'm not. I'm here for you, whatever you need." I hope my smile conveys that no weakness will ever make me respect him less.

He pulls me in, kissing me fiercely, as if my lips can erase the memory of the way his father treated him. We spend the next few minutes forgetting about the outside world and losing ourselves in each other. After the initial urgency subsides, I slide into the curve of his shoulder, laying my head on his chest. We lie there, content at being together in this calm, safe place.

Eventually, Jorden sits up and runs his hand through his hair, smoothing it down this time.

"I'm hungry. Are you hungry?"

"Yep. I'm starving." Jorden's tongue is the only thing I've had in my mouth all day.

"Come on," he declares. "Let's go to the dining hall."

The dining hall is a large, wooden building further down the hill near the gates. It's one of the largest buildings in the compound. Voices, laughter, and warm light spill out of the open windows, illuminating the path as we approach.

Jorden stops in the doorway, surveying the room. There's a lull in the conversation as every head in the room swivels towards us. I want to hide behind Jorden, but he squeezes my hand and pulls me forward. The stunned silence passes and the room buzzes with conversation again, louder than before.

Long wooden tables run the length of the hall, flanked by wooden benches and chairs. The walls are a rich golden-brown timber. At one end, a large fireplace crackles with actual flames, radiating heat. It makes the place feel warm and homey. The atmosphere reminds me of the mess hall on the station. A large family, joined by circumstances, if not by blood. Comfortable in each other's presence.

At the other end of the hall, serving tables span the width of the room, heaped with all kinds of natural foods. Corn on the cob and steaming potatoes. Vegetables I've never seen before. Jorden guides me to join a line where we take plates and cutlery. He heaps my plate high, insisting I taste everything, until I tell him to stop before it spills over. We choose a spot, placing our plates at the end of one of the dining tables, but we can't eat because people are coming over to greet him. This is his home, his family. Everyone beams at him, claps him on the back, welcoming him home. I sit down after a while, but Jorden remains standing, a huge smile on his face, surrounded by an ever-changing circle of people.

A group of younger girls that look about my age hang around him for ages. One girl hugs him as though he were her long-lost love. He keeps stealing glances in my direction, but he can't get away. When we make eye contact, I raise my eyebrows.

When he finally sits down, I blurt, "Aren't you

going to introduce me to your girlfriend?"

He laughs. "Allie? Before I left for the station, she was a trainee of mine. She was like, twelve."

"A-ha," I say, and keep eating.

He scoots closer and bumps me with his shoulder, smiling. We're sitting on a long bench with people on both sides. We don't have any privacy, but he takes my hand under the table and squeezes it. I smile, knowing it's not his fault he's being mobbed by girls, but my heart is slowly sinking. Ever since the station, I've had Jorden's undivided attention. But I was his only choice, for whatever reason. Now, suddenly, he's the returning hero, surrounded by people who know him and admire him. He could have his pick of the girls here, so why on Earth should he settle for me?

As I'm having my crisis, his father rises, lifting a glass, and the room hushes.

"This is a most joyous occasion," he announces. "My son, Jorden, has returned to us from an unfathomable distance, against incredible odds. Tonight, we celebrate," he raises his glass. "To Jorden."

The entire room answers, "To Jorden," and cheers.

The people close by clap Jorden on the back.

I'm surprised at his father's warm words after treating him so harshly before. But Jorden's tone is bitter as he whispers in my ear.

"Once you get to know my father, you learn there's the performance for the audience and there's what goes on backstage. Right now, he's working the crowd, playing the concerned, loving father."

I squeeze his hand in sympathy.

When the meal is over, the people work together to clear the long tables and push them to the sides of the hall, leaving room to dance. I stay by Jorden's side as we help, and people greet me as if they know me. Word travels fast around here. Jorden is different tonight. He's relaxed, more laid back, and he laughs more. The terrible strain he's been under has finally lifted.

I'm so glad I get to see him in his element. He's surrounded by people who know about his mission, know what he was willing to sacrifice, and they still love him. He looks so happy. It makes me happy too.

A little girl beckons to me. I kneel so she can whisper in my ear.

"You're Haley? The girl Jorden brought back from space?" I nod. "I love your hair. You're so pretty," she murmurs.

I don't know how to respond, so I ask, "What's your name?"

"Anna," she whispers behind her fingers, and runs off giggling.

Jorden touches a strand of my hair, wrapping it around his fingers.

"I liked the blue, but red is definitely your color. It's so natural on you. It looks right." His gaze is intense. I almost wish he'd dial it down because his attention feels so strong, so undiluted. He won't be able to keep it up. Eventually, he'll lose interest and I'll feel the sting of its absence.

As I watch, a beautiful blond girl runs into his arms, hugging him.

"You came back," she cries.

"Rachel?"

Jorden stares at her as if he's seen a ghost. Patting her back like he can't believe it.

Realization hits me like a punch: she's the girl from the photos he took with him. She's even more beautiful in real life, with her long, straight hair and big blue eyes. The kind of lithe, slim girl I could never compete with.

Hovering behind her is a tall boy with dark skin, black hair, and startling, light-blue eyes. Aaron, the roommate, the boy from the photo. I was wondering when he would turn up. He hangs back, looking nervous. Jorden turns to him.

"Aaron? Is that you, man? You look so old," he cries happily.

Aaron grins and hugs Jorden. "You look so young. As if you haven't aged a day."

Jorden pulls back, still holding Aaron's arms. "Where's Dale? I haven't seen him all night. And where's Dusty?" he looks around expectantly.

Aaron looks uncomfortable.

"Dale left. Not long after you went to space... and took Dusty with him. He'd been taking care of him and the kids got attached." Aaron lets out a long breath. "Dale wasn't the same after you left for space. He took it hard. You were like a son to him."

Jorden's smile loses its brightness. He keeps staring at Rachel.

"Wait. When did you come back?"

She glances back at Aaron before replying.

"When I turned eighteen. I heard the news, through our Earther contacts, about how you volunteered, sacrificing yourself. My parents were hiding in the city, turning their backs on everything we believed in. I wouldn't do the same. I came back to honor your memory. And I—" she steps back and takes Aaron's hand, "we... both missed you so much. It brought us together at first."

Jorden's gaze drifts from Rachel to Aaron, his face sliding from surprise, through hurt, into anger. He rounds on Aaron, fists clenched. "What the hell? We're best friends. You knew how I felt about her."

My heart breaks a little. He's forgotten all about me. I want to melt into the floorboards.

Aaron looks adamant. "Don't look at me like that. We *were* best friends. We were all sure you were dead." He shakes his head. "You've been gone for over *three years*, Jorden. Things change. Weirdly you haven't, but we have. Life went on. We respected your memory. We missed you so much for so long. But eventually we grew up, and we let go. You can't be friends with a ghost."

"But I came back," Jorden whispers, almost to himself.

Aaron shrugs, but his tone is soft. "You came back too late."

Jorden's shoulders slump and he turns away from them both. Turning his back to me, too. I slip away, unable to watch this anymore.

As the evening wears on, I sit on a chair in the corner. I'd be outside, but it's too cold and I don't have anywhere else to go. Pulling my knees up to my chest, I huddle in my seat, as if making myself smaller will help me disappear.

Jorden is nowhere to be seen. Is he even trying to find me?

A man is playing lively music on an ancient wooden piano. People are dancing and, despite my mood, my feet tap to the rhythm, making me feel a little better. Dancing looks fun. Looking up, I notice a boy with sandy hair and green eyes weaving his way towards me through the crowd. For a moment I think it's Jorden and my heart leaps; then I realize he's younger, about my age.

He stops before me. "You're Haley? The girl from space?" he asks.

"Yes?" I'd rather be left alone, but I don't want to be rude.

"I'm Terry, short for Terrance," he smiles, and sits down in a nearby chair. "Are you all by yourself?" he sounds surprised.

I shrug. "My escort disappeared."

"Don't worry, he'll be back. Everyone is so excited about his return. He's a legend around here. I'm one of the few people who hasn't met him yet."

I sigh. Jorden is so well loved here. *What would they do if they knew I'd almost killed him?*

"Didn't you grow up on the Farm? I assumed everybody here knew each other," I ask Terry.

"My mother doesn't live on the Farm. We have a little cottage up in the mountains. She likes it there. It's quiet. We're long time Earther supporters, but she wouldn't let me be active until I turned fifteen. I came here for training last year. After Jorden left."

"Don't you miss her?" I ask, as a wave of missing my parents overtakes me. I can't imagine what they are going through right now. For me it's been a few weeks, but for them it's been over 18 months. *Will I ever see them again?* Even if I left Earth today, over three years would have passed. Everything would be different.

Tears brim in my eyes and I stare at my lap, trying to compose myself.

Unaware of my distress, Terry replies, "I visit my mother now and then, but mostly I'm here." He holds out his hand. "Would you like to dance?"

I wipe my eyes discretely and look up, trying to smile. He seems sweet and sincere.

"I don't know how," I admit.

"Come on then, I'll teach you." Taking my hand, he pulls me out of my seat and onto the dance floor. I resist, hesitant about putting myself in the middle of the crowd, but he's strong and insistent.

Once we're there, I decide to cooperate. "Okay, what do we do?"

He grins, his teeth pearly white against his tanned skin.

"Just follow my lead." Still holding my hand, he places his other hand on my waist. Terry spins me around and I squeal, afraid he'll pull me off my feet, but his hands keep me steady. We go around and around, in time to the rhythm. Soon, I'm breathless, but enjoying myself.

Laughing up at him, I notice he has the same intense gaze as Jorden, as if he's trying to hypnotize me with those green eyes. *Is it a Farm thing?*

The music ends and a slower song begins. Couples move closer together but I hesitate, my cheeks reddening. I don't know Terry well enough for this kind of dance. Luckily, Jorden finally appears out of the crowd.

"Hey, man," he claps Terry on the shoulder in a friendly manner, but maybe slightly too hard, judging by his wince. "Thank you for taking care of her for me."

For a second, it seems like Terry will object. He darts a fleeting look in my direction before releasing me. Stepping back, he gives a little bow.

"Thank you for the dance. It was lovely."

I smile. "Thank you for teaching me."

Terry melts into the crowd and Jorden faces me, his expression unreadable. "Would you like to dance?" he asks softly.

I nod and he takes my hand, curling his arm around my waist, pulling me close until we're chest to chest. My body wants to melt into his, but my mind resists. I don't want to fight, but I can't leave it alone.

"What about Rachel?" I mutter.

"What about her? She's with Aaron now." He sounds hurt. Obviously, it's a painful subject. It's hurting me, too, but I must know.

"Who is she? To you?"

"She was my girlfriend. I haven't seen her since I was sixteen." His voice is strained.

"Did you love her?" The words fly out before I can stop them. I tense, bracing for the blow. My words stop Jorden in his tracks. He stops dancing and looks down at me, blinking, as if he suddenly noticed I'm there.

"Yes. I did," he murmurs. Instinctively, I recoil, trying to escape his embrace, but he doesn't let me go. Instead, he cups my cheek and tilts my chin up, gazing into my eyes. "It was a long time ago, *Blue*, and whatever I felt for her... It's over. You have nothing to worry about. Right now, I'm exactly where I want to be."

His gaze is warm, and I want to believe him, but I feel a pang of sadness. Déjà vu from the future instead of the past. It's been flickering at the edge of my consciousness since we got here. I thought I'd locked it away, but all the old hurt, sadness, anger, and fear are right there, keeping my brain on high alert. Preventing me from trusting him completely.

He hurt me before, and I didn't want to let him close enough to do it again, but I can't resist him. My defenses crumbled as he bypassed them effortlessly, even though I know this is a mistake.

We might be happy right now, but the end seems inevitable. My mind is screaming at me to leave while everything is still perfect. Logic says to go before he hurts me again, knowing this time I won't survive it. But I can't leave and ruin a perfect moment. I'll cherish this memory of us, like a scene frozen in amber, holding it close to my heart for the rest of my life.

Sighing, I rest my head on his shoulder as he breathes into my hair and I hold him tightly.

This is where I want to be, too.

I'll enjoy it, for as long as it lasts.

Chapter 23

The Cabin

Jorden

As the night winds down, Susan, the farm administrator, comes to find me, handing me a key.

"Your father asked me to find you a free cabin. We cleared it out today. Let me know if there's anything else you need."

So, my father is maintaining the act of welcoming me home as a hero. No more kids' dorms for me. To be honest, after tonight, I can't imagine sharing a room with Aaron, though that probably isn't even his room anymore. And by assigning me a cabin across the path from his own, it's easier for my father to keep an eye on me.

"I'm sure it's great," I answer, taking the key. "I haven't had space to stretch in months."

Susan turns to Haley. "Would you like me to find

you a bed in the girls' dorms, or—" Her gaze travels between us, questioning.

Haley blushes furiously. It's not the first time we've shared a bed since coming to Earth but, before, there weren't other choices. I don't want her to feel pressured, but Haley has been distant all evening. Ever since... *then it hits me.* Since meeting Rachel and Aaron.

I take her hand. "Maybe that's best?"

"Is that what you want? Some space?" The hurt in her eyes is unmistakable. Susan is watching us, making this harder than it should be. I shake my head.

"No. I'd rather you stay with me. If that's what you want, too."

Haley lets out a breath, her shoulders dropping. "I want to stay with you," she whispers, then she levels her gaze at Susan, expecting objections to us rooming together.

Susan shrugs. "It's your choice, my dear. I was a teenager once, myself. I'm sure you two would like some privacy." She winks, and Haley cringes.

"We're not... We haven't—" she stammers, adorably.

I wrap my arm around Haley's waist, drawing her to me, and plant a kiss on her forehead.

Susan smiles. "None of my business, dear. If you want to room together, that's fine. Okay then." She claps her hands together. "Let's get you settled."

Susan takes us to the top of the hill where a cluster of cabins are nestled by the mountain. They are just across the path from my father's cottage. Only the most highly valued members of our community occupy these cabins. Did he displace someone to favor me?

Susan opens the door and shows us around the tiny cabin. There isn't much to see. The cabin consists of one room and a bathroom. Beneath the window, a large, wooden bed piled with cushions and warm blankets looks inviting. On the other side, there's a small, blue kitchenette, a wooden table, and two chairs. A small desk with a chair and a loveseat with soft, green upholstery huddle under the other window. It looks homey.

Susan opens a closet door. "You can keep your things in here."

Haley frowns. "We don't really have many things," she says, holding up the small bag with the dress and suit we bought in the city. Neither of them is suitable for the Farm.

"Oh, well. In that case, see the quartermaster in the morning. He'll find you some things to wear."

I nod, gratefully, and Haley yawns.

"I'll take that as my cue to leave," Susan says.

I see her out and close the door, locking it from the inside. We don't usually bother locking our doors, here, but I'm paranoid after our time on the road. Then I turn towards Haley.

"Alone at last."

She smiles, but she seems reserved. I let out a long breath.

I haven't been thinking straight this evening. Seeing Rachel again, now three years older than me, was hard. Seeing her with Aaron was a punch in the gut. My mind is still reeling. Watching that unfold, and my less-than-stellar reaction, must have been hard on Haley.

Taking her hand, I lead her to the sofa.

I sit down, and she sits sideways, with her back against the armrest and her knees up like a barrier between us. Earlier today, she said she was here for me. She wasn't fazed when I broke down and cried, but then my past blindsided us. I don't blame her for being upset. She can't ignore it and I'm not sure I can, either.

I thread my fingers through hers. "Are we okay?" She regards me, chewing her lip, but doesn't reply. "A lot happened today," I continue. "We made it back, but things aren't the same. Everything has changed. The things that made it home for me, the people I was close to... The way we were... It's all gone."

I take a deep breath. *This is hard.* I trace the lines of her hand with my fingertips, waiting for her reaction. She remains silent, so I keep talking.

"Aaron was my best friend. I never expected to see Rachel again—" Haley's breath catches at the mention of Rachel. I clasp her hand tighter, trying to make her understand. "Seeing her caught me off guard. That's all. I didn't handle it well. After the way my dad reacted... He's always been tough, but I'd hoped he'd at least be happy to see me. That maybe he actually cares."

My head falls back on the cushion, staring up at the ceiling as my eyes well up again. I can't look her in the eyes as I admit, "Getting home was all the plan I had, Haley. What do I do next? I thought I'd find my feet as soon as I got here, but it feels like I'm still falling. I'm here, but I'm even more lost."

Haley squeezes my hand and, when I lift my head, her eyes are soft.

I exhale, running my hand through my hair. "The only thing I know for sure is I still feel the same way about you, *Blue*. That hasn't changed. I need us to be okay. Right now, I need you more than ever before."

Haley leans forward, finally letting down the barrier between us, and crawls into my lap. She's been getting bolder lately. Does watching me crumble give her the space she needs to be brave? She runs her fingers up my arm and slips them behind my neck, sending pleasant shivers down my spine. Her breath is warm on my face.

"I'm here," she murmurs. "We're okay. I just... didn't know where we stood. Now that you're home, I wasn't sure you still wanted me here."

I cup her cheek, looking into her eyes. "You're the only one I want, *Blue*."

Wrapping her arms around me, she hugs me. Inhaling her familiar scent, I hold her, enjoying the way she fits in the curve of my shoulder. Everything feels right when she's in my arms.

I feel so tired, so drained.

Having a cabin to ourselves is full of interesting possibilities but, right now, all I want to do is go to sleep holding her close to me.

I wake in the early hours of the morning, dread seeping into my unconscious and dragging me from sleep. It takes me a moment to register where I am. We're supposed to be safe, but I don't feel safe.

Untangling myself from Haley carefully, I slip out of the bed, tucking the covers back around her. It's not quite light outside and I'm not sure what woke me, but I decide to go check.

I open the cabin door quietly and step out onto the porch, shivering in the chilly night air. The surrounding cabins are dark, the stars faintly illuminating the path between them. My steps crunch on the gravel, sounding exceptionally loud in the night silence. I start down the hill, intending to visit the front gate and talk to the guard on duty.

Descending the winding path as I have thousands

of times before, my feet find their way on the familiar trail, almost without thought. Strangely, my skin prickles and the hairs rise on the nape of my neck. Unease morphs into icy dread slithering over my skin. Lifting my head, I catch movement out of the corner of my eye, high above me on the mountain ridge. When I turn my head to look at it directly, it's gone. But I know what I saw. Something is there. *Someone is watching me.*

Worry about Haley gnaws at my insides. I left her alone. I didn't even lock the door. Should I keep going all the way to the gate or turn back to the cabin? How did I become complacent about her safety so fast?

I'm already more than halfway down the hill. If I'm being watched, doubling back will seem suspicious. I don't want to alert them. Whoever they are. So, I force myself to keep walking at the same pace.

At the bottom of the hill, shapes huddle beneath the guard tower. I pause, suddenly cautious. What if whoever was moving on the mountain is already inside the compound?

As I hover there, a shape breaks off from the group, turning towards me, his face visible in the moonlight. Jacob, my father's second in command. Exhaling in relief, I hurry over and join the small cluster of men. Jacob claps me on the shoulder.

"Welcome home, Jorden. It's good to have you back. What are you doing here at this hour?"

"I got a funny feeling. Is something going on? I saw movement on the ridge," I whisper.

Jacob nods grimly and dispatches two men to check it out. Pride warms my chest as I realize he immediately took me seriously and didn't dismiss my information. My mission earned me that respect. The others confer in subdued tones. The tower guard above us signals Jacob to come up, and no one objects as I follow him up the tower.

From up there, we have a better view of the darkened hills around us. The secret tunnel through the mountain is a dark hole gaping like a screaming mouth. Holding out a pair of night vision goggles, the guard taps Jacob on the shoulder, pointing towards the hills. We're low tech on the Farm to avoid leaving an imprint, but we still use tech when it's important. Jacob peers through the goggles, and I follow his gaze. Even without the night vision, I make out shapes slithering down the slopes outside the compound. The black-clad figures blend into the shadows, but they are visible when they move. They're taking up positions higher on the slopes, where they have a line of fire into the compound. My heart sinks.

"Who are they?" I whisper, and Jacob whispers back.

"Trouble."

Whoever they are, this isn't a coincidence, turning up the night of my return. It's my fault.

Failing my mission wasn't my last screw up.
Now I've brought trouble home with me.

Chapter 24

Siege

Haley

A sound wakes me, and it takes me a moment to figure out where I am. We're on the Farm. I'm alone in a dark room in a warm, soft bed. Moonlight paints a silver line across the floor, illuminating Jorden standing pale and silent in the doorway.

"Hey," he says, sitting down on the edge of the bed, "I didn't want to wake you."

"What's going on?" He looks undecided, as though he doesn't want to tell me. Dread settles over me like an icy cloak as I sit up. "Jorden?"

"It looks like we'll have company soon. We spotted forces taking up position on the hills above the Farm."

"Who is it? The ESC? The Conglomerate?"

"We don't know yet, but the timing isn't a coincidence."

"You think we brought them here? That they followed us, somehow?" I ask and he nods, his eyes full of guilt. Cupping his cold cheek, I just want to hug him. "They can't blame you for this."

He shakes his head. "My father already does, and he's right. This is my fault. I should never have come back. This was a mistake."

An eerie wail pierces the dark, rising and falling, sounding like a thousand ghosts moaning together. I jump and press my hands over my ears.

"What is that?"

"Warning siren. We've got incoming. Come on, we've got to go." Jorden grabs my hand and I scramble out of bed, pull on my boots, and we sprint out the door.

"Where are we going?" I ask.

"Mess hall. We'll convene there and await instructions."

Outside, the sun is just peeking over the hills. The temperature difference between our warm bed and the frigid air outdoors makes my teeth chatter. Jorden pulls me under his shoulder, wrapping me up in his arms. It helps, but I'm so tired of being scared and under attack. I'd hoped we could rest now, if only for a day, but the blows just keep coming.

People stream out of the cabins all around us. Adults carry weapons or sleepy children. Everyone looks scared. Reaching the dining hall, we find a place to sit on one of the long benches. A group of teenage kids converge around us, drawn to Jorden. They're trying to look brave and composed, but there's fear in everyone's eyes. I spot Terry across the room and he nods, making his way over to us. Rachel and Aaron are in a group near the door. Younger children cry softly, after being grabbed out of their beds at the crack of dawn. I feel like joining them.

Jorden still has his arm around me, his muscles tense. I squeeze his hand and he peeks at me, offering a reassuring smile. Hopefully, nobody else accuses him of causing all this. He blames himself enough already.

The room falls into a tense hush as Jorden's father steps into the center of the room, holding up his hands for silence.

Before he can speak, the lights in the hall go out. A hum like thousands of angry bees suffuses the compound as dozens of drones drop around us, visible through the large windows. The blue ESC emblem blazes on their sides. Red lights slash through the windows, as sighting beams flicker over the walls, then onto the people inside. The lights creep through the petrified crowd, picking out targets in the silent hall. People pale and stiffen as the lights cross their bodies.

A girl behind me murmurs, "Will they attack us without warning? Can they do that?"

My blood freezes as a red dot crawls up Jorden's body and stops over his heart. I'm afraid to speak. Afraid to breathe. My heart is pounding; my ears are ringing. The dots swim before my eyes. Jorden is holding my hand so tightly it's cutting off my circulation.

A low-pitched whine emanates from the drones as if they're powering up. I'm afraid to watch, but I lock eyes with Jorden. *Is this the end?*

The silence inside the hall is deafening as the drones' hum rises in pitch to an awful squeal. Then the red dots drop to the ground. A moment later, the drones lift their lights towards the center of the hall, projecting a 3D image. It's a man in his late fifties, with neatly brushed hair, a dark blue uniform, and polished boots. He looks far more put together than the last time I saw him, and my heart drops.

It's the bastard that tortured Jorden. The one I'd promised to help. But I haven't told Jorden about the deal he offered me, and now it might be too late.

Staring into the camera, he addresses the crowd of Earthers.

"I'm Commander Rogers of the ESC. Who's in charge here?"

Jorden's father steps forward. "I'm Peter Lund. I'm in charge here and you are trespassing on our grounds."

Rogers smirks. "I assure you no ESC forces have set foot inside your compound, but as you can see, we can pick off multiple targets without touching the ground if we so choose. So, I suggest you hear me out."

Jorden's dad bristles, clenching his jaw in silence.

"We believe you are harboring a wanted criminal, accused of committing sabotage on VOR space station and kidnapping one of its residents. Our sources detected both parties inside your compound. In the interest of justice and to prevent bloodshed, we respectfully request you turn them both over to us."

Jorden's father flashes him a scathing look, visible even in the darkened hall, but his voice is firm. "We're an independent entity, residing on privately owned land, out of your jurisdiction. Anyone already on our land is out of your reach. You are welcome to check with your superiors." Rogers blinks, rendered speechless by this answer. Lund takes a confident step forward. "Do you have a warrant to retrieve any individuals currently on our land?"

Rogers looks confused, as though he's not equipped to deal with such a reversal. "Well, I—"

"I thought as much," Lund snaps, cutting him off. "Consult your legal department before making any further demands. Return only after you possess a warrant or better yet – don't come back at all."

I turn to Jorden, whispering, "Can he do that? Tell them to just go away?"

Jorden drags a hand through his hair, letting out

a slow breath. "Well, he just did."

The commander tightens his jaw, fury burning in his dark eyes. "We will come back, and God help you when we do."

"God favors the righteous," Lund says calmly. "We have nothing to fear."

The drones drop their beams, and the image disappears. I clap my hands to my ears as the whine intensifies. Then, just as suddenly as they arrived, they rise above the buildings, flying away from the compound.

The tension around me doesn't dissipate so easily as families huddle together in distress. We've been given a temporary reprieve, but this matter is far from over.

Chapter 25

Green eyed monster

Jorden

The tension in the air is so thick you can cut it with a knife. My father steps forward and, with a smile intended to release the strain, announces, "Since everyone is already here, we may as well eat."

The breakfast shift springs into action, relieved for something to do. Everyone pitches in, working off the nervous energy.

With this stress, I thought I'd find it hard to eat, but I've been up half the night and fear must burn a lot of energy: I'm starving.

The cluster of kids around us has solidified, including that kid Terry, the one Haley danced with last night. *Was it only last night?* It feels like a million years ago. I'm surprised he has the nerve to approach Haley when I'm here, but he's trying to talk to me as well. Must be the *returning hero* aura.

People are talking and joking now, drawing courage and support from numbers. Terry is cracking jokes, making Haley laugh. It shouldn't bother me, but he's staring at her a bit too hard. A bit too long. *Should I be worried?*

Grasping her hand under the table draws her attention. When she turns, her eyes soften, and she gazes at me like I'm the only person in the room. I shouldn't worry, but I can't help it.

There's something familiar about Terry. Then I realize: obviously, with those green eyes and sandy hair, he's like a smaller version of my father. Probably another result of our fearless leader's many indiscretions. I thought I knew all my father's unofficial offspring, but I've never seen him before. Though if Terry is my father's son, he's one of the oldest. I wonder where he's been all these years.

While we're finishing our food, the head instructor calls the junior instructors to her to hand out assignments.

Terry walks back over to us, a mix of fear and excitement sparkling in his eyes. "Okay, so to be on the safe side, we're going to accelerate training in the upcoming days. I'm training the juniors on sound guns in the barn after breakfast. Why don't you come by?"

"Can we?" Haley looks at me for approval.

I nod. "Sure, why not?"

Terry studies me curiously. "I heard you were an instructor too?"

"Yep," I confirm. "I taught self-defense from the time I was sixteen. My specialty is hand to hand combat, but I handed over my duties when I left for the station. I should probably ask the training master for a new assignment now."

Haley raises her eyebrows. "You taught other kids how to fight?"

I realize how strange that must sound to her. "Learning to defend ourselves is as normal to us as learning history or math is to you."

Terry lowers his voice and leans forward. "Hopefully we'll find a peaceful solution, but we're still preparing for a fight. It's only a matter of time till they attack us. Especially since—" He gestures at Haley and her face falls. I squeeze her hand.

Bringing her back here made the trouble worse. We've poked the bear. The authorities might have monitored our actions from afar, waiting months or even years before taking action, but now our time is up. They won't let this slide.

As we're leaving the hall, my father motions me over. "Jorden," he snaps, "I want you at the operations meeting. It's important the men see you there, as a symbol of our determination and tenacity."

Of course, he spun my failure into his win.

"Okay, what about—" I glance at Haley, by my side. She's holding my hand, but almost hiding behind me. Smart girl. He won't hesitate to use her if it gives him an advantage.

"Only you." My father glowers, ignoring Haley.

I bob my head in compliance and leave before he can say anything else, keeping myself between him and Haley. I hate the way he looks at her. Like an annoyance to be removed.

"So, what about me?" Haley asks as soon as we're out of earshot.

"You can join the juniors in training if you like," I suggest. She nods quickly. Obviously, she's as reluctant to be around my father as he is to tolerate her presence. "Okay, so I'll drop you off at the barn and come get you after the meeting."

When we reach the barn, Terry is training the younger kids to use sound guns, the same kind Destiny used at the governor's building. They shoot a concentrated blast of sound, knocking a person off their feet. Non-lethal, but effective in stopping people at close range.

The kids, wearing noise-canceling earbuds and safety pads, take turns firing at each other, blowing the target back six feet into a mound of hay. They're laughing their heads off every time somebody gets shot, as if they've all forgotten we're under siege.

I squash my annoyance, reminding myself that it may look like goofing around and having fun, but it's an effective means of defense in close quarters. When they use these to stop attackers, it won't be a laughing matter. Besides, there's nothing wrong with releasing the tension.

"Can you show me how to use the gun?" Haley asks with a glint in her eyes. "I don't want to be defenseless if something happens."

Hopefully she won't be so close to danger again, but it can't hurt to learn. I check the time. "The ops meeting is about to start, but I'm sure Terry would be happy to show you?" I end in a question directed at him, and he grins, turning to Haley.

"Sure thing. Stick with me and I'll have you firing like a pro by lunchtime."

"Thanks, man," I say and clap him on the back.

When I return an hour later, I spot Terry on the other side of the barn, showing Haley how to use the gun. While demonstrating how to hold it, he smiles down at her. Then, stepping behind her, he surrounds her with his arms, lifting her hands into the proper firing position. His fair hair and tanned arms stand out in sharp contrast to her auburn hair and ivory skin as he says something in her ear that makes her laugh.

A white-hot rod of rage pierces my gut. My fists clench.

I exhale, telling myself to relax. I'm being stupid. He's just teaching her the proper position to shoot. But the rod is twisting, burning.

Drawn towards them, moving faster than I should, I storm up, attracting their surprised gazes.

"Jorden, what's wrong?" Haley asks.

I huff out a breath, reminding myself that she has next to no experience with guys. She doesn't even know when a guy is putting the moves on her. But Terry picks up on my vibe fast. Backing away from Haley.

"Oh, hey man," he squeaks. "I didn't realize it was like that. My bad."

Haley's confused gaze slides from him to me. "What's going on?"

Terry raises his palms in surrender. "This one is all yours, pun intended," he says to me, then turns to Haley and gives her a little bow. "You were an excellent student. Come back anytime."

"Don't count on it," I mutter as he retreats.

Haley looks at me as if I've lost my mind, and I feel a bit crazy, but I can't help it. Taking her hand, I lead her out of the barn to the quiet, open field outside.

The barn was shady and filled with the noise of gun blasts and kids laughing and shouting but, out here, the racket is silenced as if someone flipped a switch. It's so bright. They have harvested the field, leaving trampled yellow straw reflecting the sunlight. The sky is a wide, blue canopy overhead and the wind whispers through the trees by the barn. Bales of hay are stacked in the middle of the field. Leading Haley over to the pile, I grab her waist and help her jump up onto a hay bale.

Her expression is still perplexed as I lean forward

on the bale, standing between her legs with my arms around her waist, looking up at her for a change.

"What is it?" she asks softly. Her hands tangle in my hair, tickling the nape of my neck and sending shivers down my spine.

I feel weird admitting it, but I don't want to lie, and what other explanation could I give?

"This sounds bad, but the way Terry was touching you, seeing his arms around you... made me want to punch him. Even though I know he was teaching you and he probably didn't know..."

Her brow creases. "What didn't he know?"

"How I feel about you," I whisper.

A smile lights up her face. Haley pulls me forward, wrapping her arms around my neck, and whispers in my ear. "I don't want any other guy to touch me, either. I only want you."

My heart soars and does a loop around us like a bird in flight. "Hold on," I tell her. Then I pop back into the barn and return with a blue-checkered blanket from one of the horse's stalls.

"What are we doing?" she asks.

Taking her hand, I lead her across the field, walking uphill to the meadow beyond, near the apple grove. It's higher up and we can see the Farm and the road approaching so, if any ESC forces make a move, I'll spot them.

Right now, I don't want to think about them or their threats. Instead, I spread the blanket on the grass and take a stance.

"Okay, so this is our practice mat. You want to learn how to protect yourself, right? You don't need a weapon, only your hands. I'll teach you."

Haley nods, shivering and hugging herself. "I never want to feel helpless again. Like I was in that alley."

Seeing her attacked was one of the worst moments of my life. I'm sure it was worse for her. I draw her into my arms, hugging her close. If only I could protect her from anything happening again. As if reading my mind, she says against my chest, "You won't always be there to protect me."

She sounds determined, but her words make me crumble.

"Yes. I will," I murmur into her hair, knowing that's a promise I can't keep, as much as I want to. Before she can protest, I add, "but I'll still teach you."

She leans back, looking me in the eye. "I won't go looking for trouble. I just want to defend myself if trouble finds me."

"Trouble seems to find you a lot," I mutter, and she chuckles. "Let's begin."

"There are several ways to get out of a hold," I say, "including the one I used when the men attacked us in the alley."

I show her the moves, and Haley picks them up fast. She's more athletic than she looks, and we have fun, twisting and swerving. Soon we're both hot and panting.

Though I'm using the same methods to teach her to fight as I've used with dozens of people before, with her it's intimate. It feels like we're dancing, not fighting. The press of her body on mine as we go through the exercises is beyond distracting.

Demonstrating how to sweep a person's legs out from under them, I end the maneuver and drop her carefully onto her back on the blanket.

"Okay?" I ask.

"Okay," she nods, out of breath. She holds up a hand, so I can help her up, but she looks so beautiful lying there, all flushed, with her hair strewn about her head, that I lie down next to her and kiss her.

"We're supposed to be training," she scolds me teasingly. "Is this what you do with all your trainees?"

I kiss her some more, then answer. "Yep, but none of them kiss as well as you."

She laughs and punches me on the arm.

Lying on her back, she stares up at the heavens as I play with a strand of her hair. "The sky here seems endless. It's so deep and wide, so blue. Staring up, I almost forget we're under siege." She has a wistful expression. "You know, I lost track of time. In two days, it's my seventeenth birthday."

I bite my lip, knowing I won't like what she says next.

"It must be hard on my parents... Missing my birthday." She sighs. "My whole life, I've wanted to leave the station. Being here with you, right now... despite everything, I'm the happiest I've ever been, but still—" She turns over on her side, looking at me. "Imagine if I'd left with you, like we planned, we'd be together on New Horizons right now." I'd almost forgotten. It seems like years ago. Another lifetime. "Would I be missing my parents just as much? Maybe because I didn't have any say in it this way and now... I miss my parents. Part of me just wants to go home."

She stops, nervous of my reaction.

I don't know what to say. Am I even allowed an opinion on this matter? The station is a million miles away. I want to be understanding but, if she goes back, will I ever see her again? Can I ask her to wait for me until I figure something out?

Turning over, she buries her face in my shoulder, and I stroke her hair. "Let's stop talking about this. It's making me sad," she murmurs into my shoulder. I nod.

"We'll have to talk about it, eventually. But it doesn't have to be today."

She sits up, tugging on my hand. "Come on, teach me some more moves."

We get back in position, but I'm distracted by movement in my peripheral vision. Black-clad soldiers are moving into position on the range above us. Too late, I realize my mistake. We're the ones they're looking for and we're up here all alone. We're too exposed. They may try to grab us.

"Haley," I say quietly, flicking my eyes towards the mountain. She follows my gaze, paling as she notices the soldiers.

"We should get inside," I say. She nods and I bend to grab the blanket off the grass, heading back towards the barn. A drone lifts off the hillside buzzing towards us.

"Run," I cry. We sprint down the path, skidding small stones and kicking up dust. Haley struggles to keep up with my pace, but I keep hold of her hand. The buzzing gets louder. I'm afraid to turn my head to see how close the drone is.

Haley stumbles when we're in sight of the barn. I pull her up and drag her closer to me, discovering the drone right on our heels. They could shoot us easily if that's what they wanted, but they haven't fired. Finally, we reach the barn, and the drone stops just outside the entrance, hovering in the opening, and searching the dark barn with its laser-guided beam.

The kids inside turn as we dash in, startled by our haste and panicked gaze.

"I need a sound blaster," I yell to Terry without slowing down. He tosses me one without hesitation and I swivel back to face the drone, yelling, "Back off!"

I'm sure it can hear me. Whether they're autonomous or human-operated, if there's a person operating it, they must think picking off a few kids will be easy.

It doesn't retreat, instead it emits a high-pitched whine, powering up a weapon, its laser scope aimed firmly at my chest.

"Jorden." Haley's panicked voice sounds behind me.

"Three, two, one." Someone chants to my left and I fire.

Terry and his trainees flank me and let loose with all the weapons they have, buffeting the drone. Its weapon's system squeals as it's crushed. Its sides crumple from the force of the hits. Then it crashes to the ground, sparking.

A kid rushes over to douse it with fire repellant before the barn catches fire.

As soon as we lower our weapons, Haley throws herself at me. "That was too close," she gasps. I swallow, trying to catch my breath as the remains of the drone smolder in front of us. "Tell me again why hand-to-hand combat is better than having a weapon?" Haley grins, cocking her head at me.

I shrug, slinging the sound blaster over my shoulder.

"Sometimes it isn't."

Chapter 26

Promises

Haley

After we escaped the drone, Jorden spent hours at the command center.

I kept busy visiting the quartermaster's and getting a selection of clothes for the both of us. They also assigned us internal communication units to talk or message other people on the farm.

With nothing else to do, I returned to our cabin, arranging the clothes in the closet. Despite a lingering sense of unease regarding the ESC threat, I enjoy playing house. Now that I have Jorden back, I wish I could stay here a little while longer. If only things would calm down enough for us to enjoy a few minutes of feeling safe.

I curl my hair into a bun to keep it out of my face as I fold the soft, fragrant clothes. They smell like herbs and wildflowers, so different from the aroma of the auto-cleaned clothes on the station.

My clothes always came back from cleaning neatly folded, so I don't know how to fold properly. Though I try my best, the end result isn't as tidy as the piles in my station closet, but I still feel like it's an accomplishment.

I turn as the door opens, admitting an exhausted-looking Jorden.

"Hey." He smiles, coming over to where I stand.

"Hey. I got us some clothes." I point out my little piles.

"That's good." He examines the closet, sliding his hand around my waist. His touch feels like coming home on a cold, dark night. I can't believe we're finally back together after all this time. It feels familiar but, somehow, more real, though it's hard to navigate relationship stuff when we're running for our lives. The thought makes me grin.

Jorden catches my smile and smiles back. "What is it?" He quirks an eyebrow at me.

"It's just nice playing house," I admit.

He grins and runs his fingers into my hair, releasing it from its knot and threading his hand into my curls, sending pleasant shivers down my scalp.

"Yes, it is," he murmurs against my mouth as his lips hover over mine. "I like coming home to you." As we kiss, he walks me backwards till my calves touch the bed, and my body tenses. The kiss sends a wave of heat through me as I realize he was holding back on the station. He never pushed to go any further than kisses, but here... There's an unfamiliar heat in his eyes that could burn me up if I let it.

My body sparks with sensation, but I'm not ready to follow through with my desires. Not right now. *What am I waiting for?*

So, I deflect. Breaking the kiss, I ask, "Are you hungry? Want to go down to the mess hall?"

Jorden sighs and tugs his hand through his hair. "Yes. I guess we should. Just let me change my shirt."

Turning back to the closet, he tugs his grimy T-shirt over his head and flings it towards the hamper. My cheeks heat as my gaze wanders over the sculpted lines of his back, noticing a patch of rough skin on his shoulder. I step forward, letting my fingers glide over it.

"What's this?"

He freezes, then turns. My fingers trail around to his chest. His gaze burns brighter again and his eyes drop to my lips. *Oops.* I should remove my hand before we're right back where we were a moment ago, but I don't.

"My Earther tattoo," he says, and the heat in his tone fades into something more thoughtful. "We removed it before going to the station. I should probably get it renewed." But he seems unsure.

"Maybe I could get one too. We could do it together," I offer.

At first, his eyes light up. "You'd want to?" he asks, but I barely have time to nod before he shakes his head. "No. That's a bad idea. You shouldn't get in too deep. If things go south, they'll accuse you of being my accomplice."

A strange disappointment grips me at his words. "I know I've only been here two days, but I'm already involved. Let me help. I want to be a part of your life here," I insist.

"Can I talk you out of it?"

I shake my head. He sighs.

"We're in this together, now. If you wanted to leave me out of it, you shouldn't have brought me here," I say, and he recoils as if I've hit him. Before he moves too far away, I grab his hand, pulling him back. "Sorry. No. That wasn't an accusation. It came out wrong. You asked me to come with you, and I made that choice. Now, like it or not, I'm a part of this."

Jorden exhales, his shoulders deflate, and he bows his head.

"All right. We'll talk about it later. Meanwhile, I'm starving. Come on, let's go eat."

Grabbing a pale, blue baseball shirt that I'd painstakingly folded, he pulls it on. *Oh well.* It hugs his shoulders so nicely, it looks better on him than in the closet.

Taking my hand, he tugs me towards the door. I follow willingly.

Later that evening, Jorden sits at the desk by the window studying a pile of printed images. I cross over to him and wrap my hands around his neck, peeking over his shoulder.

"What are you doing?"

"Just going over some plans of the compound before the operations meeting. Even though I failed my last mission, they're willing to let me participate. Maybe I can redeem myself."

"What?" I yelp. Somehow, I'd assumed his mission on the station would be the end of it. "I thought..." I falter. Did I think because we're together now, everything would change? That Jorden would never need to do anything dangerous again?

He turns and pulls me down into his lap. "What is it?"

"We've never actually talked about what you'd do once we got back. I guess I assumed that you'd done your part in going to the station, and now you'd be... free. I didn't think you'd still be involved in the fight.
"

His eyes narrow in confusion. "Haley, I grew up here. The Earther movement is a part of me. I have to be involved. Besides, it's my fault we're under siege." My mouth pops open to protest, but he raises his hand and I wait. "The ESC came here looking for me. I didn't complete my mission, and took you with me, and now they're after us. The Conglomerate might still kill us all in retaliation. All that is on me."

My stomach sinks as the terror takes over. He blames himself for absolutely everything. Will he deliberately put himself in harm's way to prove himself to his father or the people on the farm? When is enough, enough?

"I'm scared, Jorden," I say. "I don't want to lose you."

His eyes fill with emotion, but he doesn't say anything for a few moments, staring at my face as though he's committing me to memory. I take his hand, placing my other hand on his cheek.

"What are you thinking? Tell me."

"This whole situation is spiraling out of control. Risking my life never worried me before, but now—" He turns his head and kisses my palm. "I have something to lose."

My heart overflows with warmth for him. "Promise me you'll be careful? Try not to put yourself in too much danger?" I beg.

"I don't have a choice," he whispers.

My heart sinks. I just got him back and I'm going to lose him again. I know him: his instinct is to leap first and weigh the consequences later. He'll get himself killed.

"Well, I do have a choice. I can't face you throwing your life away again," I cry, pushing against his chest. Squirming, I struggle to get up, trying to escape his arms. Needing some space between us, because my heart is overflowing with fear. But he doesn't let me go. Instead, he holds me tighter.

"Wait, wait, stop." He takes my chin, forcing me to look at him. "I didn't understand you felt so strongly about it."

"About losing you?!" I'm furious. I care for him so much and it isn't enough to keep him safe. "You aren't expendable. I need you."

His eyebrows crease in pain as he studies me as if, in his mind, he's already gone. I smooth the crease with my fingers and lower my forehead to his. His voice is a warm whisper in my ear.

"What would you have me do, Haley? Tell me."

I lean back and search his face. "Don't take point in the fight. Stay out of it if you can but, if you can't, at least don't put yourself in unnecessary danger. Will you do that for me?"

He nods. "I'll do my best to stay out of it. For you. But I'll have to do something. Now that I'm eighteen, I'm not a kid anymore. I can't just hide. They expect me to step up and be counted."

"You did step up! Volunteering to blow up the jump ship almost cost your life. Isn't that enough?"

He runs his fingers through my hair. "Let's hope it is, at least for the time being."

I fix him with a stern look. I need to hear him say the words. "Promise me you won't throw your life away."

Instead of answering, he wraps his hand around the back of my neck and pulls my mouth to his, kissing me deeply, melting my resolve. I want to stay stern, but I can't resist him.

Only after he leaves for the meeting do I realize that he never actually promised.

Jorden returns from the meeting with the news. His expression is less than thrilled.

"What's up?" I ask carefully.

"Well," he shrugs. "It's not exactly bad news, but—"

"Tell me," I urge.

"They're putting together a training group to bring new kids up to speed. Including you." He holds a palm up at my gasp. "I know you want to defend yourself, but I'm still worried about putting you in harm's way. It'll be a small group of kids your age. Two girls. Glory and Beth. And..." he pauses and sighs, "Terry."

I laugh, moving in to catch his face in my hands, and he rolls his eyes.

"Yeah, I know. I'm not jealous. I just wish he wasn't

everywhere, all the time."

Pulling his head down for a kiss, I say. "This will be good practice for you. Trusting me to take care of myself. And trusting me in general. "

"I do trust you," he insists.

"Good, so you can walk me to training in the morning and prove it."

The next morning, Jorden walks me to the training hall, which is located halfway down the hill. When we reach the long, wooden building, we find a slight girl with long, silky brown hair and freckles sitting on top of a picnic table. Her eyes track us as we approach, surveying Jorden with too much interest for my liking. *Oh, God, not her too. I'll have to start carrying a stick.*

Huh. Guess we both need to work on our jealousy.

When we reach her, she smiles at us like a Cheshire cat. "Are you here for training?" she asks.

"Yep," I say. "I'm Haley."

She smirks even wider. "Oh, I know. You're famous." My cheeks heat. "I'm Glory, by the way."

She's interrupted by the arrival of a girl with frizzy blond hair, blue eyes, and glasses who, despite those promising assets, looks a bit like a squirrel. That must be Beth. She's followed by Terry, who gives me a big smile as if we're already old friends. His green eyes twinkle. He's such a Jorden lookalike it's confusing. I smile back instinctively, as Jorden's arm tightens around my waist.

"Easy," I whisper in his ear but, instead of loosening his grip on me, his arm tightens even more. "Jorden?" I ask. I turn towards him to see him grinding his teeth, though his gaze isn't on Terry now, but further up the path. Following his gaze, I see Rachel and Aaron approaching.

"Looks like our instructors are here," Beth says in a mild tone.

"Oh. *Oh no*," I breathe as Jorden goes very still.

"I'm off," Jorden mutters, turning his back on his childhood friends. Planting a quick kiss on my lips, he hurries away. But his retreat doesn't go unnoticed.

"Jorden—" a male voice calls from further up the path.

I turn to see my dismay echoed by both Aaron and Rachel, but Jorden doesn't look back.

Oblivious to the drama, Glory sighs again for dramatic effect. "You're so lucky."

"Huh?" I respond.

"Jorden..." she sighs. "He's so dreamy."

As I follow her gaze, he peeks back over his shoulder, meets my eyes and smiles his gorgeous smile. It's strained, but my heart still flip flops. *I know I'm lucky.*

"So lucky," she repeats.

"He's taken," I snap, a bit too sharply.

"Yeah, I know." She grins at my snappishness. "Don't worry. I wish somebody looked at me the way he looks at you."

Rachel and Aaron reach the hall and the other two follow them in. Deciding to play along and be friendly, I nudge Glory.

"You can't have Jorden, but Terry is like a carbon copy of his..."

Her eyes track Terry's retreating figure critically. "Oh, so you get the original and I get the copy? Anyway, they aren't identical."

"Well, no," I admit. "Jorden's bigger."

Glory does a double take and smirks. "Wait, bigger how?"

I gape at her, open-mouthed, turning tomato red as I stammer, "I meant older—"

Seeing me so flustered, she laughs, bending over double as she cackles like a witch. When she finally catches her breath, she says between giggles, "Oh, so you two haven't—" I punch her on the arm. "Ow." She snickers again. "Well, that's a waste."

"Shut up." I roll my eyes. But when we follow them into the hall, Terry catches us looking at him and winks, and that sets off even more giggling.

During the morning, Aaron works with us on weapons and, that afternoon, Rachel starts training us on self-defense.

I don't want to like her, considering her role in Jorden's past and her impact on his feelings, but I do. Despite our bizarre situation, with me dating her ex-boyfriend who is now three years younger than her, she's friendly to me. Radiating calm and self-assurance, I hope I'm so confident when I'm her age.

But I can't help wondering if she still loves him. They parted suddenly and against their will, probably scarring them both, and then having him "return from the dead". Now she's with Aaron and I'm with Jorden.

I have to believe it's over between them, or I'll lose my mind.

Rachel teaches us a few moves using Aaron as a partner. Watching how perfectly in sync they are with each other, it's obvious they're a team. That calms me down a bit.

Afterwards, she has us pair up to practice.

With three girls and a boy, it's kind of awkward. Despite her lewd comments earlier, Glory immediately pairs up with Beth.

"*Chicken!*" I hiss as I walk past her to join Terry. Glory shrugs, leaving me to deal with the situation.

Terry and I face each other awkwardly. He gives me a lopsided grin.

"It seems we're dance partners again," he murmurs and my cheeks heat. He looks over his shoulder, then asks, "What are the chances of Jorden turning up right now and beating me to a pulp?"

I glance towards Rachel and Aaron, who are leaning against the wall, talking quietly.

"Pretty slim, actually."

He exhales and laughs. "Good, because I like living."

I smile conspiratorially. "Let's do the exercises and, if he shows up, I'll distract him while you escape."

"Okay," he huffs.

"Okay."

We both laugh.

Working with Terry is better practice than working with another girl. He's stronger and taller than I am so, if I can hold my own against him, it's a bigger win than flipping a girl half my size.

I look him in the eye, estimating how tough he is. "Don't go easy on me," I say.

"As you wish." He bows.

The next thing I know, I'm staring at the ceiling. "Wow. That was fast."

"That's what she said," Glory yells from behind us.

"Shut up!" We both yell back. Terry gives me a hand up and we try again.

By the end of the day, I can actually flip him, and he swears he's not going easy on me.

I'm kind of proud of myself.

Now I'm better equipped to deal with what's coming and I might even fit in here with these kids.

Chapter 27

New Friends and Old

Jorden

My father's command center hums with activity as security becomes top priority and they reschedule all other activities. Guard shifts double. The kitchen staff takes inventory to calculate how long we can stretch our supplies. Luckily, we're mostly self-sufficient up here.

My father's advisors crowd around the table full of maps of the area. We have old-fashioned data pads streaming news coverage of the imminent standoff. Internal comms squawk, reporting the ESC's movements, or lack thereof.

At the moment they're just sitting there, watching us, lurking like a bad dream at the edge of our consciousness, waiting for us to nod off.

Today, Haley spent the morning training, and I

spent my time here at command feeling useless and underfoot. Haley begged me not to get too involved. She seems to think I'd request the most dangerous assignment, but, at the moment, she has nothing to worry about. Most of the time, I feel invisible.

As far as my father's concerned, I'm an inconvenience to be tolerated. When he looks at me, it's with tight-lipped fury. I didn't hold up my end of the deal; I was supposed to die and become a martyr for the cause. Now he's forced to acknowledge me and have me front and center for appearance's sake. Anything else would look odd, but he obviously resents it. Still, he'd never turn me over to the ESC because of how bad that would look to his supporters.

Haley is another matter. I'm reluctant to leave her alone, but my father won't allow her in his war council. She's an outsider, she doesn't belong here, and everyone knows it. I want her to stay, but I don't know if that's possible.

Neither of us really belongs here.

In the end, Jacob takes pity on me and assigns me guard duty in the tower, just to get me out from underfoot. It's better than feeling useless; at least, this way, I'm doing something.

When I swing by at the end of the training session, Haley is sitting on the table outside, with Terry and the two other girls. Her back is to me and she's laughing. I barely recognize her for a moment. *Who is this girl?* The Haley I knew on the station would be off in a corner drawing.

Walking up behind her, I press a finger to my lips. The other girls notice me, but keep my secret. Slipping my arms around her waist makes Haley freeze for an instant, until I say "Hello beautiful," in her ear.

Relaxing, she leans back, tilting her face up to me for a kiss, which I give her despite our captivated audience.

The slight, brown-haired girl grins at us when we break apart. "I'd say get a room, but Haley said you two have a cabin so—" she waggles her eyebrows.

I give Haley a look.

She shrugs. "Glory has no filter between her brain and her mouth." Glory nods in assent.

Meanwhile, Terry seems nervous, as if he thinks I'm going to kill him for sitting next to Haley. But I'm over my fit of jealousy from the other day, or at least working on showing Haley I trust her. Obviously, we can't avoid him now that they're in the same training group. So, I won't make a scene every time he's within three feet of Haley.

He catches my eye and bobs his head. He's a funny kid.

"Hey, man." I nod back but keep a stern face, just to keep him guessing.

"Ready to go?" I squeeze Haley's hand and she hops off the table, waving goodbye to the group.

"I'm glad you're making friends," I say. That was hard for her on the station.

Wrapping an arm around my waist, she peeks up, giving me a hesitant smile. "Yes. It's fun. And speaking of friends, you should talk to Aaron."

"I walked right into that one, didn't I?" I laugh, then gulp. "Isn't my life weird and complicated enough?"

Haley means well, but talking about him is like a punch in the gut.

"He's your best friend," she reasons.

"Correction, he *was* my best friend. Now I have nothing to say to him."

"Because he's with Rachel?"

I run my hand through my hair, searching for a response that doesn't make me sound like a sulky five-year-old. "It's not that, or not only that. He's three years older than me, now. He lived through those years, all those experiences I know nothing about. And yes... that too. You don't date your best friend's ex. It's like guy code."

"Even if you think he's dead?" she asks innocently.

"Especially if you think he's dead." My voice rises. I hate getting annoyed, but Haley knows how to calm me down. She stops and faces me, looking up at me with those big honey eyes. Threading her fingers through mine, her other hand strokes my hair and her touch soothes me. I take a deep breath and let it out.

"You know you're not making any sense, right?" she asks.

"I don't need to make sense. It's just the way I feel."

"Okay."

She doesn't press the issue. She doesn't have to: my mind will gnaw at it like a dog with a bone, because I want things to be okay with Aaron.

I *miss him.*

Chapter 28

TANGO

Haley

Even before I open my eyes, my nose alerts me to a wonderful smell in the cabin. My next clue that something is going on is Jorden, sitting on the edge of the bed.

"Hey, you're up. Happy birthday," he smiles, leaning in to kiss me. I can't believe he remembered. With everything going on, I barely remembered. Today, I'm seventeen. The happy thought comes with a tug of sadness. My parents always made a big deal out of my birthday. It doesn't feel the same without them. I take a deep breath. At least I have Jorden to celebrate with me, even with everything going on.

He's wearing a big grin. "Remember, I promised you an apple pie?" I vaguely remember a conversation, like, a million years ago. "I got into the mess hall early before breakfast and made you one." He holds a golden-brown pie up, proudly. If it tastes anything like it smells, it will be amazing.

Throwing off the covers, I bounce out of bed and hug him, wrapping my arms around his waist. "Have I told you you're the most perfect boyfriend ever made?"

He gives me a lopsided grin. "Not that I remember."

"Well, you are." I pull him down so I can kiss him, almost squashing the apple pie. Jorden carefully places the pie on the bedside table before I squish it, and takes my hand.

"That's good, because I've got another surprise for you. Don't move." He leads me over to the couch, sits me down, and goes outside. When he returns, he's wearing a sheepish grin and holding a medium-size box wrapped in green wrapping paper that matches his eyes. It's topped with a big, golden bow and looks kind of heavy. Kneeling on the rug at my feet, he holds the box carefully. "Happy birthday."

"What is it?"

"A surprise. Open it."

His excitement is catching. He looks so pleased with himself; it has to be something phenomenal. Reaching out, I'm about to lift the lid when it gives a little hop, as if something butted it from the inside. I pause, startled. What could make a box pop from inside?

Sliding off the couch, I kneel beside him and Jorden places the box on the rug by my knees. The box gives another little hop, as if it's trying to escape, and I giggle. "This is weird."

Reaching out gently, I lift the top off of the box.

A soft yellow head pops up. Two small floppy ears. Fluffy yellow fur brushes my hand as tiny paws scrabble, trying to climb out of the big box. I want to pick it up, but I'm terrified. I've never touched a real puppy before. It's looking around with huge brown puppy eyes, sniffing the air, and I desperately want to hold it, but I don't want to hurt it or do something wrong.

Jorden senses my distress and lifts the puppy, placing it in my arms. It squirms, getting settled, scratching my arms with its tiny claws, and then it butts me with the top of its head.

Like Nano used to.

I stroke it gently, marveling at how soft and how warm it is. It twists, placing its puppy paws on my chest, and licks the tears streaming down my cheeks.

I can't speak. I can't say anything at all.

Jorden touches my hand. "I know I can never make it up to you, what I did to Nano... but maybe in some small way, this can be a start."

I nod, crying, laughing. Jorden kisses me through my salty tears and I kiss him back as the puppy still grasped in my arms licks us both. Jorden laughs and cups my face in his big, warm hands. "I love seeing you smile." His eyes linger, his finger tracing a line from my eyes to my lips. He takes a deep breath. "I love you."

I kiss him again. I'm still unable to speak, so I let my lips do the answering, kissing him deeply, letting him know how much I love him, too.

Later, we sit on the couch, the puppy licking pie crumbs off my fingers. I'm thinking how wonderful Jorden's mouth tastes after eating pie, when he asks me, "What will you call her?"

The puppy chews my fingertips, the sensation both pleasurable and painful. The dual nature of the moment brings me full circle, reliving the joy of having a dog and the fear of losing one again. My new puppy won't be Nano, or Nano 2.0, but I want to remember him somehow. To honor the memory of my first dog in my second dog's name.

"You know that saying *it takes two to Tango*? That's what I'll call her. Tango."

Chapter 29

GHOSTS OF THE PAST

Jorden

The ESC goons are still hanging around without taking action but, now that I'm pulling guard duty, I don't feel as useless.

Leaving Haley alone for hours on end is not my preference, but she's begun hanging out with her training friends when I'm not there, and now she has Tango to keep her company. I'm glad she isn't alone. Even if it means she's around Terry more than I'd like.

We're finally together after hours apart, when my comm broadcasts a summons to a briefing. I don't want to leave her again so soon, so I thread my fingers through Haley's. "There's a briefing at the command center. Come with me. It won't take long."

When we arrive at the briefing, Haley slips into a

seat beside me as the watch chief drones on about protocols.

He's just finishing up when Brittney walks in, and I stiffen in my seat. She's older, but she looks the same. Long curly hair, tight-fitting clothes, her walk screams, "*Look at me*" and I can't help looking. She approaches the chief, handing him a piece of paper and, when she turns, our eyes meet and she freezes. Energy fizzles through the air between us like an electrical current. I'm aroused and nauseated at the same time.

"So, it's true. You came back." She struts towards me. I'm frozen in place, like a fly caught in a spider's web. Brittney reaches me and bends down, drawing my gaze to her low-cut top, running a finger down my neck. "It's amazing. You look exactly the same."

I gulp. "Well, that's how FTL travel works..."

"Hmmm," she hums. Her breath is warm, and she smells of a sweet, heady perfume. "If you like, we could find a time to reconnect. Celebrate your homecoming."

My senses register Haley prickling beside me. Her hand touches my arm lightly, just enough to remind me of her presence. I know she hates these situations.

"Who's your friend, Jorden?" Haley asks mildly, trying not to sound annoyed, but she's rattled. *Damn.*

Brittney smirks at Haley, with her hand still on my

chest. "Oh, I'm just an old friend who said a very special goodbye to him before he left."

Brittney loves to flaunt her liaisons. Everything is for show. Her "special goodbye" was for bragging rights: it was never about me. I dart a glance sideways at Haley's horrified expression, then glare at Brittney while removing her palm from my chest.

Haley pales. Slipping out of her seat, she's out the door in a moment, Tango following at her heels. I push Brittney away and she laughs. She got exactly the reaction she wanted. Darting outside, I catch up to Haley around the back of the cabin.

"Stop." I take her arm. "Where are you going?"

She looks sideways, at the ground, anywhere but at me. I feel dirty. Brittney just smeared her need for attention all over me, tainting me with the stains of my past mistakes, and there's nothing I can do now to remove them.

"I can't... watch her touch you. I don't want to hear about it, much less see it."

Crossing my arms, I exhale. "I'm not going to take her up on the offer!"

Haley huffs. "That's nice of you, but then again, maybe you should. I've been making you wait till I'm ready and maybe you're tired of waiting. I won't stand in the way of your *reunion*."

Is she for real? I'm trying hard not to roll my eyes, because that will get me into more trouble. "There's not going to be any reunion. As far as I'm concerned, she's part of the past. She means nothing to me. It was just sex."

By the look on Haley's face, that was the wrong thing to say. *Big mistake. I'm handling this all wrong.*

"I had no idea it meant so little to you," she whispers.

I take her hand. "If you're talking about us, it's not the same thing." I whisper, trying to explain. "With her, it didn't mean anything. I had no feelings for her. She had no feelings for me. I was a trophy. All she wanted was to say she'd slept with *the hero* before he left on the mission. I know it's hard to believe, but it had almost nothing to do with me."

"Then why did you do it?" She doesn't get it and she probably won't until she's much older. There's no suitable answer, so I go with the truth.

"I thought I was going to die soon, and she offer ed...?"

She wrinkles her nose like I'm giving off a bad odor.

"That's kind of worse."

I know it sounds bad. There's no way I'm telling Haley the gory details of how Brittney turned up in my room the night before I left for the station wearing nothing but a smile. How I was tired and scared and sick to my stomach before and even worse after. How the smell of her perfume lingered in my room all night, making me gag. It was nothing like it had been with Rachel. I'd no idea it could be so wild and soulless and ecstatically raw. It felt like I'd already died, and this was both my reward and my punishment.

How could I even begin to explain that to a girl like Haley?

She pulls away from me, climbing the hill towards the cabin. For a moment, I consider leaving her alone, waiting for her to calm down. But then I imagine her stewing on it. Making it worse in her mind.

Nope. I have to fix this now.

I catch up with Haley further up the path and draw her into the shade of the trees between the cabins. There's a wide pine, tilting slightly downhill, shielding us from the path. Thankfully, she doesn't resist too much. Tango busies herself sniffing the bushes by the cliff.

Leaning on the tree, she looks up at me defiantly, daring me to try to excuse myself and to damn myself in the process. There's nothing I can say. I lean in to kiss her, but she turns her face, evading me.

"Blue... come on," I beg.

To my dismay, when she turns back, her eyes glimmer with tears. "I can't compete with these girls, these women, from your past. They are all beautiful, and bold, and I'm not like them. I don't look like that, or act like that."

"Hey." I wipe away the brimming tears with my

thumbs. "You don't need to be like them. You're beautiful and perfect for me just the way you are. And this... us... is about the way you make me feel. I love you, *Blue*." I place my hands on the tree on both sides of her, caging her in. "Don't be mad at me about something I did before I met you."

"Why not?" she whispers, but she's softening.

"Because I was a different person before I met you. You can be mad at past-Jorden, but not at me, because I love you. That other guy didn't know..."

"What didn't he know?" she asks, a smile finally blossoming on her lips.

"That kissing you is better than anything past-me had done or could imagine."

Haley inhales sharply, placing her palm on my cheek. I bend down and kiss her, pressing her back into the tree bark, the smell of pine mingling with her scent. Her fingers tangle in my hair and her arms circle my neck as I deepen the kiss. Running my hands down her body, I slide them under her thighs and lift her, pressing her between me and the tree. She gasps, wrapping her legs around my waist, which only increases my arousal.

I break the kiss to whisper in her ear. "If kissing you feels this good, can you imagine how amazing other things will feel?"

Her hot breath flutters on my neck. When I raise my head, her gaze is intense and penetrating, locking us together. Her touch on my back tightens, setting my skin on fire.

"Do you want me as much as I want you, *Blue*?"

She shivers and nuzzles my neck, whispering, "I do."

I'm not sure how we got from fighting to here, but I'm more interested in how we can get from here back to our cabin. In the midst of this insane situation, the only thing I'm certain of is Blue. And if she doesn't want to wait anymore, then we really, really need to go somewhere private.

I promised to be patient until she was ready, but the look in her eyes tells me she is. Or is that just the reflection of my own desire?

Chapter 30

First Time

Haley

The tension in the cabin fills the room like a living thing, stealing the air.

Earlier, I told Jorden I want him, and I do, but now I have to put my body where my mouth is and I'm terrified.

Jorden doesn't press me, even though we hurried straight back, and so we circle each other as we move around the room. I put away my jacket. He tidies the already-made bed. We're stalling, as we watch each other out of the corner of our eyes.

Finally, I can't take the tension any longer.

Jorden is washing a cup in the sink with his back to me. I admire the movement of his shoulders, the way his muscles ripple in his strong back. Then I approach him, threading my arms around his waist.

He places the cup in the drainer and turns to me, smiling. "My hands are wet."

"I don't care," I say and pull him down to me, his dripping hand creeping into my hair, cool and wet on the back of my neck. He kisses me, slowly, passionately, making my body stir and ache, but then his lips part with mine. I want to grab him back, but he pins me with a serious look.

"Are you sure you want to?"

"Yes."

I want to connect with him every way I can. Because I love him, and I want to be with him. More than I've ever wanted anything in my life. But also, a small, insecure piece of me realizes the girls from his past hold power over him. By sleeping with him, they've bound him to them forever. He says it was just sex, but it's obvious each encounter rocked him, marked him, and I want to leave my mark, too. If I don't, they'll always have me at a disadvantage.

Instead of answering, I kiss him again, but I can't stop my nervous shaking. My nerves are making him nervous.

Jorden pulls back and murmurs, "We don't have to do this now. It can wait."

I shake my head. "No, I don't want to wait, just... go slow."

He nods and kisses me, walking me backwards towards the bed. When we get there, he stops and cups my face in both hands.

"I love you, *Blue*." His green eyes are soft and his look is so tender.

"Love you, too," I whisper against his mouth, brushing my lips to his, then pulling him down with me.

He keeps his promise. Slowly letting his hands explore my body, peeling off layer after layer of clothing as we discard everything keeping us apart.

"Wait... do you have protection?" I ask.

"You don't know what I went through to get this..." he chuckles. "But I didn't assume. I just..." His blush as he fishes around in a drawer is adorable.

I wrap my hand around his as he fumbles, waiting for him to meet my eyes. "It's good that you were prepared."

We explore each other gently, studying the ways we fit together until time becomes a blur and being separate is just a memory.

Later, I cuddle against his chest, my eyes following the line of his jaw as it connects to his neck and meets the firm line of his shoulders. Kissing the base of his throat, I taste the soft skin with my lips. I never want to stop touching him. He smiles down at me and sighs, kissing my hair.

"What am I going to do with you?"

I draw his head towards me. "I think you should probably just kiss me."

Chapter 31

Secrets and Lies

Jorden

The world feels brighter this morning.

It's hard to keep my mind on the security meeting. My thoughts keep drifting back to the events of last night. We have the worst timing in the world. If the ESC attack, they'll probably kill us all or, at the very least, capture and separate us, but I'm still glad it happened.

I refuse to stop living just because we may die soon. I've already lived past my expected expiration date. It's funny that the girl who almost killed me makes my life worth living.

Thinking about Haley as I walk down the hill towards the mess hall, I'm so in my head that, at first, I don't notice him. Then I feel eyes on me; it's like a subtle pressure, sending a tingle down my back. I glance behind me, spotting several people at different points up the path.

Terry is a way off, not close enough to talk to, yet I'm immediately suspicious. I'm not threatened by his friendship with Haley anymore. I'm over my jealousy. Then again, he hangs around me just as often.

I don't know much about him. He's new to the Farm, and he's probably one of my father's kids, but I don't know much else. He's always around, but is he really following me?

To test my theory, I veer off the path, heading into the narrow gap between the girls' dorms and the training center. If I'm right, he'll follow me. But I chuckle at the ridiculous thought; I'm probably being paranoid.

I duck behind the end of the cabin and wait for him to walk past...

...and wait

...and wait.

Okay. This is stupid. Preparing to return to the path, I tense when footsteps crunch on the gravel between the cabins.

Terry peeks around the corner of the cabin and, without thinking, I grab him and slam him up against the wall. He raises his hands, eyes wide with fear, and squeaks like a little mouse. It would be funny if he weren't being a creep. I raise my fist to scare him a little more, holding it inches from his face.

"Why are you following me? Are these my father's orders?"

"What? No, I—" he stammers, turning red. "No. He didn't. I'm not."

I raise an eyebrow. *Does he think I'm stupid?* We're tucked behind the cabins, off the main path, where there's absolutely no reason to come unless you're hiding or following somebody. He stares at me defiantly. For a second, it's like I'm looking into a mirror at a younger version of myself. There are a lot of kids with an inkling of my father in them, but this is more than an inkling. I wonder what his mother looks like.

He shakes himself, like a dog shaking off water, trying to dislodge my grip on his shirt, but he keeps silent, refusing to implicate himself. Smart.

"Why do you turn up everywhere I go?"

"It's a small compound," he mutters.

Drat. If he won't confess, there's nothing more I can do. Hopefully, I've scared him enough to make him back off. Maybe he'll tell my dad I'm on to him. At least if he wants me followed, he should use someone stealthier.

Taking a step back, I release him but, instead of bolting, he hangs there, shoulders scrunched, chewing his lip as if he wants to say something.

"Tell me what's going on," I ask, trying to sound more sympathetic.

Terry pushes his shoulders back as if coming to a decision. "I can't tell you, but I can show you. But not now. Meet me at the top of the orchard at eleven pm. Come alone, don't bring your comm device, and don't tell anyone, not even Haley. If you tell her, I'll know."

I narrow my eyes at him, wondering how he could possibly know. Then again, they've been getting closer, spending hours training together while I was in ops. Maybe he's telling the truth. I can't risk it.

"I'll think about it. Maybe I'll come, maybe I won't. I'm not making any promises," I say.

He grunts as I take off, leaving him lurking behind the cabin.

That was weird. Do I want to know what he's up to desperately enough to break Haley's trust? Especially now. I'd promised no more secrets, but I really want to know what's going on. I postpone my decision till the very last moment. At ten thirty, I get up and put on my jacket.

"Where are you going?" Haley asks.

I hate lying to her. "Emergency ops meeting. They just sent me a message," I mutter.

"At this hour?" She crinkles her eyebrows.

I bend and kiss her on the forehead. "Everything is fine. Don't wait up for me."

"Okay. But wake me up when you come in, whatever time it is."

I nod and, seconds later, I'm out the door, moving down the path. If she looks out for any reason, she'll see me going the wrong way, but I have no choice.

Heading towards the valley on the other side of the hill, the path winds down past the barn and through the meadow till I reach the orchard.

It isn't eleven yet, so I sit under a tree hidden in the shadows and blow on my hands. An owl hoots somewhere nearby, its wings flapping as it takes flight.

The whole situation is unnerving, the location rekindling memories of the longest night of my life. A few minutes later, Terry's steps crunch on the path. He looks nervous. I rise and creep through the trees, coming out farther up so it looks like I just arrived. Then I stomp loudly so my steps ring out.

Shoulders deflating, Terry seems relieved I came.

"Okay, show me," I order as I march up to him.

He shakes his head. "Not here, come on."

I follow him as he winds his way through the orchard to its other side. We emerge from the trees, following the base of the cliff surrounding the valley.

"There's nothing here, Terry," I huff. "Why are you wasting my time?"

He grins at me and disappears behind a crag of rock. I follow and, to my surprise, we're in a narrow cave. I've lived here most of my life, but I've never seen this place. Terry holds a light, but it only illuminates a short distance in front of us. The dank, earthy crevice runs into the mountain, delving deep into the rock. At least it's warmer than outside, and it's growing warmer still as we continue, leaving the chilly night air behind us. My breath constricts as if bearing the weight of the entire mountain above us. We walk in silence.

Dread rises, brushing icy fingers across my neck, and my skin prickles. Why am I trusting him? What if he has other plans for me? It would be so easy to jump me from behind in this confined space. Nobody knows I'm here.

I reach out and touch his shoulder. "Where are we going?"

"We're almost there," he huffs.

"Almost where?" I challenge but he doesn't answer me.

The air tastes fresher now and, soon after, we emerge from the passage. We're on the other side of the mountain. This cave's entrance is equally well hidden. I wonder if it's natural or man-made. A few hundred yards below us there's a road winding between the mountains. Terry leads me down the other side of the mountain towards a car parked beside the road.

"Where are we going?" I ask again.

"Not *we*. *You*. It's time you learn the truth, but I'm not the one who needs to tell you." He opens the car door. "It's an auto drive. There's a destination programmed. You're going further up into the mountains."

"I can't leave. Haley is waiting for me. I can't just disappear."

He fixes me with a steady look. "Do you want to know the truth?"

"Yes." It seems dumb to come all the way out here and not find out.

"Then don't worry about Haley. I'll take care of her till you get back."

I don't want to disappear on her, but I don't have a choice if I want to know what's going on. My gut tells me this is important, so I get into the car, buckle up, and press GO. With a hum, the car starts its journey, zipping silently on the dark roads towards its unknown destination.

Chapter 32

Breach of Trust

Haley

A bad feeling wakes me from my sleep.

Something is wrong. Tango is curled up by my feet, but Jorden's side of the bed is cold to the touch and his pillow undisturbed. Sitting up, I look around the dark cabin. There's no sign of him; he never came back.

A cold snake of fear uncoils in my stomach, slithering towards my heart. Has something happened? To calm myself, I reach for my Farm comm, intending to send him a message. My hand brushes his comm on the bedside table. It's not like him to forget it. Nothing about this situation seems normal. Can the meeting be running this late? It's past 1 am.

Pulling on my coat and boots, I head down the hill towards operations. Tango runs at my heels, surprised at this unexpected walk. When I reach the top of the path, it's obvious the building is dark. Shivering, I stand there looking in every direction. Where could he be?

For a cold second, I wonder if he's with somebody else. Brittney or Rachel or one of those trainee girls who were batting their eyelashes at him. Is that why he hasn't returned?

The thought makes me sick.

I don't believe it, but there's nothing else I can do right now. Picking up Tango, I'm heading back towards our cabin when I see someone coming up from the meadow. He looks familiar and, for a moment, I hope it's Jorden, but the shape isn't tall enough or sturdy enough to be Jorden. Stepping into the shadows of the porch, I watch as they come closer.

To my surprise, it's Terry. I stay perfectly still but Tango yawns noisily, wagging her tail and wriggling to be let down. Terry turns towards me, stepping on to the porch.

"Haley?" he asks. "Why are you out here in the middle of the night?"

I let Tango go and she runs over to him, whimpering to be picked up, wagging her tail till it looks like it might fly off. He bends down and scoops her up, carrying her back to me. He laughs as she licks his face before handing her back to me. "Thanks, I needed my face washed."

I smile, but ask, "Where were you?"

He yawns and stretches. "I couldn't fall asleep, so I took a walk up to the meadow and back. I like the smell of the grass at night, all moist and dewy. In the summer, when it's warm, I sometimes take a blanket up and sleep in the meadow, under the stars."

He steps closer to me, a bit too close, smelling of mountain grass and something musty and earthy. "Why are you up?"

"Jorden didn't come back from the operations meeting. I don't know where he is. Have you seen him?"

He shakes his head without looking me in the eye. I get the feeling he's lying. As I turn to walk back to our cabin, he falls into step with me, a bit too close, his shoulder brushing mine as we walk. When we reach the door of the cabin I share with Jorden, I turn to say 'goodnight'.

"You know," Terry says in a low voice, pinning me with an intense gaze, "I'm glad we're friends. I haven't made many friends here on the Farm. Everyone knows each other too well. I always feel like the newcomer."

"Well, that makes two of us. We should stick together."

He grins, his green eyes reflecting the light in the cabin window. "I was hoping you'd say that." He leans towards me and I try to step back, but he's too close and I'm stuck between him and the cabin wall. "I like being your friend, Haley. But I—" he takes a deep breath. "I want to be more than that."

His hand slides up my arm, fingers brushing my neck. Pushing me back against the wall behind us, his hand creeps behind my ear and he kisses me. For a moment, I'm too stunned to react. Then I push him away.

"What are you doing?" I touch my lips, as if he's tainted them.

He's panting, looking pleased with himself.

Wiping my mouth as if that can erase the kiss, I glare at him. I like him, and it wasn't a bad kiss, but I don't want him to kiss me or touch me like that.

"You know, Jorden will kill you when he finds out," I hiss.

He grins. "I'm not worried."

My confusion turns to anger, and I step forward, shoving him hard in the chest. "Where's Jorden? I know you have something to do with him disappearing."

He doesn't answer, staring at me obstinately and I shove him again.

"Tell me."

I take a step forward. Before I can do it a third time, he grabs hold of my wrists and yanks me towards him, my face inches from his. I glare at him furiously.

"Stop it," he snaps, then gulps, staring at my lips again. Somehow, this feels almost as intimate as the kiss, but he looks scared.

"Then tell me the truth."

His voice is strained. "He's gone."

My mind isn't registering the words. "Gone where?"

"Can't tell you, but I don't think he's coming back. I know I wouldn't."

Shaking my head, I insist, "No. No way. If you think he won't come back to me, you really don't know Jorden."

I'm confident as I say it, but a small voice in the back of my mind asks, *are you sure* you *do*? I've been wrong about him before. Apparently, he lied to me tonight about the meeting. Can I be sure of anything anymore? But even though he's lied to me before, I always knew his true heart.

I stomp down on my doubt. "Where is he?" My voice falters as tears claw their way up my throat.

Terry lets go of me abruptly, stepping away. Turning his back on me, he plops down on the edge of the porch, shoulders slumping. "I'm not supposed to tell you. Or anyone," he mumbles. "It isn't safe."

That isn't a refusal; it's a negotiation. He must be dying to tell someone. Terry needs encouragement so, even though I don't want to encourage him, I sit close enough for our shoulders to press together. "Tell me."

He studies my face, then exhales a long breath till he runs out of air.

"I'm his brother."

Duh. As far as surprises go, it isn't a big one. The proof is written on every inch of him. If he were older, he could have been Jorden's twin. Several of the Farm kids are Peter's children. Why is this such a big deal to him?

"So, you are one of his father's kids?"

Terry looks hurt. "From one of these women at the Farm? No. Jorden and I are true brothers. Same mother, same father."

I shake my head. "How's that possible? His mother died when he was five. You're only two years younger than he is, and he's never met you. No way that's possible."

Terry smiles at me like he's sharing a wonderful secret he's been waiting to get off his chest.

"Technically, I'm five and a half years younger than him. But he lost three years in transit. So now, I'm only two and a half years younger."

"Oh, wow. I forgot about the time loss. So does that mean you never knew your mom? Jorden told me she died when he was five years old.

Terry shakes his head. "Well, about that..."

Chapter 33

New Beginning

Jorden

The car drives for what seems like hours, climbing higher and higher into the dark mountains.

At first, I'm too tense to relax but, as the trip continues, I start dozing, rocked into a light sleep by the gentle movement of the vehicle.

I awake with a start when the car announces. "You have arrived at your destination."

The clock on the dashboard says 2:23 am. We could be anywhere. Rubbing my eyes, I get out. Cold mountain air envelopes me, rousing me into wakefulness. The car stands in front of a small log cabin, much like the ones on the Farm. Dim light spills from its windows. It's a bizarre time to turn up at someone's doorstep, especially if they don't know I'm coming. Climbing the porch steps, I knock on the door. It swings open with a creak.

Creepy.

From the entrance, the inside of the cabin doesn't seem sinister. It's actually quite homey: logs burn in the fireplace; the furnishings are bright and inviting; a pink sofa and table, with two matching armchairs, face the fire. On the other side of the room, there's a small, round table covered in a white lace tablecloth. The tiny globe spinning in the window draws my eyes. So, whoever lives here is an Earther. But who? And why are they so far away from the Farm? Why the secrecy?

As I watch, a woman steps into view, her back to me in the dim firelight. She looks vaguely familiar, like a person I knew in a dream. Her soft, blond hair is shot through with strands of gray. The way she moves reminds me of someone. She pulls her shawl tighter and turns around. Her eyes open wide when she notices me, as though I'm the ghost and not her.

I recognize her at once.

I want to run to her, but I'm frozen in place. How can she be here, alive? I've missed her so much for so long. This is unbelievable.

"Jorden?"

I find my voice. I don't know how. "Mom?" I cry, finally stumbling towards her.

She collapses into a chair as if her legs can't hold her anymore, and I fall at her feet, burying my face in her lap. Stroking my head like she did when I was little, her hand flutters like a ghost's touch. Like a dream come to life. It reminds me of how she'd comfort me after I skinned my knee, or on one of the many occasions my father punished me for a violation of his rules.

Soaking in her touch, I'm scared to lift my head and open my eyes for fear she'll fade away. When I do, I'm shaking uncontrollably. "How is this possible?"

"My beautiful, beautiful boy. Let me look at you. You're so big. A grown man. I missed you so much," she says as she takes my chin in her hand, her eyes shining with tears. Then she places her trembling palm over her mouth, overcome with emotion.

I hug her, and she feels so small. I remember a tall woman, big enough to hold me on her lap, carry me up to bed. Of course, I was five. I'm the one who's grown and changed, while she stayed the same. After a while, she releases me, or I let her go, and she rises, pulling me to my feet. She's still tall, but now I'm taller and she looks me up and down approvingly.

"I'm so glad you returned. There's so much to tell you, but it's late. You need to rest; we can talk in the morning."

Incapable of arguing, I nod. I'm physically and mentally exhausted. My mind needs to process.

She leads me to one of the two doors off the main room. It's a boy's bedroom. I wonder why she has a room here, and where the room's occupant is right now, but I'm too tired to ask. Removing my shoes and my jacket, I get into the bed. After I lie down, she pulls up the covers, tucking me in. For a weird second, I wonder if she's going to read me a bedtime story. Instead, she sits on the side of the bed, stroking my hair.

I take her other hand, solid and warm in my grip, as if making sure she's real. "Will you still be here in the morning?"

She smiles. "Of course," and pats my hand. "Go to sleep, Jorden. We'll talk in the morning."

I smile up at her, so happy that I can't think of anything else as I drift off.

When I wake up, I lie there for a moment remembering where I am. Recalling the wonderful, impossible dream I had last night.

I dreamed my mother was alive, and older.

Was it a dream? Outside the unfamiliar room, plates and cutlery chime, and a wonderful smell of food wafts in. I'm ravenous, scared, and exhilarated.

Hopping out of bed, I straighten my rumpled clothing, run my fingers through my hair to tidy it up a bit, then stop. I want to go out there, but I'm scared I'm still dreaming, and this will wake me up.

Slowly, I open the door. My mom is in the kitchen wearing a blue apron, cooking eggs. Her hair is up in a knot. When she sees me, a smile lights up her face. "Jorden."

It's like I got kicked into the past, as though I'm five again. Suddenly I'm shy. "Mom."

She points to the table with the spatula. "Sit down."

She's set two places at the small, round kitchen table. Blue China plates on a white tablecloth. I pull out a chair.

"How do you eat your eggs?" she asks, and I have another moment of uncertainty. *Shouldn't a mother know how her son eats his eggs?* "Do you still like them sunny side up?"

I smile, because she remembered, then shrug. "Since we moved to the Farm, nobody really asks me how I like my eggs anymore. I just eat them the way the mess hall serves them."

"Well, I'll make them any way you want." She crosses over to me, putting a hand on my shoulder, and bends to kiss my temple. "You've gotten so big."

Her eyes are misty. Mine too.

I smile up at her. "Sunny side up would be great."

Finishing the eggs, she adds them to my plate with fresh bread and butter, then pours me orange juice. The whole thing feels unreal. It's every fantasy I've ever had about getting my mother back rolled into one perfect moment.

"Go on, dig in," she says as she takes the seat beside me.

I shake my head, giving half a laugh. "I keep expecting to wake up."

She smiles. The crinkles beside her eyes have gotten deeper, her blond hair is mixed with gray. "You're not dreaming. Though I know what you mean. It's been a long time."

"It's been forever."

I'm not complaining just... What do you say in a situation like this?

Pain flashes in her eyes. "Finish your eggs, Jorden, before they get cold, and then we'll talk."

After we finish eating, I help with the dishes, and we move to the living room. I wait for her to speak as she brushes my hair away from my forehead, chewing on her lip.

"Why only now? I almost died on the station, mom. Almost didn't make it back. Why wait this long to let me know you're alive?" I cry.

"Jorden, I'm sorry. I didn't know you were going until it was too late. Back then, I had a few sources in your father's compound, but I found out too late. When I discovered he sent you, I was furious. I never thought he'd risk your life."

I huff. "It was never a suicide mission, but we all treated it as one. I never believed I'd live and nobody else did, either. And now I've made a mess of things by not dying when everyone expected me to."

She gives a wry laugh. "You came back. Against all the odds. Nobody imagined that." Her eyes tear up again. She grasps my hand. "I'm so glad you survived."

"We're going to need some tissues to get through this conversation," I say.

She laughs and fetches a box, wiping her streaming eyes. "Did you know I started the Earther movement?" she asks.

I nod. "Father never mentioned it, but I met someone after my return to Earth who told me how it started. Judith... I don't know her last name."

She nods. "I remember her. She was with us at the very beginning. You were probably too young to remember my job, but I'm an environmental scientist. While working on the New Horizons terraforming project, I discovered that using the same new technology on Earth could clean up our atmosphere; we could save everybody still living here. But my employers didn't want to hear about it."

"Why not?" I can't believe what I'm hearing.

"Because it isn't profitable, Jorden. When they develop a new planet, they have an endless stream of revenue rolling in. They own it, every resource, every tax, forever. If they used their technology here on Earth, all they'd get is cleaner air, a longer lifespan for people already living here, better health. But they won't profit from it. It won't be cheap, or easy, and they won't make nearly as much."

My fists clench at her words. "It shouldn't be their choice."

"No, it shouldn't, but who's going to force them? They own everything. Earth's governments are weak; the leaders are practically figureheads. The Conglomerate calls the shots."

"So, you and dad agree on that?"

"On that, yes. Not much else. On the goal, but not on the methods. We shouldn't become worse than the people we're trying to stop; the ends don't justify the means. I never believed in terrorism. Peter was willing to sacrifice your life. Worse, he was prepared to sacrifice your soul. If your plan had worked, you'd have been a terrorist. A mass murderer."

Now it's my turn to count the colored rings of the rug beneath our feet. "He didn't make me go, mom. I volunteered. It was my idea," I whisper.

She shakes her head. "That doesn't matter. You volunteered after years of indoctrination. After years of being force fed sermons and propaganda. Of years of him tearing you down and making you feel worthless unless you earned his approval."

I gasp. "How do you know that? You weren't even there." I say it in surprise, not accusation, but she winces before she replies.

"Because he did it to me, too, from the moment we met. After the honeymoon period was over, he began chipping away at my confidence. Making me feel stupid and worthless. I had to grovel for his attention, his approval. Be grateful for every tiny scrap of affection. It took me years to scrape myself up off the ground and remember that I was worth more than his opinion of me. Only then was I able to find my feet again and leave."

Taking her hand, I use a tissue to wipe away her tears. Her expression is more angry than sad. My own cheeks are hot and wet.

"Why did you leave, mom?" I ask, then shake my head. *No. That's not it.* I understand why she left. "Why did you leave me behind with him?"

She looks down at her hands. "He wouldn't have let me take you. I'm sorry Jorden, I wasn't strong enough to take you with me and I needed to get away before he found out."

"Found out what?"

"If I'd stayed longer, he'd have found out, and taken both of you."

"What do you mean?"

She stares at the floor, then looks up at me, her eyes shining. "You have a younger brother, Jorden. When I left, I was two months pregnant, and I faked my death. "

"What?" My head is spinning. This is too much to take in all at once.

"You've met him." *Way too much.*

"I've met him?" I can't believe my ears.

"Terry, Terrance, is your brother, Jorden. You

slept in his room last night."

I shake my head. "No, no. That doesn't make sense. He can't be my brother, mom. I'm almost eighteen, he's like sixteen. How could he be my brother if you had him after you left dad? I should be five or six years older than him."

"You are, Jorden. Technically, you're almost 21. You lost three years in transit. Space travel really complicates things...."

"Wait, then why is Terry on the Farm? If you wanted to get away from dad so badly, why send Terry to him?"

"Terry wanted to meet his father. He was fifteen, and I was furious after I discovered Peter sent you on a suicide mission. I wanted to avenge your death, but first I needed better information."

I get up and pace back and forth, running my hands through my hair. Trying to get a grip on the new situation. Till I stop and face her again.

"How did you get Terry onto the Farm?"

"I've been sending donations to the Earther cause, under a pseudonym, for almost a decade now. Peter was glad to accept him, along with another sizable donation."

It's strange hearing her refer to my father as Peter. I'm used to people talking about him with respect, even reverence. She says it casually, almost with contempt.

"Didn't he notice the resemblance?" Now that I

know the truth, it's ridiculous that I didn't see it myself. "The kid is practically a clone."

She smiles, bitterly. "Luckily, your father has so many unrecognized offspring, one more close resemblance would only flatter his ego."

My mind is churning, trying to accept what I learned. I open my mouth to say something, but I can't think of anything. I might be having a breakdown. After a minute of silence, I blink. "I have to go back. Haley will be going mad."

My mother smiles at me, her mouth quirking up on one side. "Haley? Your little acquisition from the space station?"

She really does know what is going on. Thanks to Terry, her little spy. *My little brother. I can't process that right now.*

"She's not an acquisition, mom. Haley is my girlfriend."

Her smile widens. "Do you love her?"

This is strange. I've never had a mom to talk to about these things. I certainly couldn't talk about girls with my dad. "Yes. More than anything."

My mother nods, but her eyes are sad. "That complicates things a bit."

"Why? How?"

"You need to keep her in the dark. Your father will be keeping tabs on you. He may have your lodgings bugged. Don't tell her about me until you are certain you aren't being overhead. I'd rather you didn't tell her at all. Everything is riding on him not knowing about me or Terry."

"I'll keep your secret, but I have to tell Haley. If she ever speaks to me again."

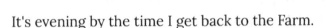

It's evening by the time I get back to the Farm.

The first thing I see when I enter our cabin is Haley, curled up on the couch with Tango in her lap. Her eyes are red.

I've been gone almost 24 hours and she must be frantic, but she stays seated. Placing Tango on the couch beside her, she hugs her knees, her back stiff and her face strained.

"Where have you been?" she asks in a clipped tone.

"It's complicated."

She stands up, her arms crossed. "It really isn't. You promised you'd never lie to me again."

I want to tell her everything, but I can't. There might be cameras here and microphones. It isn't safe to talk where they can overhear us. I try to tell her with my eyes, to make her understand some-how.

"Haley."

She shakes her head, drawing closer to me, but

holding back, just out of arm's reach, her arms crossed tightly. "I love you, but I can't go through this again. Do you have any idea what I've been through since last night, not knowing where you are? Knowing the last thing you did before you left was lie to me?"

I try to close the gap between us but she backs away, so I stop, lifting my palms in surrender. "Haley, just give me a chance to explain."

She circles around me to the door, putting on her coat and picking Tango up. "I'm going to spend the night in Glory's room."

"Haley. Please, wait."

The door closes, and she's gone.

While I consider chasing her, finding a place to tell her everything, I don't know where it's safe to talk. I've missed her every minute we've been apart. The need to tell her what's happened churns in my gut. I want to respect my mother's request, but Haley is my top priority. If our cabin is bugged, maybe it's better to wait. I wince, imagining my father watching us. Probably best we don't spend the night here together right now.

I hate being apart from her when I don't have to be, and that she thinks she can't trust me, but she's forgiven me for worse. It's not like she can go anywhere. Hopefully, she'll calm down overnight. I'll find her and speak to her first thing in the morning. We'll sort it out together. She has to forgive me.

Crawling into our cold bed, I hug her pillow to me. It's a pitiful substitute for holding her. Then I fall into a fitful sleep, tormented by the smell of her hair on the pillow.

Early the next morning, I head down the mountain towards the girls' dormitory. As I approach, Glory emerges from the cabin, yawning and tugging on her jacket. I smile carefully. I don't know how much Haley told her.

"Good morning. Early practice?" I ask. She nods, returning a yawny grin.

"Haley still asleep?"

She looks puzzled. "Shouldn't I be asking you that?"

My heart skips a beat. "Didn't she spend the night in your room?"

Glory narrows her eyes at me. "Did you guys have a fight?"

"Yeah, you could say that." I'm trying not to panic, and failing.

She gives me a dirty look. "Sorry, I haven't seen her." She shrugs. "She'll probably show up at training later. You'd better have a good apology ready. It must have been some fight for her to want to spend the night with me instead of you."

Glory turns away, heading down the hill, and I run both hands through my hair, searching the path.

Where could she be? Glory is probably her best friend here. Could she be with Terry? Would she go to him? I need to talk to him, anyway.

Turning towards the mess hall, I only take a few steps before a small shape uncurls from a doormat outside one of the cabins, and dashes towards me.

It's Tango.

Dread unfurls in my chest and icy fingers grip my heart.

Haley wouldn't leave Tango alone out in the cold. Something has happened to her.

Chapter 34

Taken

Haley

When I wake up, it's dark and my head hurts.

I try to turn over, slowly, but my left arm is chained to the bedframe with a cold metal bracelet, clamped like a vice around my wrist. I'm on a military-type cot in a room lit by a single lightbulb in the hallway outside the open door. Apart from the bed, the room is bare, with no windows in the gray, concrete walls.

Where am I? After my fight with Jorden, I remember leaving our cabin, trudging down the hill towards the girl's dorms to Glory's room carrying Tango. My heart drops. Tango. Where is she?

"Tango, here, girl," I call out quietly, but there's no snuffling or the swish of soft paws running up to me. No wet nose. Please let her be okay. If only I knew that whoever took me didn't hurt her.

The crucial question is, who took me? Did the ESC storm the compound and grab me? I don't remember anything. Sitting up gingerly, I feel my head for bumps. Nothing. My mouth is dry and my tongue feels and tastes like a fuzzy caterpillar. My head aches. Did they drug me with some substance, maybe? Gas?

What time is it? My Farm comm isn't in my pockets. I flick on my station comm, more out of habit than anything else, and it lights up, searching for a signal. Sorry pal, not going to find one.

With nothing else to do, I lie there torturing myself, rehashing our argument and the last words I said to him. Did Jorden try to find me this morning? Does he know I didn't spend the night at Glory's? If he finds Tango, he'll be as worried as I was about him yesterday. My heart sinks. Maybe he thinks I'm hiding somewhere, sulking just to punish him.

Time passes; I don't know how long. I've definitely missed training. I make a few futile attempts to remove the bracelet, but it's solid and tight against my skin with no chance of prying it off. Still, I strain the wrist cuffed to the cot, trying to pull my hand out. Dragging the bed away from the wall is impossible; it's bolted tight. There's nothing else in the room I can use.

Finally, a dark shadow fills the opening, standing there silently. I cringe instinctively. The light in the room snaps on, blinding me. I screw my eyes closed and let them adjust before opening them again. When I do, Jorden's father is sitting in front of me, having dragged a chair in from another room.

Peter Lund. Earther leader, and all-round narcissistic asshole who treats his son like dirt in private while applauding him in public. Oh, how I hate him. His cold, green eyes crease as he studies me, judging my expression.

"You must be wondering what you are doing here," he states. I glare at him, as I have a feeling he's going to tell me. "I'm going to negotiate your return to the ESC. Don't think for a second that I'll let the actions of one stupid boy tear down everything I've built here."

Even if I'm mad at Jorden for lying to me, I can't stand the way Peter talks about his son. Did he notice Jorden was missing the past day? That's why he felt confident to take me now. He knew Jorden couldn't stop him.

"Don't you think Jorden will notice I'm gone?" I spit.

"By the time he does, it will be too late. I won't engage in a public showdown with him. I'll notify him after you're gone." He exhales, his forehead etched with deep frown lines. "I should have known he wasn't up to the task he took on. He's always been weak, like his mother."

My lip quivers. "Jorden is the bravest boy I've ever

met. He's tougher and stronger than anyone should have to be at his age. He took on an impossible task, and he almost succeeded." I'm the one who stopped him. "Even though you asked the unthinkable of him."

If I could shoot laser beams out of my eyes, he'd be dead.

Lund raises his eyebrows at my passionate rant. I'm surprised, myself. Since when do I yell at grownups? Especially scary ones.

But he seems more amused than angry, as if I'm just a yapping puppy. "You think you know him?" he snarls. "Because you two have been swapping saliva for a few months?"

"It's amazing he's even capable of love after growing up with a father like you."

"Love?" he laughs, but there's no humor in it. It's a frozen word in his mouth. "Is that what you think you two have? As far as I'm concerned, you are just one of Jorden's many mistakes. One that I must now rectify."

He gets to his feet as if we're done. If he leaves, I'm doomed. I need to give him something he wants more than turning me over.

"Wait," I plead and he pauses. His eyes are hard lumps of jade. Taking a deep breath, I gather the courage to convince him to let me stay. I need to talk to him the way Jorden talks to adults, without fear or worrying about the consequences.

I gulp, but manage to say, "They want me back because they think Jorden kidnapped me." His eyebrows rise; I got his attention. He sits down again as I continue: "But he didn't."

Now his eyebrows rise all the way up.

"We planned the whole thing together. I was with him in the med lab, every single day from the moment he woke up. Everyone on the station knew we were a couple, long before the explosion. I was, and still am, in love with him. He didn't take me against my will; I helped him get away."

Lund is listening intently. Best way to lie, stay as close to the truth as possible.

"That's why I came here with him when I had a dozen opportunities to get away in the city." True.

"Did you try to help him complete his mission?"

"No, he didn't tell me anything about it. I only found out after he'd rigged the pod to blow." I lower my voice, even though we're alone. "And they need me to testify against him. They don't have any footage of what happened in the pod bay. The station was in disarray." Nobody knows I begged him to stop, or that he locked me in the control room. I couldn't stop him. "The pod blowing up was an accident. So, I vented the air to reduce the blast, but I overdid it. I never wanted to hurt him," true, "because I love him." True. "I want to stay with him here." True.

Lund's eyes glisten with excitement.

I continue, driving my pitch home. "Let me talk to the ESC, or the media if you like, and tell them. I can speak on his behalf. I'll tell them I'm here of my own free will, and I want to stay. If I tell them the explosion on the station was an accident, do you think they'll listen?"

"You're very convincing." I can see the gears in his head turning as he thinks about it. "And you are willing to speak publicly?"

I nod.

He claps his hands together. "A daughter of the void, who spent her whole life in the bowels of a space station, speaking up to defend an Earther. Yes. That is better than handing you over and admitting his guilt." He pauses, leveling his gaze at me. "They still may demand I return you to their custody."

I nod. "I understand, but it's a step in the right direction. As long as they don't attack to save me. Not if I say I'm here of my own free will."

He shakes his head. "No, probably not. Let me think about it. I'll let you know my decision."

Lund lets me stew down here for the rest of the day, becoming more and more convinced he won't accept my offer. The hours wear on and I keep rehashing my last conversation with Jorden.

I should have gone to him when he returned and let him explain. I should have told him I loved him, and missed him, and how worried I was. Instead, I stormed out like an idiot and now I may never see him again.

I'll never even get to kiss him goodbye.

My frustration makes me want to scream, cry, and shout. Good idea. Maybe someone will hear me... or maybe Peter will decide I'm too much trouble, shoot me, and get it over with.

When Peter finally returns, I'm tied up in knots. Exhausted from imagining the worst possible outcome. He pulls a blindfold over my eyes before releasing my cuff, but it doesn't cover my right eye properly. As he marches me out, I glimpse the next room. Dozens of monitors light the space, showing scenes from all over the Farm. To my horror, one of them displays our cabin. Jorden is clearly visible sitting on the couch holding Tango.

No wonder he wouldn't tell me where he was last night. Did he know we were being watched?

My stomach twists and I shudder as I think of what else his father might have seen. He's not only invading *our* privacy. He's watching everyone. So much for trust and a low-tech, down-to-Earth community. We were never safe here. Nobody was. We're all pawns in Peter's game.

There's a closed door opposite the room with the monitors, but Peter marches me along a dark hallway and then up a flight of stairs. When he removes the blindfold, I blink.

We're in his office in command. I've never been in here before, but it's obvious from the framed photograph on the wall of him, his late wife, and a young Jorden. The perfect family man. The perfect liar.

Peter pulls my Farm comm out of a drawer and throws it onto the desk in front of me, then lounges in his seat and steeples his fingers. "If I accept your offer, I assume my son will corroborate your version of the events?"

"Of course," I lie to his face, hoping my voice doesn't tremble.

Now all I need to do is forgive Jorden for lying to me and get him on board with this lie I've concocted to protect him. We need to find a way past this. I'm willing to lie to protect him, if I have to. I'll lie to stay with him.

His father studies me as if he's trying to read my mind. "I will set up a call for you to explain what happened. It may take a few days to contact the right people who will listen." I nod. "For now..." he pauses dramatically, "you are free to go, but do not tell Jorden where you were. I can make it very uncomfortable for you." I don't doubt it. "He almost died once. I wouldn't want there to be any accidents now that he's back."

Did he just threaten to hurt his own son, to keep me in line?

Hate rears its head like a cold-blooded snake un- coiling in my stomach. I hate him. I hate this man so much. He may look like Jorden, but he's nothing like him. I clench my fists as I say, "I understand."

Jorden wants his father's approval so badly, but he's never going to get it. Peter sees him as a tool. An instrument to be used and discarded as needed.

I emerge from the Command & Control building blinking, my eyes adjusting to the late afternoon light. I've been gone since last night. My mind reels trying to decide what to tell Jorden, but we need to talk somewhere safe.

When I open the cabin door, Jorden is where I was sitting last night, holding Tango. I take a hesitant step into the room, scared he'll give me the same treatment I gave him after disappearing for 24 hours. Before I can take another step, he leaps out of his seat, leaving Tango blinking on the couch.

In seconds, his arms are around me, crushing me to his chest, as a torrent of apologies and words of love pour from us both.

"I'm sorry."

"I love you."

"I was so worried."

"I missed you so much."

"Don't ever do that to me again..."

"I won't, I'm sorry."

"I love you."

...and I don't know who said what. We're both desperate to reconnect, to close the rift that opened between us, and make things better.

I wrap my arms around his neck and pull him

down to me, pressing my lips to his, begging forgiveness for my absence and my impatience. After we break apart, I wrap my arms around his waist, reluctant to let him go. Remembering the cameras, I stand on tiptoes so I can whisper in his ear.

"We need to talk, but not here."

He nods. His eyes convey he knows it isn't safe here.

Pulling him closer again, I turn my face up for another kiss. I know now that we're being watched, but I don't care. Let them look.

After I've kissed my fill, I say, "How about we take Tango for a walk?"

"Yep. Good idea. I need to stretch my legs."

Hand in hand, we walk down the hill towards the pasture. It's cold and will be getting dark soon. It's warmer inside, but they could bug any structure. By mutual assent, we left our Farm comms behind.

"How paranoid is your father? Would he have cameras in the barn? Up in the hayloft?" I whisper.

Jorden looks around us, scratching the back of his neck. "I'm not sure. I thought I knew how he operated, but it turns out I didn't know much of anything."

"We should get out of sight," I say, and Jorden nods.

We trudge uphill to the orchard, ducking in under the trees till we're deep inside the shade, even though it's colder here. Tango sniffs amongst the leaves and Jorden sits, leaning on a tree trunk, and I lean on him, snuggling close as he wraps his arms around me. His chest rises and falls, his breath ghosting warm on my neck. I can't see his face, but maybe it's better for the conversation we need to have. So many secrets have pooled between us. We need to be careful we don't drown in them.

"Do you want to start?" I ask.

For a moment he's quiet, then he exhales. "I don't even know where to start." I wait, giving him time, till he starts talking in a rush.

"Two nights ago, Terry asked me to meet him. I didn't think it would be more than a few minutes, but he sent me... to meet my mother." He pauses, waiting for my reaction. So Terry was telling the truth. Unbelievable.

"She's alive? Oh, Jorden. I'm so happy for you. What was that like?" I twist to see his face. His eyes are shining, full of emotion.

"Amazing. Strange, like a dream come true. I still can't believe it."

"Where was she all these years?"

"Hiding overseas from my father, and the crazier thing... Terry is my younger brother."

Blowing out a long breath, I admit, "I know."

His breath catches. "What? How do you know?"

"Terry told me the night you disappeared. About five minutes after he tried to kiss me."

His muscles tense. For a moment, I think he'll

jump up and go looking for Terry. "That little shit. I'm going to kill him," he rasps.

I laugh. "That's what I told him when I shut him down. But before you do, hear me out. Strangely, I don't think it was about me... It was about you. Admittedly, it's a weird way to show it, but I think he looks up to you. He wants to be like you, in more ways than one."

"I don't care. You're mine." He buries his face in my neck, pulling me closer, and I sigh in relief, thankful he won't let jealousy divide us.

Covering his hands with mine, I twist so I can see his eyes. "Okay, caveman. Calm down. Yes. I'm yours. And you're mine. And nobody can come between us, unless we let them."

His eyes are dark green in the shade, as his brow creases in thought. "Wait, so, when you asked where I was... you knew? Was it a test?" He sounds hurt.

Things are so complicated with all these secrets and lies.

Placing my hand on his cheek, I say. "No. I knew his version, but I didn't know if Terry was telling the truth. I just wanted you to tell me."

"But I would have. I was going to," he stammers, "only I couldn't do it in our cabin. I was worried we were being watched."

Now it's my turn. "It is. We're being watched. They bugged our cabin."

"How do you know? Where have you been?" Jorden asks.

"Your father grabbed me last night after I left our cabin. It's all my fault. I should have stayed and let you explain." Jorden squeezes my hand. "He knocked me out somehow, then kept me somewhere underground, near C&C. Then he led me out through an underground control room with dozens of screens, with footage from all over the Farm. I saw you inside our cabin."

Jorden pulls me tighter, his hands clenching around me. "That bastard. How did you get away from him?"

"He threatened to return me to the ESC, to cut a deal. I needed to offer him something better than giving me back, so I told him you never really kidnapped me. That we planned it together, so you could escape. I promised I'd testify to the ESC or the media or whoever he wanted because I want to stay here."

I tense, waiting for his reaction. He sounds doubtful. "And he bought that?"

"Even he can see I love you, Jorden. Why wouldn't he believe I'd do whatever I can to save you?"

He squeezes me so tight I squeal. "You're brilliant. I love you so much."

Dipping his right shoulder, he slides me onto his arm and kisses me full on the mouth. I thread my fingers into his hair and take a moment to savor the feel of his lips and get lost in his kiss. I wish we could leave it at that, but... we can't, so I break off our kiss gently.

"There's one more thing I need to tell you." I chew my lip, hesitant to tell him. His eyebrows crease again and I want to reach up and smooth them, but I don't.

"When we were in custody at the ESC. I said I'd help Inspector Rogers bring the Earthers to justice for trying to blow up the station. Not you. He knows I'd never testify against you, but the others, the leaders."

His frown deepens. "Why didn't you tell me?"

"There was a lot happening that day. Guards surrounded us immediately after it happened. Then we were on the transport and we jumped in the freezing lake, and afterwards we were kind of busy," I smile sheepishly. I can tell he wants to be mad, but he can't help grinning as he recalls our night in the cabin by the lake. "And I guess after that... I just kind of forgot?" I bite my lip, awaiting his response.

Jorden huffs. "I can't believe you, Haley. You were so mad when I lied to you, but not telling me the truth about helping the ESC is almost the same thing. Do you get a free pass? How could you promise to turn on us?"

I try not to think back to that night, but I have no control over the images playing in my head. A tear escapes my eyelids and rolls down my check.

"I'm sorry. That was the only way I had to stop

them torturing you. They were making you relive suffocating on the pod deck. What I did to you."

Reliving that moment in my mind, watching him gasp for air, makes me tremble in his arms and another tear rolls down my cheek. The moisture hangs on my chin for a moment before it plops off onto his hand. The tiny drop of liquid melts Jorden's anger completely. His voice softens.

"Letting the air out wasn't your fault. It was mine. I didn't leave you a choice."

"I didn't let you go," I whisper. "When I could have just let you—"

"What? Blow up the jump ship? I'm glad you didn't. Don't ever feel bad about that. I'm glad you stopped me, no matter the cost. You saved everyone on that ship. You saved me from the worst decision in my life."

He wraps his arms around me, pulling me nearer. I rest my cheek on his chest, listening to his heart thrum. For a few moments, we sit in silence, tangled in memories of the horrible day that almost changed everything. When he speaks again, his voice is thoughtful.

"What did he ask you to do?"

"He didn't say. He said he would let me know, and then we escaped—"

"Okay." He exhales, and I sit up straight again. "Is there anything else?" He sounds scared to ask.

I take a deep breath. "While we're coming clean...

I also ate the chocolate chip cookies you had under your sweater in the cupboard, the ones you thought I didn't know about."

"That's fine." He laughs. Breathing out a warm puff of air onto my neck. "I love you."

"I love you too," I say.

He squeezes me tightly and, though nothing around us has changed, the light suddenly seems brighter, the air warmer. His voice is lighter and more hopeful.

"Okay, so things we now know. My mother is alive, my father is watching us. They bugged our cabin. The ESC probably won't attack us if we convince them you weren't kidnapped... though they may still be mad we stole and crashed their ship."

I take a deep breath. "So, more or less, things are working out okay. Except now we can never... you know... in the cabin again. Like ever."

He snickers, nibbling on my neck, and waggles his eyebrows at me. "It would look suspicious if we just stopped cold turkey. "

I tilt my head up to look at him. "So, you want us to... With the cameras there and your father watching? Are you insane?"

He threads his fingers through mine. "Well, at least we'd need to make him think we're still at it."

"How is that any better? Oh my God, I can't believe you."

But I can't help smiling. He has this huge goofy

grin on his face.

"What do you want me to say, Haley? I'm just a guy, in love with a girl, trying to get her to sleep with me."

"Oh, that's all, is it?" I wrap my arms around his neck. "Or you know, maybe instead of faking it in the cabin we can just—" I pull him down to me.

"Hmmm," he murmurs, "you make an excellent point."

Chapter 35

Decoy

Jorden

Haley has decided talking to the ESC and taking responsibility for our escape will solve all our problems. There's no talking her out of it. She thinks this will protect me, but I'm not so sure. My father wants to make Haley a spokesperson. It's typical for him to twist the situation in his favor, but what happens when the world is no longer watching?

Right now, Haley is in the C&C conference room. While a woman gives her a light touch of makeup before going on camera, I go to my father's office to try and talk him out of it.

"Can I talk to you?" I ask as soon as I close the door behind me. His gaze hardens.

He clenches his jaw. "You're here. Talk."

I let out a breath. "Don't make her go on air

with this confession. In taking responsibility for my crimes, she's tying her fate to mine. Haley believes everything will be okay after this, but it won't be. If she shoulders the blame, she can't go back to her life. It isn't fair to make her pay for my mistakes."

His eyes are ice, his posture steel. "Then who would you suggest pay for them?"

Haley will hate me for this, but I have to try. "Turn me over."

"I can't do that," he snaps. For a moment, hope glimmers that paternal feeling prevents him from giving me up, but hope fades as he continues. "It won't satisfy them. They demand her return and will continue wanting her as long as she's an innocent bystander taken against her will. True or not, they won't want her back after hearing she's your accomplice."

"The entire world will see her as a traitor and collaborator. Please, keep her out of this," I plead.

He rises to his feet, his taut patience finally snapping. "I don't take orders from you. You brought back a liability but now, through her own admission, the daughter of space sides with our cause. That makes her an asset. This gives us an advantage."

The fire flashing in his eyes tells me he's not going to back down. He doesn't care about the damage this causes Haley. Striding towards me, he places his hands on my shoulders, and I try not to flinch. His tone softens.

"Stop fighting this. You made a mistake bringing her back here, but this is your chance to redeem yourself. Let her speak in your favor."

I bow my head and nod my agreement.

"Anyway, it's too late to stop it now. In a few minutes, we'll be going live on an international news broadcast with a leading anchor. I got in touch with the network and they were happy to pick up the exclusive story. We're being smart. The ESC won't like the exposure but, as a governmental entity, after it's aired publicly, the public will hold them to their word."

Rising, he strides out the door, and I follow reluctantly. He's set up a conference call inside his HQ, the camera capturing Haley on a neutral background that could be anywhere.

I squeeze Haley's hand before the broadcast starts. It's cold and clammy. Despite the makeup, she's pale. This was her idea but, now that she actually has to talk on camera, I can tell she's absolutely terrified. *I hate this.*

"Do you want me to cancel? Tell them we're not doing it."

"No." Her voice trembles, barely a whisper. "I want to do this."

Haley is stubborn. Once she's given her word, she won't back out. It's one of the many things I love about her.

"Okay. I'll be behind the camera. If you get scared,

just look at me."

I retreat to a spot off camera just as it comes to life, blinking with a baleful red dot. There's a monitor facing me where I can see the broadcast.

They split the screen between the news anchor and Haley.

"Good evening, Haley. I'm Kelly Travers. Everyone here on Earth has been following the story of your kidnapping from VOR space station. Tell us how you are?"

Haley stammers in response. "I-I'm fine. Nobody hurt me, and Jorden didn't kidnap me. It was my idea."

The reporter blinks in surprise, but then her eyes crease with concern. Staring into the camera, she leans forward, as if only Haley can hear her.

"Are they coercing you? Forcing you to say these things? Tell me. We can help you."

Haley's eyes find mine. Her distress is clear. They aren't buying this. My father appears at my side and grabs my elbow. "You need to get on camera. Sell them on the fact that you two are a couple."

"What? No!" Panic surges through my chest as he yanks me forward. I dig my heels into the floor, try to grow roots, anything to stop him dragging me in front of the camera. Millions of people are watching this broadcast. I'll be exposed once and for all. Haley's eyes, pleading with me for help, are the only thing that breaks through my fear. *Get a grip,* I chide myself. Haley is exposing herself to criticism by lying for me. I can sacrifice as much for her.

My father stops off camera and shoves me. I stumble to the other side of the room, thankfully catching myself before I fall, embarrassing myself in front of the entire world. Taking a deep breath, I straighten my shoulders, step forward, and take Haley's hand.

My father raises his hands, mouthing, "Introduce yourself". I gulp and face the camera, taking strength from Haley pressed into my side, praying I don't look as terrified as I feel.

"My name is Jorden Lund. Three years ago, Earth time, I was passing through VOR space station on my way to the colony of New Horizons. During my time on the station, Haley and I met, and we fell in love." I gaze down at her and she nods, encouragingly. "On the day the jump ship arrived we discovered a bomb in the pod bay. We tried to stop it but failed. The bomb exploded and severely injured me. I was in a coma for a month while Haley nursed me back to health. After I woke up, they accused me of planting the bomb. I panicked."

Unsure how to continue, I glance at Haley. She squeezes my hand and takes over. Now that I'm by her side, she sounds more confident.

"We had to do something," she says. "They were going to charge him. I suggested we stage the kidnapping and escape to Earth together."

"Why would you do that?" the reporter asks.

Haley looks into my eyes and says without hesitation, "Because I love him."

Her honey eyes are on me, filled with genuine emotion, brimming with so much love it takes my breath away. Forgetting about the camera and the millions of eyes watching, I lean down and kiss her. Haley caresses my cheek, returning my kiss for much longer than is necessary to get our point across. For a moment, the room fades away. Then my father coughs loudly, bringing me back to the moment. Breaking our kiss, I ignore the camera for another moment, focusing on Haley, her gentle smile, her loving touch.

"Well, I'm sure everybody saw that," Haley whispers.

Touching my forehead to hers, I whisper back, "Good. Let them look."

When I face the monitor again, the reporter is beaming. Dozens of enthusiastic viewer comments in our favor fill the bottom of the screen. The segment will probably go viral.

The reporter clears her throat. "That was adorable. I'm convinced, and obviously, our viewers agree. Now I'd like to introduce Inspector Rogers from the ESC. The screen splits again, so that Rogers is visible in his own little box. Kelly looks pointedly at Rogers. "Well, after what we all saw, I assume you will drop the kidnapping charges?"

Rogers scowls at us, his fists curling. If he had the technology, he'd probably reach through the screen and choke the life out of me with his bare hands. After a moment, he remembers he's on camera and admits reluctantly,

"Based on this evidence, we will drop the kidnapping charge against Jorden Lund. Nevertheless, he's still accused of other crimes, such as stealing and destroying a ranger ship, for which we still intend to pursue justice."

The reporter gives us a big smile. "So, what's next? Haley, your parents must be so worried. Are you planning to return home soon?"

Haley gulps and glances at me. That's a tough issue for us both.

Then Inspector Rogers speaks up. "The ESC has been in contact with Haley's parents since the beginning of this incident, and we're working on reuniting them as soon as possible. We will ensure Haley's safe return."

Haley's breath catches and her hand squeezes mine harder, but she just smiles at the camera till the reporter thanks us and the signal cuts off.

As soon as we're off the air, I pull her into my arms.

I kiss the top of her head, shaken and trembling, while she clings to me, repeating, "We did it, we did it," breathlessly into my chest. I can handle being shot at, but being on TV is way too scary for me.

It seems like a win, though. They withdrew the

charges on an international broadcast. Now will they keep their word and pull their forces away from the Farm?

Thirty minutes later, an ESC drone hovers into the compound and heads into my father's command center. Inspector Rogers conducts a far less public call this time as the drone floats in front of my father's desk. I crowd in the back of the room with the Farm's leading personnel.

Rogers seethes while my father lounges in his chair looking smug. "You may have won this round, Lund, but we're not finished."

My father smirks at him. "Oh, we're finished, my friend. Withdraw your forces from my area before I alert my new friends at the broadcasting agency."

Rogers curses under his breath but replies in a curt, professional tone. "My forces are withdrawing as we speak."

"Good," my father snaps. "Then we're done here."

The drone retreats and one of my father's men follows it out to make sure it has left. Once he returns to confirm the drone's departure, the tension around the table breaks. The men clap each other on the back in relief. But not everyone is rejoicing.

"Do you think this is over?" Jacob asks as he regards my father grimly.

My father sits up, dropping the smug air. "Not in the slightest. They won't let up till we're all behind bars or dead."

Chapter 36

BLACK OPS

Haley

Despite the ESC forces' retreat, Jorden's dad keeps the Farm on high alert. They rescheduled our training session to the evening after the broadcast and summoned Jorden to a logistics meeting at C&C.

Six of us are in the training hall. Glory and me, Terry, Beth, Aaron and Rachel. Towards the end of our session, as we're getting ready to head over to the mess hall for supper, all the lights go out. Before we can react, a loud bang shakes the windows of the training hall. Then there's a "ratatatat" sound outside.

Instinctively, I crouch, locking eyes with Terry next to me as his face pales.

"Gun shots," he whispers.

More gunfire erupts outside and another explosion lights up the night.

"I thought the ESC left," I whisper.

He shakes his head. None of us know what's going on right now.

Aaron is the first to snap out of shock. "We're under attack. This is what we've trained for. We're a unit now." His voice is level as he hands the sound guns to Beth and to me. Aaron takes one of the three rifles in the hall and hands the other two to Rachel and Terry.

"Glory, can you use a handgun?" he asks.

"Yes." She nods, but her hands are shaking so badly she almost drops it.

Rachel crouches by the window, peeking out into the night. Across the path, the infirmary is burning. By the light of the flames, I see black-clad figures darting between the buildings. Thick smoke hides their features, casting the scene in a surreal and ghostly atmosphere.

My Farm comm comes to life, making me jump. Turning the sound down low, I hold it close to my ear.

"Haley, it's Jorden. Where are you?"

I'm so relieved to hear his voice. "In the training center. Where are you?"

"In command. Stay put, don't go outside. Whoever it is, they're inside the compound. They're dressed in black, and they have night vision. I'll come to you."

"No. Stay indoors. I don't want you to get hurt. Is

it the ESC?" I ask.

"We don't know. There's no insignia. If it is them, they're operating off the books." Chills race up my spine. Black clothes, no insignia, mean dark ops. We can't count on them to follow law enforcement protocol.

"Trust me. I'll be there soon," he says and signs off.

Crawling to the window at the back of the cabin, I peer out into the night. The buildings' staggered layout enables me to see the command building from the school's back window. A figure jumps out of a window at the end of the C&C building close to the mountain, only making it a few steps away before the building blows up. The figure falls. Massive blocks of burning wood rain down. The smell of burning intensifies. He's on the ground now, but still moving feebly. I hold my breath, praying for him to get up, but with a horrifying creak, the side of the building collapses on the unmoving person.

Silence.

He's gone, buried under the burning building.

I don't even register I'm screaming before Glory pounces on me, hugging me to keep me quiet before I draw the attack force down on us.

Pushing her off, I whimper, "No, Jorden, no," and sink to my knees.

The rest of our group surrounds us.

"What happened...?" Aaron demands of Glory,

She shakes her head. "Jorden was trying to reach

us. The building collapsed on him."

Rachel buries her face in Aaron's shoulder as the color drains from his face. Terry slumps into the wall behind him. I'm huddled in Glory's arms. Everything is falling apart. I can't breathe. My heart is pounding so loud it's making the Earth shake. I can feel it through the floorboards.

No, *that doesn't make sense.*

I push Glory away and press my palms to the floor.

"Aaron," I whisper and point down, my breath still coming in big, shuddering sobs. With everyone quiet, they can all hear the sound. We need to take care of this first, then I can curl up into a ball and mourn.

Peeling back the edge of the rug beneath us, Glory and I reveal a trapdoor.

The others take up positions around the opening, aiming their weapons. Glory and I hang back as Aaron presses down on a hidden mechanism, sliding the door sideways. Then he retreats, aiming his weapon and light into the hole.

There's a ladder attached to the side of the hole, and Jorden is hanging on to the top rung. His eyes widen as he registers the four of them in defensive positions and my red, tear-streaked face. Without waiting for them to lower their weapons, he vaults out of the hole and is by my side, pulling me into his arms.

"What is it? What's wrong?" he cries.

"I... I saw you die. The building blew up, it fell on

you," I say, pointing at the heap of burning logs lying where the command building used to be. Then I bury my face in his chest, shaking uncontrollably.

Jorden tightens his hold. "No. No. You told me not to go outside. So, I went down into the tunnels. I'm fine. I'm okay."

I pull him down. His lips find mine, warm and full of life. Even though we need to run, hide, fight, I need this kiss more than anything else.

After a long moment, Jorden pulls back, stroking my face as he gazes into my eyes. "It's okay. I'm okay," he repeats.

My heart is still pounding, and I cling to him to reassure myself he's really here.

Aaron's eyes are awash with relief as he drags a hand down his face. "You gave us quite a scare there."

"Did anyone else make it out of command?" Glory asks.

Jorden nods. "A bunch of people. Tunnels from C&C run under the compound with access to every building."

Aaron looks amazed. "We've lived here all our lives. How didn't we know?"

Jorden runs his hand through his hair. "You won't believe how many things about this place we didn't know."

"Like what?"

A rapid burst of gunfire comes from close by.

"I'll tell you later. We should go, now."

The others climb down into the hole. Releasing Jorden, I scramble down the ladder into a dark pit below. He follows me and drags the rug over the opening, then slides the trapdoor back into place. The seven of us stand close to each other, flashlights flickering on pale faces. We hold our breaths as we hear the door of the training center being kicked in. Heavy boots stomp into the room above our heads.

"Clear." The shout comes from directly above us. Another pair of boots enters the room. "Sir, we just found a group of kids hiding in the dorms."

"Take them down to the mess hall. Shoot anyone that gives you trouble."

I inhale sharply, then clap a hand over my mouth to muffle the sound. Aaron taps Jorden on the shoulder and gestures. Jorden nods. Aaron leads the group, heading downhill till we're far enough away from the building to talk without being heard. Tapping Jorden's shoulder, I hang back for a moment.

"What is it?" he asks.

"I'm scared," I whisper.

He hugs me, whispering in my ear, "So am I, but we'll find a way out of this, okay?"

"Okay."

I grab his hand and jog to pick up the pace as we close the gap with the rest of the group, kicking up dust as we go.

It feels like the walls are closing in on me and it's

getting harder to breathe. Jorden is alive and we're all together, but I have a bad feeling about this place.

Chapter 37

IN THE TUNNELS

Jorden

The tunnel disappears into the darkness up ahead. The rough, gray concrete is cold to the touch. As we progress, motion-triggered lights spring to life around us with a sharp click. The lights click off after we pass, plunging the tunnel behind us into black, as if the dark is chasing us.

It's nerve-wracking.

At every junction, a tunnel branches off to the left. Moving to the front of the group, I signal a halt to confer with Aaron and Rachel, putting my personal feelings aside. This is life and death. We need to work together as a team.

I point into the darkened passageway. "That probably leads to the mess hall. That's where they're taking everybody."

"They might have my parents there, and my little sister," Glory sniffles behind us.

"We can't rush in," Aaron replies. He sounds so grown up. "First, we need information. We don't even know who's attacking us."

"Black, unmarked uniforms..." I muse. "The ESC don't operate like this, shooting people and blowing them up. They'd arrest us, not kill us. Especially not on the same day they told the world they're withdrawing." I shudder at my next thought. "But with the ESC out of the way, it's the perfect opportunity for the Conglomerate to get rid of us."

"It doesn't matter who they are," Rachel says. "We should find an exit, get to the vehicle shed near the main gate."

The younger kids hang back, waiting for us to decide on a course of action. As if we have all the answers. For once, I'm glad Aaron's older than me. Maybe he really does know more.

"I wish there were signs," Beth whispers, almost to herself, and Glory snickers.

"Would you like a lighted EXIT sign?"

Haley elbows Glory. "Don't be mean."

Terry hangs back, away from the girls, quiet and tense. His eyes follow me, darting away whenever I catch him. I don't know if I can trust him. We never got a chance to talk after I got back, and this is such a bad time to become a big brother.

I nudge Aaron, pointing up. Thick cables and pipes

run along the ceiling, with cameras placed at regular intervals. Here and there are large, gray capsules and other weird metal containers.

"He's watching us," I whisper. If my father made it to the control room. His own secure panic room, where he can see everything, and control everything.

I'm having trouble breathing normally. The air in here is thick with dust. These tunnels aren't used regularly, but everything seems in good condition, waiting for the day it's called to duty. I wonder who else knew about these tunnels besides my father and now Haley and me.

"We need more info. Let's keep going and find out what's happening before we rush in," Aaron suggests.

At the bottom of the hill, we reach a T junction. Another tunnel meets ours, going both left and right. Ahead of us is a vertical shaft with a metal ladder going up into the scaffolding surrounding the guard tower. I never realized it was hollow. The narrow rungs are sunk into the wall, promising a tough climb.

"Somebody should go up and get a look. Maybe we can see what's going on," Rachel suggests.

Terry steps forward. "I'll go."

Unslinging his rifle, he hands it to Glory. She stuffs the handgun in her belt and clutches it with both hands as if she's holding a particularly nasty snake. If we weren't in so much trouble, I'd find it funny.

"Two people would be better. Support each other," Aaron says as he steps forward, but I place a hand on his shoulder.

"I'll go with him. We need to have a chat."

Terry pales and his eyes widen. I swallow a smile.

Haley squeezes my arm. "Be careful."

"I will." I give her a quick peck.

Grabbing the bottom rung, I pull myself up. Terry is already a few rungs higher, climbing like he's got something to prove. As we rise above the group, I wonder what to say, but climbing takes a lot of my concentration. There's barely enough room to stand on the rungs and the shaft is dark. After a few feet, we're above ground. The air is fresher and the walls surrounding us shift from concrete to a thick iron mesh. I can see through, but not much is visible at ground level. We need to get higher.

Terry is taking a break halfway up, catching his breath. I climb up next to him, wedge my feet against the side of the shaft, and lean back, taking the strain off my arms. He glances at me nervously, then does the same. I flex my arms, stretching them out before I climb again.

"I guess I should call you bro, now," I say.

"Um..." No wonder he's nervous. He doesn't know if Haley told me about the kiss.

"Meanwhile, I'm trying to decide what to discuss first. Us being brothers or you kissing my girl-friend?" I crack my knuckles and he gulps. I stifle a smile. Scaring kid brothers is fun. "I'll take that as an admission. Pity. We won't have time to get to know each other better, since I have to kill you now. Good thing I'm used to being an only child."

Terry's expression is priceless, unsure if I'm seri-ous or messing with him. I'm not a hundred percent sure, myself. "Is there any excuse that would make you less mad?" he asks.

"Relax. Haley made me promise not to rip your arms off and beat you to death with them," I say, laughing to break the tension.

"That's very specific," he mutters.

I climb till we're face to face, keeping my expres-sion stoic long enough to freak him out. "Yeah, well, I specifically described to her how you were going to die."

He laughs nervously, but I don't join in. "It was nice of her to make you promise," he says.

"Yeah, well, she's pretty amazing."

"Do you know how lucky you are?" That's probably the only thing to say right now that won't get him killed.

"I do." He huffs as if I got the right answer.

"Did you really think I wasn't coming back? That I'd just leave her here? Man, you don't know me at all."

He grins. "No, but if you let me live, I'd like to."

"Good answer." I clap him on the shoulder hard, almost dislodging him. "Let's go."

We climb higher until we're parallel with the guard tower. I cling to the side, facing the farm buildings. The flames engulfing the infirmary are waning. Lights are on in the mess hall and, as we watch, a squad of dark figures marches down the hill, herding a group of people in front of them. They are too far away for me to make out faces, but I know everyone who lives here. The group stops by a dark mound on the path. I realize with a start that it's a body. That shape is someone I know. A friend or a neighbor the intruders killed...

A member of the group bends over the body, then turns with a roar, attacking the nearest soldier. There are shouts, and others in the group turn on their captors. For a moment, chaos reigns, but then the soldier shoves off his attacker and opens fire, mowing down the brave person who attacked him and three others. The rest of the prisoners drop to the ground, dodging the bullets. Soldiers pull them up roughly, leaving the injured lying on the path, twisting and moaning in pain. A soldier aims his weapon, light crackles, and the first figure stops moving.

Terry gasps, "It's an execution."

The soldier moves on to the next person lying on the ground and the scene repeats itself. When he's dispatched all four, he aims the weapon at the people standing, huddled close together. His shout echoes off the surrounding mountains. "Move."

Terry's breathing is fast and strained. His shoulder trembles by mine as he whispers, "They aren't here to arrest us. They're here to kill us."

I nod, my mouth dry.

The group reaches the mess hall and splits in half. Three soldiers escort the prisoners inside. Three stand guard outside. From up here, three more soldiers are visible inside the mess hall.

So that's at least nine. There must be many more. They wouldn't devote their entire force to one building.

Did they meet any more resistance? Everyone would have been in the mess hall or on their way there. They took us completely by surprise.

Peeking through the mesh into the guard tower, I'm surprised when a pair of eyes stare right back at me. Rattled, I snap back and slam into Terry, who loses his footing and bangs into the metal shaft.

"Who's there?" the black-clad soldier shouts.

I mouth frantically to Terry, "Go, go."

Terry descends in gigantic leaps. The soldier lifts his weapon and aims it right at my face through the grating. The metal melts, inches from my face, as a beam slices clean through to the other side of the shaft above my head. I know Terry is below me, but I don't have time to go slow. As the soldier's finger squeezes the trigger, I let go of the rungs, lean back, and drop.

After a few feet of free fall, I slam into Terry, almost knocking us both the rest of the way to the bottom. Above us, the soldier yells into his headset. At ground level, another soldier turns and fires towards the guard tower. Fiery beams slice through the shaft just below us. We navigate our way down while avoiding the scalding metal, scrambling as fast as we can.

We're idiots, alerting them to our position. Once they follow us, they'll find the tunnels and we'll lose our advantage.

When we descend below ground level, the beams slicing through the shaft are no longer a threat. I don't know how long it will take them to cut through the iron mesh and enter the tunnels. The entire structure shakes as beams flash repeatedly, cutting an opening in the metal. As a powerful vibration rattles the rungs, I lose my grip, crashing into Terry, and we plummet the rest of the short distance to the ground. Luckily for me, he cushions my fall as I land on top of him.

The others crowd around and Aaron pulls me up, then turns to give Terry a hand. Stifling a few curses, Terry stands, grimacing and touching his ribs.

"We agreed you wouldn't kill him," Haley says, giving me a pointed look.

I shrug. "You said nothing about crushing him." She wrinkles her nose.

Sparks fall around us, joined by the stench of scorched metal.

"We've got to move. Fast. The tunnel here runs parallel to the gate. There must be an exit somewhere," Rachel says.

I grab Haley and pull her deeper into the tunnel. The others follow, Aaron bringing up the rear. "We're idiots," he whispers. "We've given away our advantage. If they get down here, they can cut off our escape route, and they will trap anyone else trying to flee through the tunnels. We need to pin them down here and prevent them from finding the rest of the tunnels."

I want to kick myself for drawing their attention. I keep messing up.

There's movement in the vertical shaft. I push Haley behind me, whispering, "Keep moving till you reach the next bend and get out of sight."

Recovering his rifle from Glory, Terry gets into position with his back to the wall. Aaron and I stand across the tunnel facing the vertical shaft, waiting for the first soldier to emerge.

With a thud, a black-clad soldier lands in the hole and the three of us open fire, surprising him. He's clad in head-to-toe body armor, but we're at such close range, the bullets ping off his armor and ricochet into the walls beside us. It's a miracle we aren't hit. After his initial surprise, he rallies, swinging his gun towards Terry.

Time slows. The color drains from Terry's face as he follows the motion. A second before the soldier opens fire, a blonde blur darts past Aaron; Rachel shoots the soldier with the sound gun at almost point-blank range, hurling him back into the shaft. His helmet slams against the concrete with a resounding crack, and he falls to the ground face-first.

The four of us freeze, waiting for motion, but he doesn't stir.

"Did I kill him?" Rachel whispers in a horrified tone. Aaron steps in front of her and pulls off the soldier's cracked helmet.

"Rachel, look away," he mutters and, when she stares at him, he asks softly, "Can you go check on the younger girls for me? Please."

Rachel retreats up the tunnel. Aaron hands me the soldier's gun and helmet and then strips him of his body armor. I try on the helmet, marveling at the built-in comms, data, vid-feed from other soldiers, and night vision.

And that's when I hear the shot.

"Go," Aaron shoves me ahead of him, herding us into the intersecting tunnel. I turn to look, but he shakes his head, blocking the view with his body. "Here," he hands me the soldier's gloves that sync to his gun and helmet. Once I have them, I can flip through menu options to control the weapon.

We only have moments to regroup before the next

soldier comes down the hole. Terry shoots him with a compressed electro burst from the first soldier's gun, frying his systems, trapping him in a dead suit. We take him out easily.

"How many men will they send down here before deciding to plug the hole with explosives?" Terry asks.

The answer comes seconds later as a smoking canister falls into the hole.

"Run," Aaron shouts.

We make it a short way up the tunnel before the blast blows us off our feet. The three of us collapse in a pile near the girls, with Terry squashed between me and Aaron. He probably thinks I'm doing it on purpose.

Haley and Rachel dart forward to help us up. I'm still wearing the helmet, so I'm privy to the attacking forces chatter.

"I can still hear movement down there," a tinny voice reports.

"Affirmative. Control, send in the hounds," comes the reply.

I repeat the message, mouthing to Aaron, "They're sending hounds."

Aaron blanches.

"Hounds?" Haley says with a smile. "I never met a dog I didn't like."

"You won't like this kind of dog," I say, and her smile falters. "Think robot dog four times Nano's size with razor-sharp teeth, programmed to seek and destroy."

Haley winces when I mention Nano. That wound will never heal. We don't have time to think about it, as we hear scuffling and a loud screeching from the passageway. It seems like something large and metallic is coming down the shaft. The sound makes my teeth ache.

"We need to run. Go, go, GO!" I shout as a huge, metallic gray shape with glowing red eyes like a hellhound darts into the tunnel. Scooping up the kids in front of me as I go, I run, pushing them forward. The smart move might be to turn and fight, but the creature triggers my primal fears. It's probably faster than us and harder to kill. All I can do is run and pray it doesn't catch up.

We haven't found an exit by the time we reach the first junction. We don't even know if there's an exit on this side. Maybe we're running into a literal dead end. Aaron is in the lead and he wastes a second swiveling around to shout, "Left or straight?"

Left will take us uphill again, the way we came. Straight, we don't know. Rachel yells 'left' and I agree.

"Yes, because it's a way forward."

Aaron keeps moving and we barrel around the corner, my calves straining as I run uphill.

Behind us, the snarls get closer by the second.

Haley and Glory are struggling, but I don't let

them fall behind. I'm the rear guard, no matter what, till I have to turn and face those things. The snarling intensifies, bouncing off the stone walls and my shaking shoulders. I don't know how close it is, but I shudder, imagining its jaws closing around my neck at any moment.

The lights in the next section of tunnel ahead click on with an audible snap and the red lights of active cameras face us on the tunnel walls. There's a rumble coming from up ahead.

"What is that?" Terry yells. I hear the sharp intake of breath from the others. As rear guard, I can barely see past Aaron's shoulders, but then he veers to the left and I see them.

A cascade of small metal balls rolls downhill towards us like a man-made avalanche, heading straight for us. The hounds are closing in and we have seconds before we're crushed between the two threats. Just as I think we're doomed, a dark opening appears on our right.

"There. Aaron, to the right," I yell, grabbing Haley's arm and hoping the rest see it and turn. We swerve around the corner just in time, the rest of the group so close ahead of us that, if they stop, we'll slam into them. Luckily Aaron doesn't stop, but progresses into the T junction. I keep moving till there's no further room. The others pile up, pressed into an alcove several yards into the tunnel. I wrap my arms around Haley to shield her, but twist to get a better look behind us.

The balls pass the opening, two of them colliding with the wall of the T. As they hit, they spring open, transforming into sharp metal spiders. They hit with such force that they embed into the concrete wall. I don't want to imagine what they'd do to a person.

We wait, listening, hardly daring to breathe. As a whining, whirring sound comes from the passage-way.

After five minutes with no movement, I crawl back to peek around the corner, hugging the wall but avoiding the spiders.

The two hounds that chased us are pinned to the wall, pierced by dozens of metal spiders. One of them is sparking, its electronics fried. The other still looks "alive": its eyes glow red, teeth gnashing helplessly as it tries to pry a spider from its side, but it's pinned and can't get free. I almost feel sorry for it. Almost.

But I don't feel bad as I aim the soldier's blaster at its core and destroy it. Then I stumble back to the short tunnel section of where the others are sitting.

"Two hounds down. No more movement in the tunnel," I report.

"What is going on? Where did those balls come from?" Rachel asks. "Was somebody trying to help us? Or hurt us?"

"Good question. We were almost spider food." Beth shudders.

"Or dog food," Glory adds.

Haley shudders. "Those weren't dogs. Nano was a dog. Tango—" She pales. "Oh my God, Jorden. Tango. Tango is still in our cabin." She turns enormous eyes on me as if I have all the answers. I want to save Tango, but I don't know how.

"I know, but... there's nothing we can do right now. The cabin is empty. She should be okay. We need to get ourselves out safely, first." Did I give her another dog just to lose it soon after?

At first, I think she'll argue, but she surprises me.

"Okay. How do we get out? What do we do?" Her voice barely shakes as she attempts to stay calm, which is good.

The problem is, I have no idea how we'll get out of this alive.

Chapter 38

Uphill Battle

Haley

Jorden runs a hand through his hair, letting out a shuddering breath. He's rattled, looking to Aaron for guidance. Though their interactions are strained, even Jorden is deferring to Aaron.

"What now?" he asks.

The ground above us shakes, walls vibrating as something heavy pounds the earth repeatedly. The sound takes on a hypnotic rhythm as the walls shake with the impact. We crouch low, scared the ceiling will drop on us, and hurry uphill, away from the rumbling.

"It's just a matter of time till they break through," Rachel says.

"They lost two men and their mechanized hounds, so they know whatever is down here is a threat,"

Aaron replies. "At the moment, they're as blind underground as we are to the events on the surface. So they don't know we're just a bunch of scared kids with a handful of old mecha weapons. They probably think we're more dangerous than we actually are. Which means they'll come in next time, guns blazing."

Rachel shudders, and Aaron pulls her into his side, placing a kiss in her hair. I peek at Jorden to gauge his reaction, but he seems indifferent to their interaction, focusing on the imminent attack.

"Hey, those scared kids took out two of their men," Glory scoffs, "give us some credit." The others smile as Glory continues. "Do you think they know where we are? Or is it just a coincidence they started to dig above us?"

"How would they know where we are? Are they watching us?" Beth asks. She casts a look at the enemy helmet Jorden is wearing.

Jorden shakes his head. "They can't see us. The helmet is broadcasting, but I covered the external camera and broke off the mike. The soldiers' locator chips are in their wrists, not their suits. Sounds like they've reduced chatter, assuming their channel is compromised. Anyway," he glances up at the nearest red dot on the wall, "I know who's watching us: dear old dad. I just don't know what he wants, yet."

He shoots a glance at Terry, who's hanging back, looking terrified and isolated, as far away from Jorden as he can get. It's so weird that he's Jorden's brother. I hate that he's in pain. Terry has been my friend since I got here, aside from that unfortunate kiss. As I step closer to him, meaning to offer comfort, Jorden's eyes snap to mine. We have a brief staring argument before Jorden sighs and relents. I move closer to Terry till I'm walking by his side.

"How are you doing?" I ask.

Terry doesn't look at me, but he doesn't move away either. "I'm trying to get my bearings in this maze," he says and points to long, gray cylinders on the walls. "Do you think those spider balls came from one of those? Are they some kind of defense mechanism?"

"They might be. The question is, who or what is triggering them?"

Aaron calls a halt at the next junction. "Did anyone pay attention to how many side tunnels we've passed?"

"Three. No; four," Terry says quickly.

"The next tunnel should lead to the mess hall," Aaron says, his words floating ominously.

"They're holding everyone in the mess hall. We need to save them," Jorden says quietly.

I return to his side, placing a hand on his arm. "There are dozens of armed men up there. What could we do?"

The headset squawks, and Jorden relays the message to the group.

"'Roundup ninety percent complete. Targets still not located'. They haven't found who they're looking for, yet." He pauses, recognition dawning in his eyes. "They're looking for me."

"You don't know that," I protest.

He sets his jaw. "I'm the one who tried to blow up the jump ship. They want me."

"Even if it's true, what will turning yourself in accomplish?"

"They won't stop till they find their targets. The longer this goes on, the more people are going to die."

"Did you stop to think they may shoot you on sight?" Rachel says quietly. He knows, but he's in hero mode, trying to save everyone but himself. Rachel is the voice of reason. Maybe he'll listen to her even if he won't listen to me.

Aaron seconds her concern. "Even if you turn yourself in, that doesn't mean they'll pack up and leave. We're witnesses. They won't let us live."

Jorden huffs. "But they haven't killed everyone, yet. They're waiting for something."

By his determined expression, I know where he's going with this. When he's faced with a challenge, he doesn't think about himself; he reacts, and it's going to get him killed.

"I have to turn myself in." Jorden finds my eyes, begging me to understand.

But I don't. I won't. His words flatten me, knocking

all the air out of my lungs.

"Can I talk to you for a minute?" I struggle to keep my composure, but it comes out fiercer than I intended. Everyone stares at me, this outsider interrupting his grand plan of self-sacrifice. My cheeks burn at being the center of attention, but I hold my head up, eyes fixed on Jorden.

"Give us a second," Jorden asks the others, taking my hand and drawing me into a dark corner where we can have a modicum of privacy. It's dark, but his eyes reflect the light behind me, burning ivy green, determined and sad.

Taking his cheeks in my hands, I kiss him, then whisper, "I love you, but your first instinct is to save everybody else and never think of yourself. It's hard-wired into your system, but please don't follow your instincts for once. You have to stop offering yourself up as a sacrifice. There are other ways to solve this without trying to get yourself killed."

His breath flutters across my face as his arms wrap around me, holding me to his chest.

"Haley, I'm not trying to get killed. I don't want to die," his rushing heartbeat thrums against my palm, "especially not now that I have you to live for." His muscles contract and release, as if he's fighting himself, struggling to reconcile my request with his impulses. "I don't... I'm not...." he sputters, then sighs. Dragging a hand through his hair until it stands on end, reaching for the tunnel roof. "I don't want to die," he repeats, leaning back to look into my eyes.

My heart cracks for him, the way he's forced to face impossible decisions time and time again. I reach up, smoothing his hair back in place, and let my hand travel down his neck, finding his cheek again.

"Make sacrificing yourself a last resort, not the first option. If wanting to live isn't your first priority," he shakes his head but I press on, "know this, you're my first priority. If you volunteer to get yourself killed, I'm going too."

He winds his hands into my hair, pulling me as close as two people can get. I tighten my arms around his waist, wishing we could stay together forever. But we're out of time. The others are waiting; the noise is deafening, pieces of rock cascade from the walls as the tunnel shakes around us.

"Promise me you'll find another solution? Don't surrender yourself unless it's the last option."

He nods, and I pray he keeps his promise.

As we return to the group, an enormous chunk of rock crashes into the tunnel, narrowly missing Beth. Cracks split open the wall around the breach and mounds of dirt pour in through the gaps, filling the tunnel with choking dust and cutting us off from the others.

"Meet us below the mess hall," Aaron shouts

through the rubble.

We circle around the collapsed area, running downhill to the parallel tunnel and doubling back. My breath is tight in my chest. They could breach any minute now. We bypass the collapsed area and find the others below the next junction.

"We need to put a stop to this, distract them, or get out of here," Aaron states. "I'll go up there and see what's going on. Get some intel."

"I'm going with you. You need someone to watch your back," Jorden announces immediately, our conversation already forgotten.

I huff in frustration.

"I'll go with," Rachel offers, but Aaron shakes his head.

"No. Stay here with the younger kids."

"I'm just as capable as you," she protests.

"I know. That's why I want you in charge," Aaron says, smoothing his hands down her arms in a soothing gesture. "I'm coming back. I don't have a death wish." He stares pointedly at Jorden. "I'll also bring back the suicide squad here." Jorden makes a face at him.

I'm just relieved Aaron knows Jorden well enough to guess what he's thinking and cares enough to stop him from doing anything stupid.

Aaron glances at me, and I nod my thanks.

Five of us crowd into the alcove below the trapdoor that leads to the mess hall. Terry has his weapon ready to cover their backs once they open the trapdoor. Rachel and I are there to say goodbye.

"This isn't goodbye," Jorden insists, as I kiss him fiercely. "I'm coming back."

"You'd better," I mutter. "I'll kill you if you die."

His lips twitch. "Love you, *Blue*."

"I love you more."

He gives me one last kiss and grasps the rungs, pulling himself up the ladder while I sink back against the wall, praying this isn't the last time I see him alive.

Only hours ago, I thought I'd lost him. I rub my chest as the phantom pain flares up, reminding me what it felt like to have a gaping hole in my heart. Thinking he was gone was pure agony. I can't survive that again.

Please come back, Jorden.

Chapter 39

FAMOUS LAST WORDS

Jorden

I don't want to die. I really don't.

Saying goodbye to Haley drove home how badly I need to see her again. I want a future with her. I can't die now. Then again, it isn't completely up to me.

We don't even know where the trap door opens in the mess hall. This could be so much easier if only my father had shared his game plan with the rest of us. Aaron and I emerge from the opening to find ourselves in the basement level where the storerooms are located. Gunfire erupts close by and we dive for the closest wall, heart pounding, until we realize the sound is coming from the floor above us. We exchange glances and hand gestures to coordinate our next move.

We leapfrog up the hallway towards the stairs to the upper level. One sticking to the wall, providing cover while the other moves. Despite the tension, it's good having Aaron beside me again. I've been so isolated since I left on my mission. If only we could naturally fall back into our easy banter. We used to know each other so well; I could tell what he was thinking without even asking. He felt like an extension of me and he had my back completely. Now, I'm not so sure. I can't get used to this older version of him and all the ways he's changed. Aaron and I may not agree on the rules regarding "dating your best friend's ex", but during combat we're still in perfect sync... until he opens his mouth.

"Why are you still mad at me?" he whispers.

I glare at him, eyebrows raised as I move forward, grinding out, "This isn't the time to talk about it, with people shooting at us."

Aaron huffs. "Well, you haven't been talking to me when people aren't shooting at us."

"What's your point?" I slam into the corner by the stairs where I have a view of the hall and the stairs leading up to the mess hall. Thankfully, both are empty.

"You're with Haley now," he whispers.

"True."

"And anyone with eyes can see you're crazy about her."

"Also true."

"So stop being an ass about me and Rachel!"

He's got a point, but I'm not letting him off easy. "I need to think about it."

Aaron groans. "What is there to think about?"

"Well, if I give you a green light to go for my ex, you might decide to make a move on Haley next." I grin, but Aaron is dead serious.

"Not likely. I'm going to ask Rachel to marry me."

I wait for it, but there's no pang of jealousy, no knotted stomach. Huh. I'm really fine with it. So, I do the only thing that makes sense. I clap him on the back as I move past him. "Congrats man."

He grins at me, his teeth shining white in the gloom. "You mean it?"

"Better you than me."

He laughs. "You say that now, but just you wait."

"Oh, I intend to wait. Haley just turned seventeen, but you old folks go ahead."

He chuckles. "I can still kick your butt, young man."

"Look forward to you trying, after..." I nod towards the stairs, "we deal with this and not get dead." I want to stay serious, but my lips twitch up, buoyed as the heavy weight of our disagreement shifts off of my chest.

When we reach the top of the stairs, Aaron winks at me. "Game time. Focus."

The top of the stairs is inside the kitchen. Aaron pushes the door open an inch to get a view of the room. It's empty. The usually clean metal counter-tops are now stained with spilled pots and crushed vegetables, evidence of the sudden attack and a hurried exit. A smear of blood mars the white-tiled floor. My grin dies as reality slams back with grue-some force.

Keeping absolutely quiet, we creep through the kitchen till we reach the door to the mess hall with its round windows. As I peek through, a black-clad figure passes the door, inches from my face. I recoil so fast I slam into a countertop, sending a pot spin-ning away across the slick, metal counter. We both watch in horror as it slides. I lunge for it, trying to catch it before it crashes to the floor, but it's too far away. It plummets, as if in slow motion, clattering to the floor in a cacophony of sound. We barely have time to turn before the soldier barges into the kitchen, pulse weapon raised.

Aaron steps in front of me. Perhaps he hoped his borrowed armor would shield him, but the beam hits just below his breastplate, knocking him back into my arms. His weight and momentum as he staggers send both of us crashing to the floor.

My hands are wet and sticky and warm, and it takes me a moment to register that Aaron's blood is pooling between us, seeping into my clothes.

"No. No, no, no, no, no," I chant as I try to stop the bleeding with my hands, but the soldiers grab us and drag us roughly into the hall. It's packed with people sitting on the floor and huddled against the walls. Five black-clad soldiers are in the room with us: three next to the doors, two more on the tables, weapons raised.

They slam us down in the center of the room and Aaron gasps with pain. His wound is gushing. Taly, one of our medics from the infirmary, crawls towards us. A soldier standing on a table raises his weapon, aiming at her wordlessly.

"Let me help him. He's just a kid. He doesn't need to die," she pleads.

The soldier's face is grim, but he lowers his weapon, allowing her to reach us. Taly kneels by us, removing her jacket to create a bandage, spreading the cloth over the wound.

"Keep pressure on it," she orders. I press down with all my strength, but the blood soon soaks the jacket through. Aaron's face is graying by the minute.

The doors to the hall open with a bang and two more black-clad soldiers march in, flanking a woman dressed in white.

No. This doesn't make sense.

It's my mother.

My heart almost implodes from shock. Gone is the motherly figure I met recently. She looks like a different person with her hair pinned up in a severe bun, wearing a fitted jacket, form-fitting pants, and high boots. What looks like a business version of the soldiers' tactical headset sits behind her ear.

Our eyes meet as she surveys the hall.

"Bring them," she barks at the soldiers. Even her tone is different.

The soldiers' drag us to our feet and out into the entrance hall. Aaron can barely stand; his forehead is drenched in sweat, his dark face drained of color, his warm skin tone gone.

"Mom?! What's going on? You're with them?" I whisper.

She shakes her head, tight-lipped, as though she'd rather not speak in front of the soldiers. Flicking her gaze to the men behind us, she demands, "Give us a minute."

It's obvious she holds some authority here, but it's fragile. They start to leave but I grab her arm, my hand leaving a bloody smear on her white suit.

"No, wait. Please help Aaron first. He needs medical attention."

Her startled gaze snaps to the bloody print, then to my eyes. If she mentions her wardrobe malfunction while my best friend is bleeding to death, I don't know what I'll do.

She hesitates. I don't. "He's my best friend. Please."

Her look is dark, but she nods and gestures to the soldier next to her. "Get the medic."

I help Aaron lie down and keep pressure on the wound while my mother stands above me, impassive, waiting, and all I see is a stranger.

I've lived almost my whole life without a mother and, now that I've found her, I realize I know nothing about her. Who is this person in front of me? The ideal I had in my head may never have existed in real life. In her current stance and demeanor, I see echoes of my father. They weren't together by coincidence: they're both driven, idealistic and, apparently, they'll stop at nothing to get what they want.

"Where is Terry? Where's your father?" she whispers as soon as the soldiers leave.

"Why do you need them?" I hiss back.

My mother raises her eyebrows. "Terry is my son. I'm not leaving here without him, without both of you. And your father will finally pay for everything he's done."

I would like to say that bothers me, but it doesn't shock me as much as I expected. "What about everyone else?"

"My employers would like to see you all dead, but I have negotiated a stay of execution for your father's misguided followers if he turns himself in."

"He won't surrender easily."

The door opens and the soldier returns, leading another black-clad figure carrying a big bag. Blue eyes peer at me from under the helmet. A woman's soft voice says, "You can let go now. I'll take care of him."

I hesitate, but she lifts my hands away gently and I stand up. My hands are sticky with blood. Without thinking, I walk over to the basins by the restrooms and wash my hands, my friend's blood mingling with the water. This whole situation doesn't make any sense. I feel numb as I stare into the running water.

"Jorden?" My mother presses. "Where are they?"

"Terry is safe and I think I know where Dad is. If you release me, I'll find out."

She frowns. "Can you bring them here?"

"I'll try, if you get your men to stop shooting people."

"This isn't what I wanted." Her shoulders slump. "I tried to find a peaceful solution to this situation."

I turn around to see her eyes as I snap, "You call this peaceful?"

"If I hadn't come, they'd have sent someone else with no ties to this place. Someone who'd wipe you all out without hesitation. Peter never understood, but if I hadn't worked for the Conglomerate... I couldn't have saved anyone." She hangs her head and I understand what went wrong between my parents.

"He wanted you to leave your job. Fight the Conglomerate's actions from the outside."

"Your father never understood why I had to stay and try to change things from the inside."

"I'm not sure I do, either."

"After years of being under your father's influence, I wouldn't expect you to. He was just using you to get what he wanted," she remarks bitterly.

I don't want to defend my father, but how can she not see the parallel here?

"Don't you see it's the same thing? You're using Terry and Dad is using me. Why can't you just treat us as your sons instead of using us as pawns in your game? Is that too much to ask?"

I guess it is. She said goodbye to me fifteen years ago, her time, and I'm nothing more than a memory of the boy she once gave up. I see it in her eyes as she realizes she doesn't know me anymore, either. My mother leans back, crossing her arms and narrowing her eyes as she disconnects. She didn't expect me to talk back to her, but I'm tired of being used and manipulated. All I want is to get away from both of them.

"I was hoping to get your support on this matter," she says, giving me every opportunity to relent and go back to being the loving, malleable son. The one who was willing to do anything, sacrifice anything, for his parents' love.

"I'll help you find Dad, and I'll let Terry know what you asked me to do."

She grimaces as she clutches her arms tightly. "What about you? I want the three of us to be a family again. You, me, and Terry."

"The three of us were never a family," I snap, and she rears back as if I've slapped her. But antagonizing her isn't smart. Softening my tone, I carefully avoid making any promises. "Look, can we talk about it when this is over? I just want to make it out of here with everyone I care about still breathing."

Her eyes cloud, hope and sadness tugging at her face. "Yes. Afterwards we'll talk." She takes a deep breath, drawing a mask over her features, back to business. "How are you going to get there?"

"Same way I got here."

She raises her eyebrows, but I don't explain.

"Can you tell your men to stop shooting people until I get back?" She nods. I hope I can trust her. "Take care of Aaron. If he dies, our deal is off..."

"I can't guarantee—" she protests, but at my furious stare she amends, "I'll do everything I can to save him."

Without another word, I walk back into the kitchen and stumble down the steps till I reach the trapdoor into the tunnel. The group is sitting huddled together against the wall. Terry's weapon snaps towards me as I open the door. My kid brother. If only mother knew he was here all along. He lowers the weapon as I climb down. There's relief in Haley's eyes, and panic in Rachel's.

"Where's Aaron?" Rachel cries, getting to her feet. "Jorden, where is he?" She stares into my eyes, fearing the worst.

Sinking back against the wall, I slide down till I hit the floor. My legs just quit their job. Haley immediately moves to my side, taking my hand. I press my forehead to hers for the space of three breaths, taking just a moment to recharge. Touching her helps me breathe again, enough to say, "He got shot." Rachel's hand flies over her mouth, stifling a sob. "They're taking care of him."

"Who is?" her gaze slides up the ladder I just came down.

"My mother's people."

The whole group gapes at me.

Beth is the first one to find her voice. "What does your mother have to do with this?"

"She works for the Conglomerate." Terry is the only one who doesn't seem shocked. "You knew," I accuse him.

His face is pale. "I knew she worked there. I didn't know they were going to attack us."

Before I can unpack that, Rachel announces. "I'm going to him. I have to."

For a moment, we lock eyes. This girl I used to love. We both know she belongs up there with Aaron. Just like I belong down here with Haley.

"I can't stop you," I say. It's what I would do if the girl I love was up there hurt. "Just be careful."

Rachel nods, grasping the bottom rung with white knuckles, and then she's gone.

Chapter 40

DISILLUSION

Jorden

Now we're five, and they're all looking at me. Shit.

I force my legs to resume their function, pushing myself back up. "We need to go."

"Where are we going?" Haley asks.

"I need to find my father. Terry, take the girls. Find an escape route."

"What about you?" Terry asks.

"I need to find my... our father," I need to get used to saying it. "If I'm right, he's in the command room under his cabin. The tunnel probably continues uphill past the entrance to C&C. Maybe I can still get through to him. My... our mom said they'd hold their fire for now, but it still may not be safe."

Terry squares his shoulders. "Then I'm going too."

"Why?"

"He doesn't even know I'm his son. Maybe if I tell him, it will make a difference."

Doubtful, but he still has hope. I can't take it away from him. Maybe it will make a difference. I don't know.

"Glory? Can you at least go with Beth?"

They look at each other. "Heck, no"; "We're staying with you," they chorus.

Haley threads her fingers through mine. I know she won't leave despite the terrors facing us in the dark tunnels. Are there enemy soldiers lurking in the gloom, more hounds that like to snack on people?

"I'm going up ahead. There might be more traps," I inform the four scared faces in front of me. I only get a few yards up the eastern tunnel when one capsule on the wall releases a puff of sweet purple smoke in my face. Haley gives a little scream. But I smile.

"It's fine. Nothing is wrong." I take a deep breath, tasting the fragrant night air in the meadow.

Funny. I don't remember how we got out here from the tunnels.

I lead them up to the orchard, dipping under the trees, the apple blossoms fragrant on the boughs, perfuming the night air.

Haley touches my arm. "Where are we going?"

"You'll see in a minute."

Terry doesn't ask because he knows what's up here. We creep along the base of the cliff until I find the outcropping. Taking Haley's hand, I duck inside. Terry follows us. It's dark and musty inside the cave, but warmer.

Weren't there more of us? I can't remember.

Tango shuffles around at our feet, sniffing the unfamiliar cave smells.

When did Tango get here?

Haley presses close to me. "What's going on?"

I put my hands on her shoulders. "I'm going to go back and find my dad, so I want you to go with Terry, now. He'll take you somewhere safe." I look over her shoulder at Terry. He nods, but Haley shakes her head, like I knew she would.

"No, I'm not leaving you. Come with me."

I love her all the more for it. I bend down and kiss her. "Haley, I can't run away from this. These people are my family. I need to be here." Haley clings to me, weaving her hands together behind my back, and it breaks my heart to peel her off. "Please don't make this any harder. I'll come back. I promise."

There's a sound in the narrow pass, from the direction of the mountain. Someone is coming. They're trying to be quiet, but their breathing is too loud to miss.

"Terry, does anyone else know about this passage-way?" I ask. He shrugs and raises his hand, holding some kind of metal cylinder.

A shadow appears outside the cave on the Farm side. Someone is waiting there. We can't go forward, and we can't go back.

We're surrounded.

Blood pounds in my ears. I don't know which way to turn. There's almost no room to move in the narrow passageway. Haley is between Terry and me so, if we need to fight, we can protect her, at least for a little while.

"Terry, someone is coming. You need to protect Haley."

"Sure, bro. I'll take care of her." His tone is off. Something is wrong.

"Thanks." I put my hand on his shoulder, and he grabs hold of my arm and sprays something right in my face. Haley gasps and tries to grab the canister but he fights her off, blocking her with the arm that's holding mine.

I want to react, but everything slows down to a snail's pace. The spray is disrupting my reflexes. Movements that should be as easy as breathing seem almost impossible. Like dislodging his arm. But my hand moves so slowly it feels like it will never make contact.

Haley hits him, trying to break his grasp on me. Steps echo through the cave as the stalkers in the darkness rush towards us. I turn away and then I'm falling. I hit the ground and even the pain arrives slowly. My head bounces on the stone path. Dust motes rise and float in the air above me, dancing in the beam of the flashlight that falls from my hand.

Terry stands over me. Black shapes behind him hold Haley. Sound reaches me slowly, drawn out, as if from afar. "I'm sorry, bro."

Moving through a thick fog I lunge for him, focusing all of my rage on Terry. "You're his spy. I knew it," I cry.

Struggling off of the floor I grab Terry and pin him against the wall, my forearm crushing his windpipe. Rage burns its way up through my chest, turning my fists into iron. His fingers claw at me, his face going purple, but I don't relent. This time I'll kill him. Nobody can stop me.

"Jorden, no. Stop. No." Haley's panicked voice is by my ear. "Jorden, stop, you're killing him."

"Good. Lying, backstabbing creep," I tighten my fingers and hear his wheeze. *But something isn't right.*

The image in front of me wavers. It's Terry. Crushed against the wall. But we're not in the crevice in the mountain. We're in a tunnel. Haley claws at my arm, trying to drag me off him. Glory and Beth stand huddled close. Terry is pale, eyes wide with terror. *Something is wrong. This is wrong.*

Releasing his neck, I step back, and he slumps down, coughing.

"What happened... where are we?" I ask Haley as I clutch my head and blink, slowly getting my bearings back, realigning myself in space and time. "We were escaping. He turned me in to my dad... he hit you and betrayed me."

Haley shakes her head. "No. No. We've been in the tunnel the whole time. You were scouting up ahead, and a gas trap went off in your face, some kind of hallucinogen. The next thing we saw, you were completely out of it, trying to kill Terry."

Terry is bent over, his elbows on his knees, breathing in big rasping gulps. Glory and Beth hover close to him, watching me apprehensively as if worried I'll go for him again. My world tilts. I sway, and Haley puts her hands on my arms to steady me.

"Are you back? Are you all right?" she asks.

Dazed, I nod, taking a step towards Terry. He backs away quickly. How do I apologize for this? The feelings I felt were so strong. The anger, the mistrust. They didn't come from the gas; it only amplified what I already felt.

"I'm sorry," I offer weakly.

"I thought we were okay." Terry regards me like a bomb about to go off.

"We are... I...."

Haley touches Terry's shoulder. "It wasn't Jorden, it was the gas..."

He brushes her hand off, his voice rising as he turns towards her, eyes flashing. "Don't make excuses for him. It wasn't a coincidence that he went for me out of the four of us. He knew it was me."

"Hey!" My hands curl into fists. The anger rises again, threatening to break loose. "Don't touch her."

Terry takes a defensive stance, ready to protect himself. Before the situation explodes, Haley gets between us, staring each of us down. "Stop it. Snap out of it. Both of you."

I'm breathing fast. My eyes are fixed on Terry, daring him to make a move. He holds my gaze until Haley turns to him again. "Terry, please."

At Haley's insistence, his gaze softens, his shoulders slump and he finally relents. Turning his back on us, he moves up the tunnel.

"Wait... it isn't safe," Haley shouts, but he doesn't stop. Just puts as much distance between us as possible. I can't blame him for being mad, but I can't fix it either. So, I follow him, the girls falling in around me. We'll deal with our issues when we get out of here. *If we get out of here.*

Marching uphill at a steady pace, we creep along, skirting other suspicious cylinders as the tunnel gets steeper. We're almost there.

"Let's stop a minute to catch our breath," I suggest.

The girls sit down in an alcove beneath a trapdoor to a building. Terry continues around the corner. It's too dangerous to keep charging off alone. Haley pins her eyes on me. She doesn't need to say anything. *I broke him. I need to fix him.*

"I'll get him," I say.

"Talk to him," Haley mouths.

Great. This will be fun.

I huff, but follow him around the corner. He's standing alone close by, obviously trying to keep his distance from us, but he starts moving again when he sees me. "Will you wait up a minute?" I whisper-shout.

He rounds on me. "What, Jorden? What do you want?"

I can't imagine what's going through his mind right now. As if he can read my thoughts, he blurts out, "You don't know what it's like. Hearing about my older brother my whole life. Hoping I'll meet him someday, wondering what it would have been like to grow up together. For the past three years, I thought you'd died, and I'd missed my chance. And now suddenly, you're back, and I've finally met you... and you hate me." His voice breaks and my heart breaks a little, too. *I can't imagine what that's like.*

"Wow. I don't hate you."

His face is red and scrunched up, bottom lip quivering like he's going to cry. "Oh?" he retorts, "So, why were you trying to kill me?"

"That wasn't me," I repeat Haley's argument, lamely. "It was the gas."

"How about threatening to kill me while we climbed the tower? That was you."

"I was just messing with you." *Kinda.* But now I feel bad about it. He stares at me accusingly, but I won't feel guilty about that. "Okay. Wait. About the threat in the tower... how did you expect me to react? You kissed my girlfriend, and even now you look at her the way a dog stares at a bone."

He drops his eyes and studies the floor as if he's trying to burn a hole through it, mumbling, "I can't help the way I feel."

"Yeah?! Well tough, mate, because I'm not sharing," I snap.

"Don't worry. She made it very clear I never had a chance."

His mopey face makes me want to laugh. Good that she made it clear. Strangely, I still feel sorry for him. This is so weird. *Would a good big brother console him? Or beat the crap out of him?* I've never been in this situation before. My little brother wants to talk about girls, which is kind of cool. But it's not cool that we both want the same girl.

I grab his shoulders, turning him to face me, and he flinches, looking up at me with eyes like my own. "Listen to me," I say. "I don't hate you. Sadly, I don't know you well enough to hate you. Give me a little time to wrap my head around the idea that we're brothers. But if we're ever going to get along, accept that Haley is off limits and get over it. There are 10 billion girls on the planet–find somebody else!"

His lips quirk up. "There are 10 billion girls on the planet and you brought one from space."

I laugh. "Yeah, well, she's one of a kind. Find your own, and you and I will get along just fine."

He grins, the tension between us diminishing.

Glory pokes her head around the corner. "Are you boys done braiding each other's hair? Because, you know, life and death situation... We need to go."

"Coming," I say, then whisper to Terry, "How about her?"

He makes a face. "Ugh. No, thank you."

"Okay, we'll just keep looking, then."

Chapter 41

SAVING TANGO

Haley

After ten minutes more climbing, we reach the lateral tunnel that runs from Peter Lund's cabin to the group of cabins by the mountain.

"Do you think there are exits in the individual cabins?" I ask, thinking of Tango alone in our cabin. I didn't insist on trying to reach her when we were running downhill, but now that we're going back...

Jorden takes my hand. "Probably not," he says. "If there's an exit at all it will be in one location. That means going outside, twice."

"They've finished rounding everybody up and taking them to the mess hall," I whisper insistently.

"No," he says in a final tone. "I love her too, but it's too dangerous."

My lip quivers, but I don't argue with him. I'll just

do it after he leaves.

"Haley?"

"What?" He steps closer, catching my eyes. "Wait for me to get back. I promise we'll go together." He gives me a quick kiss before vanishing into the dark opening to his father's underground control room with Terry.

I count to five... ten.... sixty... then peek at Glory and Beth sitting side by side in the tunnel. "Take care of each other—"

Beth shakes her head without waiting for me to finish. "Haley, don't."

"I wouldn't have made you all come up here, but we're so close..."

Glory screws up her face. "You know I like you, and I like your puppy, but I like me more. I'm not getting killed with you."

"I wouldn't ask you to. It's not far. I'll get her. Get in, get out. It'll be five minutes." Beth shakes her head, but I don't back down. "If I don't get back first, tell Jorden... tell Jorden that I love him, but I love her too. I have to go get her. We may not have time later." *He'll understand. It's what he'd do.*

"Haley!" Glory's shout echoes down the tunnel, but I don't stop. Taking a sound gun, I race down the tunnel. The gun has a light attached to the top but, strangely, there's another light glowing blue. My station comm just lit up. Back from the dead. I didn't even activate it. Maybe something in the tunnels is messing with it.

There's a ladder at the end of the tunnel. Slinging the sound gun over my shoulder, I position it across my back so my hands are free to climb. It would be better to hold it ready, but that's too difficult. Climbing up the four vertical rungs, I fumble for the latch to release the trap door. It's the same as the one in the training center. Underneath, there's a handle to pull it down and then it slides easily sideways.

The cabin's interior is dark. Moving the rug above the trapdoor enough to climb through, I pull myself up and into the room, crawling along the floor. My hand lands in a wet patch. Ugh. It smells metallic and slightly sweet...

I flick on my station comm, and the faint bluish light illuminates my surroundings. To my horror, I'm face to face with a man lying motionless on the floor. His face is pale and spattered with blood. Blue eyes stare sightlessly into mine. He looks surprised, as if he didn't expect them to shoot him. A scream bursts out of me, but I stifle it half way, ending in more of a whimper.

My right hand is sticky with blood. My palm and my forearm are soaked, the blood staining my sleeve up to my elbow. A low buzzing sound fills my head as dots swim before my eyes. *I'm going to be sick.*

The cabin is empty except for the body, lying face down in its pool of blood. Clambering to my feet, I make it into the bathroom before I fall to my knees and lose my lunch.

Afterwards, I wash my trembling hands and face in the sink, trying to make as little noise as possible. My sleeve is soaked, and I still feel the phantom sensation of blood on my skin.

Taking a few deep breaths before I return to the room, I skirt the body without looking at it. When I reach the window, I press against the wall, surveying the moonlit path outside. It's mostly dark between the cabins. Which is useful right now. Porch lights cast small pools of light that dot the path. There's no movement outside. It's as silent as the man lying behind me. A chill runs down my spine. That could be me, soon.

I try not to think of him lying there. Who he was.

I can't see anyone or hear anything.

There are two rows of five cabins. I'm about three cabins down from ours, in the lower row. Our cabin is in front of me and to my right. I can do this.

Slithering along the wall till I find the door, I ease it open, then slide the gun off my shoulder, holding it to my chest in case anyone arrives. At least I practiced when I wasn't scared to death. Maybe I'll even get a shot off.

Holding my breath, I step onto the porch. It's quiet. The C&C building is burning to my left. The smoke blowing in this direction makes it hard to breathe. If the sparks carry, other buildings will catch fire too. Are there people in the other cabins? Have our attackers done a sweep here recently?

The gravel crunches under my feet as I leave the bottom step, as loud as an avalanche in the deathly stillness around me. Pressing to the side of the cabin, I wait in a pool of darkness for anyone to come investigating, my finger on the trigger of my gun as my heart beats a staccato rhythm.

Suddenly, my station comm lights up with an incoming message notice blinking on the display. *What? How?* The bright light flickering in the darkness could get me killed. I pull my sleeve down over it to hide the light, diminishing the glare, but it still shines through. *What a time to go haywire.*

I need to move, but going fast would be reckless. With my arm pressed to my chest to conceal my comm, I dart between the cabins, staying in the dark as much as possible.

Two more cabins to go.

One more.

I'm in front of our cabin.

Crouching low as I cross the path, I pray there's no one out here to see me run up the steps and open the door, almost falling into the room.

Thankfully, we never lock the door when we leave.

I'm shutting it as quietly as I can when I hear feet crunching loudly down the path.

"I saw movement, further down," a voice says.

A comm squawks. "Roger that. Targets located

and secure. Consider all others non-essentials."

'Non-essentials'?

As I crouch by the door, panting, Tango raises her head sleepily from her basket near our bed and tumbles out, yawning and wagging her tail. She trots over to me, hopping up on her hind legs to lick my cheek. I pick her up and bury my face in her soft fur.

"Hey, puppy." I'm not sorry I came, even though this may be over for me in a few minutes. All I can do is slide down with my back to the door. Cuddling her, I wait as the soldiers' crunching footsteps approach slowly, cautiously. As if I'm dangerous. Ha. I guess they're not expecting a terrified seventeen-year-old girl armed with a sound gun and a puppy.

Just then, my station comm comes to life again, flashing an urgent message. I stare at it in amazement. What's wrong with it? It shouldn't be working at all. I'm one and a half light years from home. This is insane. Concealing the light with one hand, I tap the display. There's an actual message from an unknown sender, identified only by a mess of numbers and letters.

Short but chilling.

> Get out. They're coming >

>> who is this? > I reply.

> Inspector Rogers with the ESC >

What? How?

>> who is coming? >

> Conglomerate kill unit >

> Get Out. NOW! >

>> yes, I know. They're already here. I'm trapped >

>> how did *you* know? >

> had a drone onsite. They took it out just before the attack started >

I crawl over to the window. Tango is squirming. The soldiers are drawing closer, three black shapes against the night. I have my sound gun, but I can't shoot all three of them. Crawling back, I crouch by the door. There isn't anywhere to hide.

>> how are you on my comm? > I ask.

> Noticed you wearing it during interrogation. Took us a few days to locate the frequencies. Device is two-way comm. I... we've been listening >

>> OMG. Dying here >

>> you mean you heard everything... O_o >

> Believe me, we didn't mean to eavesdrop on your private life >

>> NVM. I need help. Now! >

> sending help, en route. pinpointing the location of your transmission. we had a hard time finding the signal earlier >

>> I was underground >

>> What about everybody else? >

> Our sources say they won't hold back. They're going to hit with everything they have. They don't want Earthers behind bars – they want them dead >

>> don't they know there are families here? Little kids? >

> they know, don't care. Earthers are terrorist cell, Conglomerate will say they committed mass suicide, blew themselves up. public will believe it >

>> no. pls. stop this. there are innocent people here >

> you are my responsibility. the Earthers I couldn't care less>

>> I'm not leaving without Jorden. So, stopping the raid is your problem >

> my primary concern is retrieving you. My second goal is bringing Earther leaders to justice >

>> I'll come in. I'll testify if you like. Promise. just let the kids go free. Grant Jorden a full pardon >

> do you think you're in a position to make demands? >

>> no. I'm in a position to get shot, very very soon. how would that look to your bosses? That u didn't save me >

The comm is silent for a few moments. Moments I don't have.

Maybe I should surrender. Just let them take me down to the mess hall with the others. Then I remember the dead guy in the other cabin. *The non-essentials.* They aren't rounding people up anymore. Something has changed.

Softly, I give Tango a kiss and put her down, then grip the sound gun. I'm sure I can get at least one of them. After that, I have no idea.

Feet crunch on the gravel right outside. Heavy footsteps tread on the wooden stairs.

They're outside the door.

Chapter 42

The control room

Jorden

The exit from the tunnels under my father's cabin isn't a trapdoor but a regular door, as if he uses this route frequently, so he made it as convenient as possible. The door opens into a small hallway with stairs to the floor above. To our left is a room with a cot, which must be where he kept Haley the night he grabbed her. At the thought, my hands tighten on my rifle. That bastard. I'd like to wring his neck.

But no. I'm here to talk him into surrendering. I need to stay calm.

The control room is to the right. Screens cover the whole wall opposite the doorway. My father's back is to us, as he's facing a complex control panel. *So much for low tech.* The hypocrisy is not surprising, but it still stings.

Did he know we were setting off traps in the tunnels, or was he operating them? Actively trying to waylay us? He'd opt for maximum control, but maybe the soldiers running around the compound are keeping him busy.

As we watch, he touches a screen, enlarging a feed from the armory. Dan, the arms master, sprawls lifeless across the counter, blood dripping through his splayed fingers. Two black-clad soldiers lean on the wall by the body. When my dad turns the audio up, they are chatting casually.

"Do you think they'll replace us soon? I'd rather be outside with the action," one says.

The other one crosses his arms and leans his head back. "Nah. Let them finish. I'd rather they call me when it's time for chow."

My father frowns and his fingers fly over the controls. Smoke pours from a ceiling duct. The soldiers start coughing. One of them clutches his neck, retching. His face purpling, the shorter one grabs for his friend's shoulder but misses, keeling over on the floor. The taller one bends double, then falls to his knees and onto his face. They twitch violently until they stop moving. The whole thing takes less than a minute.

Terry steps forward. "What did you do to them?"

My father leaps out of his seat and stalks towards me, ignoring Terry. "Jorden, what are you doing here?"

"I came to get you."

"Get me?"

I wonder how much he knows. The audio isn't up on all the screens. Most of the images show empty rooms, but there's a screen showing inside the mess hall, packed full of our people. Before I can answer, he narrows his eyes, glaring at Terry. "Who are you?"

"Terry. I'm new here, sort of." Terry's eyes scan my father's face, hoping for a shred of recognition. A sign Dad knows who he is or senses the family connection. But my father's face is blank, and his gaze slides off Terry's face almost at once, losing interest. He turns back to me, gripping my shoulder.

"Good, you made it out. Not many did."

A camera showing a section of the tunnels displays bodies piled into a corner. The tunnels all look the same, so I don't know where it is, but I try not to look too hard in case they're people I know. I can't see the girls. They must have found a blind spot. Better that he can't see them. I point to the scene in the armory.

"You have weapons? Hidden ways to attack them?"

He nods. "Yes, but most are lethal to everyone close by. They are a last resort or come with acceptable losses."

What does he count as acceptable losses?

Terry steps forward, his eyes seeking my father's. "I need to tell you something. I'm your son too."

My father's face barely twitches. "Kid, I'm sorry to say it, but I probably don't remember your mother, and this isn't the time for family reunions."

Terry's face darkens. "Oh, you remember her. I'm Eleanor's son."

My father's face clouds over, like a storm about to burst. "That's impossible."

Terry glances at me, eyebrows raised. "I'm getting tired of hearing that." He speaks slowly, as if talking to someone simple-minded. "I was born a few months after she left you. After she got away." Typical teenage snark directed at totally the wrong person to be snarky with. Terry doesn't know yet, but he's about to find out.

Sadly, I'm too far away to stop my father as he surges forward, grabbing Terry by the shirt and slamming him into the wall, roaring into his face, "You lie!"

Terry's eyes widen in panic. He must have spent as many years thinking about this conversation as he did about meeting me. I'm guessing he didn't think it would go like this.

"Put him down," I muscle my way between them, but Dad doesn't let go.

His face is inches away from Terry's, his fists clutching Terry's t-shirt as if he can wring the truth out of him. "Where is she?" Dad snarls.

"She's here, on the Farm," I say. He drops Terry abruptly, leaving him to fold into himself, defeated.

My father turns to me, fuming as I continue. "She's in the mess hall, leading the force that attacked us. Mother is prepared to let everyone left live if you turn yourself in."

Dad turns to the screens, his face white as a sheet. Mother is in the entry hall where I left her, surrounded by her men. Dad's eyes widen in surprise, then crease in anger as he enlarges the image and presses the public address system for the mess hall.

"Eleanor?" His voice trembles as he addresses the wife he believed dead.

She looks up, as if she can see him, and addresses the camera.

"Hello, Peter. I came here for three things, you and the boys. We've rounded up everyone in the compound. My employers would like to see you all dead, but I've negotiated a stay of execution for your followers if you turn yourself in. Just come down to the mess hall and bring my boys with you."

"Your boys?" he snarls at her. "This boy Terry? You sent him here to spy on me? After all these years, this is how I find out I have another son?"

Her face is grim. "If it were up to me, you'd never know he existed."

"You hate me that much?" He sounds confused. She just stares into the camera. Then he turns to me. "You knew she was here?"

I shake my head. "I just found out."

"Did your mother tell you where she worked,

where she probably still works? She works for the Conglomerate. She stands with everything we've been fighting against." He spits out.

I shrug. "I didn't even know she was still alive until a few days ago."

"Well then, since you are used to her being dead, this shouldn't bother you too much." He says in a triumphant tone in his voice as he operates the PA.

"My dear Elanor. I wired this whole compound with explosives under every building. With the press of a button, I can liquidate you and your men."

"I have all of your people." She sounds confused, as if she didn't expect her winning move to be check-mated.

"I have your sons, so I win," he gloats.

All his followers must be listening to this exchange. After twenty years of loyalty, he wrote them off as if they meant nothing. Terry is pale, his eyes wide with horror. I had years to process the disconnect between my father's public persona and the man he truly is; Terry needs to digest it all at once. This is what the coveted backstage pass to this family gets you. Terry may have heard stories from our mother, but he's only seen our father's public face so far. Now he can see the monster with his own eyes.

The comm I took from the soldier crackles as my parents talk. *"Targets located and secure. Consider all others non-essentials."*

"What does that mean?" Terry whispers to me.

"They wanted the three of us. Now they'll kill everyone else." I step up to the microphone, interrupting my father but ignoring his glare. "Mom, it's Jorden. What about the others?"

"I can only guarantee their safety if the three of you turn yourselves in."

Is she telling the truth? I don't know her well enough to judge.

"What do you say, Dad?"

His expression is hard. "Why should I surrender? I'm holding all the cards right now. I have the three things she wants right here."

"What about all the people they're holding in the mess hall?"

He shrugs, his eyes cold. "Regrettable losses. I've been building the infrastructure for this movement for twenty years. The Farm is the hub for our activity, but I have other resources and people in places of influence. I'll continue from a new location."

"What about the people out there? They followed you. Believed in you enough to lay down their lives for this cause, including me."

"And lay down their lives they shall. As for you... you didn't go through with it, did you? You came back." He spits in contempt, and his perception of my return hits home.

"Me being alive really messed things up for you, didn't it? You were the grieving father who gave up his son for the cause. The heroic leader. But when I came back, I rewrote the story. I failed, which means you failed. You don't give a damn about me or any of us. You never did. Only about what it means for you and your image. That's why you don't care if the Conglomerate kills everyone. Rigging the entire farm to blow is proof you always intended to go out with a bang, didn't you? Getting back at Mother as you do, it's just a bonus."

He crosses his arms, waiting for me to finish with a smug expression, as if he knows something I don't. "Are you done?" he spits. "I'm not going out today. I have a way out of here, and despite your disrespectful attitude, you are still my sons. You'll both join me when I leave here, alive. Hopefully, in the future, you'll learn to treat me with proper respect."

I can't believe him. "I'm not going with you or with her." Shouldering my weapon, I turn to the door. "This is a waste of time. I need to get back to Haley. Come on, Terry."

My father shakes his head, a sneer on his lips. "Don't leave now, Jorden. Watch the feed from your cabin. Do you remember I told you bringing her here was a mistake? You are just in time to watch her die."

Now I understand his smug expression. It's *I told you so.*

He nods to the screens in front of him and I turn to see the live footage of our cabin. Haley is crouching by the door, holding Tango. The external cameras show three black-clad soldiers sweeping the cabins, going door to door. She has nowhere to hide. I turn towards the entrance, preparing to run, but my father blocks my path, standing between me and the way out. Rock solid. Unmoving.

"You couldn't get there in time, even if I allowed it," he says.

"Move. Let me go. Please." I don't try to hide the panic in my voice.

"I'm sorry." He doesn't look sorry or sound sorry. There's no sympathy in his stone-cold eyes.

Terry's gaze flicks from me, to my dad, to the screen, where the three soldiers are advancing toward our cabin. I raise my gun, pointing it at my father, as my hands shake.

"MOVE."

He raises his eyebrows. "You'd shoot your own father? To save this girl?"

"Jorden," Terry says softly, pointing to the screen behind me and I turn to see my father is right.

It's too late.

Chapter 43

LAST STAND

Haley

Crawling with Tango over to the closet, I place her on the bottom shelf and shut the door so she isn't hurt when the soldiers' storm into the cabin. Then I face the door.

This might be the end, but I'm going down fighting. My heart pounds wildly. My mouth is dry and my hands still feel sticky.

The door handle swivels, and the door swings inward. A black-clad figure fills the doorway. Taking a breath, I aim the sound gun at his chest and squeeze the trigger. The sonic gun whines and emits a concentrated blast of sound, blowing him out the door. As he flies away, he collides with the man behind him, hurtling off the porch and into the dust. I got two of them.

I can't believe my luck. But the third is still up-right, pressed against the wall on our porch.

He peeks in, cautiously, but my gun is still loading. I can't get him, too. So, I spin and dash for the window, yank it open, and throw myself out. Landing heavily outside, I keep rolling; it knocks the wind out of me, so I lie flat as the beam of his weapon cuts through the wall behind me.

The two soldiers I blew off the porch are getting up off the ground outside. I spin wildly, debating which way to run. The cliff face is in front of me, the soldiers to my left. So, I duck to my right, circling around the side of the cabin, hoping I can make it back into the tunnels. Though I know I'm not fast enough to outrun them, I won't stop trying. When I emerge on the other side of the cabin, I'm back on the small path between the two rows. But the first soldier I shot is standing in the middle of the path. A small rivulet of blood trickles from a nick in his eyebrow into his eye. He blinks and raises his gun, whistling for his buddies to join him.

"What do we have here?" a soldier behind him asks. "Should we take her down to the mess hall?"

The one who followed me into the cabin sneers. "Why bother? Non- essential." They exchange looks.

"Just shoot her," the bleeding one snaps.

"No, please." I raise my hands. "I'll come quietly."

As I lift my arms, my station comm lights up again, and the soldier in front cocks his head. "What is that?"

My comm is flashing and buzzing as a stream of messages hits it. Very slowly, I twist my wrist so the display faces me. The messages accelerate, flashing wildly in rapid succession, and I make out a single word, sent again and again.

> DUCK >

I drop, bending my knees and hit the path, the rough stones scraping my hands as the soldiers blink in surprise. They don't have time to react before an ESC drone drops from above, cutting the three men down with rapid fire.

Clasping my hands over my head, I kiss the gravel and stay as flat as possible. The men grunt, then bodies smash into the ground beside me, blood spurting towards me. A drop splashes on my wrist, warm and wet and sticky. I lie there, watching it drizzle down my arm until it falls to the path, leaving a trail on my skin.

The smell is horrible. Blood, burned flesh, and urine.

I wait till they stop moving, then roll away gagging and peek at my comm. They staggered the messages into a huge queue. As I look, another message arrives.

> All clear >

Pushing myself up on shaky knees, I back away from the dead men on the path. Gagging, but my stomach is all puked out. Then I circle back around the cabin, the way I ran, to avoid the corpses.

Inside our cabin, I extract Tango from the cupboard. She's busy chewing on one of Jorden's slippers and looks annoyed at being disturbed. I pick her up, carefully extract the slipper from her mouth, and drop it on the floor.

More drones flit across the sky as I step outside, followed by the sound of aircraft. From the porch, I watch the first ESC craft touch down in the middle of the path before Peter's cabin, blue-clad agents pouring out, their weapons raised. Signal lights guide in a stream of craft pulling over the mountains.

I have to find Jorden.

Chapter 44

THE FINAL SHOWDOWN

Jorden

I almost collapse in relief as I watch the drone mowing down the Conglomerate soldiers, and Haley gets up and retreats to our cabin. Bracing against the wall of the control room, I exchange glances with Terry, who seems as relieved as I am.

My father steps forward, eyes on the monitors as the first ESC craft lands. This won't end well for him.

"That's it," I state. "You lost. Whatever happens now, it's over for you."

Dad pushes his hair back, eyes scurrying from side to side, frantically seeking escape routes. Then he enlarges the image of the mess hall. Mother looks up when the PA crackles.

"It's over, Elanor. The ESC is here, so your little plan didn't work. You don't get to take me after all.

You aren't as clever as you thought. Then again, you never were. I have the boys, Elanor. So, in the end, you lose. Goodbye."

He thumbs the controls, priming the explosives hidden under the mess hall, prepared to kill them all just to kill her. Just to win.

"No. You can't. Everyone is in there. Aaron, Rachel," *my mother*, "all your loyal followers." I push off from the wall, lunging at him and dragging him away from the controls, shoving him towards the door. He's bigger than me, but I'm fueled by rage. Though I interrupted him temporarily, his eyes are still calculating the best way to get past me and activate the bombs.

Gunfire erupts close by. First, we hear a handgun, then the whine and boom of a sonic gun. A moment later, Glory and Beth dash in from the tunnel and run straight up the stairs, something big and metallic close on their heels: another hound.

It bounds into the hallway after them, but it notices a closer target, my father, standing with his back to the door. With one pounce, the killing machine latches on to his shoulder, yanking him to the floor. He screams as the mechanical beast rips at him with its sharp teeth.

"Jorden, help me!"

I'm frozen as his gaze shifts to Terry. "Terry, son, help!" *Now he's his son.*

I finger the trigger of my rifle. My father was prepared to let Haley die and make me watch. He was going to kill my mother. Blow up Aaron and Rachel and every other person I grew up with. I will never be like him.

But he's still my father.

I aim, and Terry joins me, firing at the hound again and again till it's a smoldering heap on the floor. My father lies underneath it, shaking, bleeding, but alive.

Crawling out from under the steaming metal, he stammers, "Thank you, son. Thank you both." For once, his eyes show emotion, since we saved the only thing he cares about: his own stinking hide.

"Keep your thanks. I don't want anything from you anymore," I spit as I step over him and grab his shirt. Dragging him up off the floor, I march him out of the room and up the stairs, away from the consoles and the triggers.

He doesn't resist. Terry follows us.

Opening the front door, I step out into the chilly night air and drop him on the porch, where he collapses to the ground. ESC agents are streaming over the mountain peaks on both sides of us, landing their crafts in the middle of the hill. The ESC insignia blaze on their blue uniforms and vehicles.

The smoke from the burning C&C building blows thickly around us. I can barely see across the path, but the smoke clears for a moment and I see Haley, holding Tango in her arms.

The gun in my hand clatters to the path, forgotten. She puts Tango down gently, but there's nothing gentle about the way she runs to me, flinging her arms around my neck. Her lips find mine.

We kiss as the world burns around us. The sound of the ESC troops rounding up the Conglomerate soldiers, the crackling flames and shouts of surrendering Earthers fade away until all I can hear is her breathing. All I can feel are her soft hands on the back of my neck, and all I can taste are her lips.

When the sound creeps back into the world, I smile down at her. "Can't I leave you alone for five minutes without you getting into trouble?"

Her smile curls up from her lips to her eyes. "I learned from the best."

"Why didn't you wait for me?" I ask.

"Would *you* have waited?" *She has a point.*

"I thought I'd lost you."

"You didn't." Her hands creep up my back, giving me chills, her eyes reflecting the flames dancing behind us.

"I said I'd protect you."

"You did protect me. When you taught me to protect myself, you made me brave enough to do it, and gave me something worth fighting for." Her voice is fire.

Is she talking about Tango? But her hand curls into my shirt and she pulls me down for another kiss. No, *okay. This isn't about the dog.* Instead of letting me kiss her as long as I'd like, she pulls back, looking down.

"Jorden, I need to tell you something important," her voice is hesitant. "I asked the ESC to come help us. We made a deal. They agreed to grant you a full pardon. They won't press any charges. Absolving all the Farm residents uninvolved in terrorist acts and any children who grew up here under Earther influence. But not your father, or Jacob, or anyone who planned terrorist attacks."

"Okay." My stomach drops. Her expression tells me there's something else, something bad. "What did you do?"

Burying her face in my shoulder, she wraps her arms around my waist, whispering. "My side of the bargain is to turn myself over to them, so they can send me home. Soon."

No. "Can he force you to go?"

She leans back and finds my eyes. "I agreed."

"Why would you agree?"

"In return for a full pardon, for you. So, you can have a life after this. Leave here, get away from him." She nods toward my father, being led away by the ESC agents. "This is how I protect you, too. I can't beat people up or pull you out of a burning spaceship. But I can do this."

I shake my head. "No."

"If I don't go willingly, there's no deal and he'll still force me to leave. I'm a minor. My parents are ESC employees. They don't care if you kidnapped me, or if I came with you of my free will, or if I want to stay here with you. They'll make me go back."

It must be the flames, or her words, that suck all the oxygen out of the air. I pull her to me, trying to get her close enough so they can never take her away, but I know no matter how close we are or how hard I hold on to her, it won't be enough.

Chapter 45

HOMEWARD BOUND

Haley

The next few days go by in a blur. The remaining Earthers rebuild the Farm, dragging away charred logs from the burned buildings. Burying the dead.

I don't know most of the people who died, but everyone is somber. Many families lost a member, either killed or incarcerated. Some families packed up and left. I'm unsure if the rest can carry on living here without their leaders.

I'm not too surprised when Jorden's mother appears on the Farm. The authorities charged the black ops team for the attack, but the Conglomerate's legal team got her off the hook. Big surprise.

Still, she's trying to help, and seems sincere about it. Thanks to her, Jorden, Terry, and I flew down to the hospital in Boulder to see Aaron. We found him with Rachel sitting by his bedside, looking much better. I'm glad Jorden made peace with Aaron. At least he'll have them and Terry once I'm gone. I don't want him to be alone.

We stay busy during the day, helping out however we can. By the time we get back to the cabin at night, I'm exhausted, but I don't want to sleep. Instead, I lie by his side, tracing his face into my mind, carving it into my memory. There'll be time for sleeping on the station.

Jorden kisses my drooping eyelids. "You're barely awake. Go to sleep."

I wrap my arms around his neck, pulling him closer, whispering, "I don't want to give up a single moment of our time together."

He holds me tightly. "I'm here. I'll be here when you wake up."

Tomorrow, yes, but after that?

I pull back just enough to look into his eyes. "You won't leave me?"

"Never." He kisses my forehead, but doesn't say the awful truth.

He's not the one who's leaving.

We're down near the barn, helping bring the horses

in for the night, when my comm buzzes. This is the call I've been dreading. Inspector Rogers let me have a few more days, but now his voice is strict.

"It's time, Haley. We can't postpone any longer. You must honor your side of the bargain if you want our agency to live up to theirs. Tomorrow morning, an escort will take you to Earth Space Control, to board the transport to VOR. They're taking you home."

Since the day we left the station, I knew that I'd eventually have to say goodbye to Jorden and go home. I've never been afraid of space, but now I feel the weight of all the space about to come between us crushing me. Stealing my breath. I want to stay on Earth with Jorden, but I can't. My parents won't allow it and I'm still a minor. I don't get to decide for myself.

I end the call and Jorden gathers me in his arms, my head under his chin, and we cling to each other as if he could save me from having to go home. But he can't.

As the light fades, I take his hand and we enter the barn. It's deserted at this hour, quiet, and warm, and dark. I lead him up to the hayloft, pulling him down into a pile of hay, curling into his chest. Placing my head next to his heart, I listen to the strong, steady rhythm.

He doesn't speak: there's nothing to say to fix this. We're about to be separated, possibly forever. I'm scared, but I take his hand, caressing it, drawing lines with my fingertips along his fingers.

"I'm leaving tomorrow... but we still have tonight... to say goodbye."

His look is so loving and so sad. He strokes my hair, whispering in my ear, "I don't want to say good-bye. I want forever with you. Can you wait for me? I'll find a way for us to be together... This can be a beginning for us. Not an end."

I caress his cheeks and kiss him. Reluctant to say goodbye, but equally afraid our love will die a slow, painful death as time and distance inevitably pull us apart. But I leave room for hope, however faint, that we'll find a way to be together again.

I nod, and we lie there, studying each other's faces, so we'll remember every little thing when tomorrow separates us.

Chapter 46

Across the Stars

Jorden

We convinced Haley's escort to let me accompany her to the Spaceport to say goodbye. They even allowed us to bring Tango so she could stay with Hayley till the very last minute.

Haley holds Tango close to her face, stroking her soft fur, her eyes glistening with tears. "She won't understand where I went. She's just a puppy."

"I promise I'll take care of her." I force a laugh. "When you come back, she'll be a full-grown dog."

Haley nods earnestly. "In a year, I'll no longer be a minor. My parents can't stop me from returning to Earth. And I've applied to Star Academy..."

I smile, smoothing back her hair, tucking it behind her ear, trying to be optimistic and smile for Haley's sake, but I'm dying inside.

A year till she's eighteen, and another three years for her to complete the return trip. Four years without seeing each other may as well be forever. I can wait that long, but who knows if she'll still want me after a year apart?

Over the past few months, she's blossomed from a timid, closed-off 16-year-old into a beautiful, confident girl that could have any guy she wants. When I first met her, only people who took the time to get to know her could see how amazing she was. Now she emits light, like a beacon drawing people in.

I guess being in love will do that to you.

Cupping her face in my hands, I gaze into her honey eyes. "I love you so much. I'd say to the moon and back, and that might be far enough if we were both on Earth, but you're going to be so much farther away. So, I'll love you as far as you go. To the ends of the galaxy, to the end of the universe. Wherever you are. Do you love me?"

She nods, her eyes brimming over with tears. "I love you so much it hurts."

I kiss each cheek, tasting her salty tears and then her lips. "Then this isn't goodbye. I'll find a way for us to be together even if I have to steal another ranger ship and fly up to the station to be with you."

Haley grins, but shakes her head. "I don't think your pardon covers future crimes. Anyway, they'll never let you back on the station after what you've done, pardon or not."

"I don't care. Do you believe me I'll find a way?"

She nods and kisses me, a kiss full of promise and hope and love. I try not to think of this kiss as our last, but it feels so final.

Haley hugs me like she's never going to let me go. I hold her until her escort grasps her shoulder and practically drags her from my arms towards the waiting ship.

Tango is straining on the leash, whimpering for Haley. I know exactly how she feels. Picking up our puppy, I bury my nose in her soft fur so nobody can see my face right now.

I told her I'd find a way, and I keep my promises.

At that moment, there's a commotion at the door. My mother appears in her business suit, waving a data-pad.

"Stop. Stop." She hails Haley's escort, striding right up to the ship. "Please unhand the young lady. I have a court order stating that Haley Ann Shavit, born on Earth on March 17th, 2164, is legally 19 years old and no longer a minor. Therefore, it is her decision and hers alone if she wants to return to VOR space station. This isn't up to her parents or the ESC. It's Haley's choice."

The stunned escort releases Haley's arm, reaching for the datapad, and Haley runs down the gangplank and straight into my arms. I hug her to me so tightly she squeals, and Tango licks her face.

I can't believe it. She isn't leaving. I haven't lost

her.

My heart is beating so fast it feels as if it could lift us both off the ground as it takes flight. My mother leaves the ship and approaches us, smiling, lowering her voice.

"We're lucky they haven't figured out the legalities of time dilation yet. We set a precedent here. Most people who leave Earth are over eighteen or are minors headed for the colonies, and they don't return. I argued that her date of birth is the standard for determining legal age in every court case to date. The laws may change in the future, but it will give them one hell of a headache figuring them out."

I can't believe our luck. We didn't even think of that.

"Thank you." Tears blur my vision.

Haley looks up at me, her eyes shining. "If I'm nineteen, you know what that means..." I nod. "That means I could go to Star Academy," she says, and I say at the same time, without even thinking, "We could get married."

Her eyes open wide. "Oh wow. Jorden. I—" She exhales, smiles and hugs me tightly. "I love you so much, and... can we make a plan and wait for a few years, till, after I graduate from the academy?"

"Of course," I laugh with relief. I'm not thinking straight right now, but it doesn't matter. Kissing Haley's hair until I can catch my breath enough to say, "Whatever you want. I'm happy as long as we're together."

My mother has a huge smile on her face as she regards us both. "Haley, you applied to Star Academy about a month before leaving the station, right? I checked, and they received your application and accepted you, so if you want to, you can stay on Earth and start your training." Haley nods happily, and my mother continues, "Jorden, if you like, I can pull some strings and get you into the Academy as well."

"Can you do that?" Haley asks breathlessly. I can't tell from her tone how she feels about the idea.

My mother laughs. "I work for the Conglomerate. There aren't a lot of things I can't do."

They both turn to me expectantly.

"Oh. Wow. Can you believe I never thought about what I'd do next? I never expected to have a future." I can't believe how lucky I am. "Would you like me tagging along to the academy with you, Haley?"

"I won't go without you."

I gather her face in my hands and plant a kiss on her lips. Another first kiss. The first since I got her back, since we can finally have a future together.

I'm overjoyed and relieved that I haven't lost her.

Whatever the future brings, I know we'll face it together.

- The End -

**To be continued in
The Children of the Stars**

DƎAR RƎADƎR

If you enjoyed this book, please leave a star rating and a review. Reviews are invaluable to independent authors and every single one matters.

Even if you hated it, tell me why. Hopefully, it's something I can fix in future books.

If you leave a review on your social media or blog, please tag me @debbieiancu or email me: debbie.iancu@gmail.com

ACKNOWLEDGEMENTS

I hope you enjoyed diving back into Jorden and Haley's world.

This book was written in 2019. Any similarities to current events are coincidental and unintended.

Once again, I must acknowledge my "book village" who made this book happen.

Thanks to Maayan Rogel for her amazing developmental edit and the notion that things that happen underground couldn't happen in the light of day.

To my many beta readers along the road, including Lisa Smith, Elise Carlson, Sarah Houck, MK Beker, and my aunt Lynda Schwartz. Apologies to anyone I forgot.

Thanks to my wonderful and meticulous editor, Lisa Smith, who understands that I don't understand commas.

Thanks to my mum, Beverly Iancu, for proofreading the huge and heavy A4 copy. And Roni London for putting in an effort despite being called in for active army duty.

My amazing cover designer Lindsay Mcdonald, from Firefly Designs – helpingauthorseveryday.com who created the gorgeous covers for this series.

Thanks to my writing support during these years, my many friends in the Twitter #writingcommunity; and my friends at the Fantasy Writers Association, including Yotam, Anat, Roni, Nati, Or, and Keren, who make book fairs far more fun for everyone.

Always last, but never least, thanks to my family; Yuval, Shavit, and Shahar. My pet writing buddies - dogs Angel (RIP) and Shugi (may he have a long life), and Spatz the cat. I love you all.

Also by Debbie Iancu-Haddad

Speechless in Achten Tan: Book 1 of The Sands of Achten Tan

Mila hasn't spoken in the five years since she became an Onra, a first-level Everfall witch. After failing the test to reclaim her voice and control her magic, her mentor sends eighteen-year-old Mila to Achten Tan – City of Dust – a dangerous desert town, built in the massive ribcage of an extinct leviathan. To reclaim her power, Mila must steal a magical staff capable of releasing it, from Bone Master Opu Haku's sky high lair. Her only resources are the magical luminous elixirs of the cursed caverns where she grew up, and a band of unlikely allies; a quirky inventor, a giant-ant rider, a healer, a librarian's assistant, a Tar-tule rider, and the chief's playboy son. But in the City of Bones, enemies & friends are not who they seem, and trusting the wrong person can be deadly. If Mila fails, she will never speak again and her bones will be added to the desert.

This book includes a kick-ass female protagonist covered in tattoos, giant ants, first-person present-tense narration, magic, banter, lots of innuendoes, and cute boys kissing.

The Bone Master

Kaii Haku has lived his whole life in the shadow of

his cruel father's magic.

Rebelling against his father- the Bone Master- by drinking and sleeping around was Kaii's main occupation for years.

But when one of his best friends is kidnapped by pirates, Kaii embarks on a perilous rescue mission with two retired pleasure house workers, a shy teen bookworm, and a feisty girl from the pirate crew.

The journey will take Kaii and his allies far from Achten Tan, to a sea ruled by dangerous conditions and ships that travel on the backs of monsters.

For the first time in his life, he has the power to make a difference, but if he wields his emerging bone magic to save the girl he loves, he risks losing himself and becoming like his father - a man who tried to kill him.

This is the second book in the Sands of Achten Tan series, but can be read as a standalone. It contains a complete adventure and no cliffhangers.

In the Heart of the Storm: An Achten Tan short story

There are worse things at sea than monsters.

Blown off course by a storm, a pirate ship carried on the back of a giant nudibranch takes shelter at an island where no island should be. Fenn, the mage in charge of their creature transport, senses something is off, but the island's uncharted location is only the first sign of an ominous presence lurking out of sight. The malevolent entity will force Fenn to make unbearable choices if he ever wants to see his home again.

This story is one of two prequel stories for The Bone Master: Book 2 in the Achten Tan series, but it's standalone and doesn't contain any spoilers for either book, so you can enjoy it even if this is your first encounter with this series.

Download free story here:
https://dl.bookfunnel.com/1nq9a7j1gb

Pirate in the Desert: An Achten Tan short story

Dagen's pleasant life in the pirate kingdom of

Janolous Cove, raising giant nudibranchs to carry their ships, comes crashing down when a demon comes to claim his next of kin.

Perfect if you like unique fantasy world-building, pirates, and relatives who make your worst uncle seem like a sweetheart.

This story is one of two prequel stories for "The Bone Master: Book 2" in the Achten Tan series, but its standalone and doesn't contain any spoilers for either book, so you can enjoy it even if this is your first encounter with this series.

About Debbie Iancu-Haddad

I'm a Jewish Israeli author living in Meitar in the Negev Desert. Writing Sci-fi, Fantasy, and a dab of horror.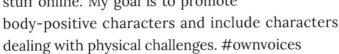

I spend my time taking part in Anthologies (ten to date with two more on the way), writing VSS on Twitter, and buying way too much stuff online. My goal is to promote body-positive characters and include characters dealing with physical challenges. #ownvoices

For my day job, I give lectures on humor, laughter yoga workshops, and chocolate workshops, and see how often I can make my kids roll their eyes.

I'm older than I look and have no intention of ever acting my age. I love to hear from readers. Contact me via my author website or buy my books here: http://linktr.ee/Debbie_Iancu

Made in United States
North Haven, CT
05 January 2024

45665803R20241